HAZARD

WEST HELL MAGIC - 1

HAZARD

West Hell Magic - 1

DEVON MONK

Hazard Copyright © 2018 by Devon Monk

Paperback ISBN: 978-1-939853-11-0

First Edition August 2018

Published by: Odd House Press
Art by: Kanaxa Design
Interior Design by: Indigo Chick Designs

DEDICATION

To my family and hockey lovers, young and old.

1

SOMETIMES LIFE AND DEATH come down to a split-second decision.

This particular decision hung over an impossible, improbable accident that would kill the rookie skidding across the ice on his back. He was already passed out and concussed. Boneless in that sickening rag doll way that made it hard to watch.

He was also about to be slammed in the side of the head by his own teammate who hadn't seen him fall, hadn't seen him slide. Taking a direct shot from a man who could knock a ninety-mile-an-hour puck into the net and slam full grown men into the boards on the regular, was brutal.

If the rookie didn't move, he'd never stand up again.

Get up, get up, I silently chanted.

He did not even twitch. Which meant that guy on the ice, my teammate—though I wasn't even sure how to pronounce his last name—was about to die.

No one could stop this shit show. It was possible no one had put two and too much together and even noticed what was about to happen.

Life and death moments, the few I'd seen—one bike vs. car and one hiker vs. edge of cliff—that stuff always played out in super-slow motion for me.

Maybe it was because I was observant.

Maybe it was because I was a wizard.

Some days I swore the only reason shit happened when I was around was because magic didn't like me hiding what I was. Didn't like me hiding that I had magic.

Magic—that non-sentient, chaotic force that had been cracked up out of the earth by drilling, fracking, earthquakes or whatever conspiracy of the week. That thing that had gotten into our air, our water, and for some of us, got into our blood and irrevocably changed us—wanted me to use it.

Magic wanted me to bend, to break. To give in to it like it was my destiny or something. To use me until I was all used up.

I'd spent twenty-two years hiding what I was. Twenty-two years fighting what magic wanted me to be.

Magic wasn't my destiny.

Hockey was my destiny. Ice, sweat, grit, and hope.

But right here, right now, this moment? This life and death choice was going down.

Choice number one: do nothing, let the guy take the hit to the head. I'd feel sorry for the guy. I would. But I would still be one of the many new rookies drafted into the NHL. My dream job. My lifelong hope.

Choice number two: do something, do *magic*. Save his life. There would be no major league hockey for me. The life I'd been chasing for fifteen years would be gone. Taken away before I'd even gotten a taste of it.

Wizards, shifters, and every other kind of magically infected marked weren't allowed in major league hockey.

Weren't allowed in the minor leagues either.

If I saved this guy it would end my career.

It would save him. *Save* him.

And what kind of a choice was that for a regular guy like me to make?

Shit.

Just like that, time ran out. And just like hockey, instinct took over.

The defenseman's stick swung back. He thought he was going to hit the puck clean, didn't realize unpronounceable-name unconscious guy was flat on his back, down for the count and sliding right into the line of fire.

I pulled on magic with everything I had in me.

And magic answered like a rebel scream.

It flew from me, from my fingers, from my solar plexus, from deeper places that might be where the heart or soul or core of me started and ended. Magic exploded into the air with heady oil-painted strokes, swirling in gold and white and midnight blues like Van Gogh's Starry Night had caught fire.

Magic, all of it visible, all of it painting me: the yellow and gold of my determination, black of my fear and anger, blue of my shame. And in that wall of colors was green, faint but visible: my hope.

Hope that I hadn't just destroyed my life.

Hope that I had been fast enough to save his.

Magic slid between the hockey stick and unpronounceable guy. The wall of solid color rippled with impact as the defenseman smashed the puck and his stick into it.

The impact set off a low, sweet sound like struck metal, and magic undulated in starry waves of color.

Everything stopped. All the players. The coaches. The scouts. The reporters. The viewers in the stands.

Everything.

I had one brief, hopeful moment that no one had noticed I was the one who had thrown that monster of a spell. Even though I was the only one on the ice breathing so hard. Even though I was the only one who had acted fast enough to do something.

It was a pretty impressive spell. Fast, precise. Strong enough to take the puck hit without letting any of the stick impact the guy on the ice.

It was kind of beautiful, really.

Pulling that much magic up out of me had the normal consequences. I was instantly exhausted, ravenous, and sick. If I didn't get some food or shut-eye, I'd hit my knees and pass out.

Have I mentioned using magic sucks?

I stood there, sweating, shaking in a way I couldn't stop, my vision fuzzing at the edges, swallowing down bile. I stared at the scene, but it was moving away from me down a long gunmetal tunnel.

"What the hell?" the defensemen yelled. He scurried away from the wall of blues, yellows, and green, green, green, that still shimmered in front of him like it was fire.

Why was magic still shimmering there?

My head felt thick, my thoughts sort of gooey.

Oh, yeah. I had to let go of the spell, cut the strings that attached me to it. Should do that before I passed out, although passing out would probably end the spell too.

Or maybe not. It wasn't like I did a lot of magic. I hated the stuff. Avoided it at all costs. Never trained 'cause I was never gonna be a wizard, right? So what did I know about spells?

Nothing, really.

"You!" a woman's voice rang out. It seemed too big to fit in the stadium, so big, it filled my skull, made it ache. She stood, and even though she was across the ice from me, I saw her light up as if someone had just snapped a spotlight on her.

"Wizard!" She pointed at me.

A sensitive. Great. Just what I needed. Someone who could zero in on marked who were using magic, or who were about to shift, which was also a kind of magic, but in a more physical, beasting-out way.

I would have answered her but my brain was slushy and I was still trying to figure out how to cut the spell. I'd done it before. Done it under pressure twice. Once with the whole bike versus car thing and once with the hiker vs. edge of cliff.

I tried to imagine a pair of scissors in my gloved hand and made snippy motions. But the imaginary scissors were made out of butter or something because they just sort of melted away.

Screw it. I was *this* close to passing out. I didn't have time to be subtle. I pulled back my hockey stick and took a swing at the ice, imagined a puck there, imagined sending that puck flying toward the spell.

Imagined the puck hitting it high glove side.

Magic hummed, then shattered, a beautiful melted chorus of color and sound that rained down on the ice in soppy, sparky colors.

Goal!

The first and last I'd made in professional hockey. And it didn't even count.

SOMEONE SHOVED A SPORTS drink at me. It wasn't enough to recover from using magic, but it should keep me from passing out. Things went by in a blur while I drank. I was off the ice, down the corridor, out of my gear—but not showered—and sitting in a chair across from a desk in what appeared to be an office.

I couldn't remember the details of any of it.

This wasn't just an office, it was the coach's office. Nice. Expensive. A pro-league office. The office of the man who ruled over the Colorado Avalanche.

The coach was there. So was the woman sensitive, and someone in a suit who looked like a lawyer.

"You still with us, Mr. Hazard?" Coach asked as he settled down behind his desk.

I nodded while finishing the drink, my whole body shaking like I was stuck naked in a snowstorm. My stomach was killing me. Yarking up everything I'd just drank looked like a real possibility. I eyed the trash can in the corner behind the coach and estimated my speed and accuracy.

"Do you have more, uh…water?"

My voice was scrubbed out like I'd been yelling for three periods nonstop.

The sensitive reached in her bag and handed me a wrapped bar, heavy with protein and carbs. I'd never tried this kind before. They were formulated for the marked: wizards, sensitives, Canidae shifters, Felidae shifters, and the others. I had made it a point to stay away from all that.

"It will help." Her voice was normal volume, and she wasn't glowing anymore. "I have more."

I shook my head, but my hands were already moving, tearing at the wrapper, shoving half the bar in my mouth.

Instinct to survive. I had it.

Oh, *god* that was good. If someone asked me what it tasted like I'd never be able to tell them, but after a couple chews the bar was gone, my stomach was on the mend, and my shaking was down to a shivery tremble.

"You pulled down a lot of magic," she said sympathetically.

I'd noticed her in the stands during the last few practices. She was in her forties, had soft, dark eyes and was wearing a hijab in the team's colors of burgundy, silver, and blue.

"You will need to rest," she said. "Hydrate. Eat."

I didn't need her pity and didn't want her advice. All I wanted was to forget that stunt I'd just pulled.

Or, better: I wanted everyone to forget about it. I frowned, wondering if there was a magical way to make them forget. Maybe? Yeah, probably.

But should I do that to someone?

"Mr. Hazard?" Coach again. "Random?"

The lawyer guy raised his eyebrows.

Yes, I had a stupid name. I blamed my dad who was probably high when he named me and my mom who didn't change my name because my father committed suicide a week after I was born.

Welcome to the world, kid. You don't have a dad, but hey, here's a stupid name you can keep for the rest of your life.

My mom had been left raising a baby on her own while holding down a couple crappy jobs to try to keep a crappy roof over our heads. The re-naming thing got shoved to the back burner and stayed there.

I'd heard all the jokes. I'd heard all the jeers. I gave the suit a look that invited him to come up with a new one.

"Son?" Coach said again.

Right. My future was at stake here, not my name.

"I'm sorry, Coach. I promise that will never happen again. If you would just give me a chance, I'll never—"

"What you did was a brave thing."

The way he said it, strong and clear, full eye contact, told me he meant it. That was nice. I felt a warm embarrassing *need* for that kind of praise. Praise for my character, not for my magic. But that kind of need was a weakness. It gave away too much of who I was. Or rather who I wanted to be.

I shoved my reaction down and hoped it didn't show on my face.

From the brief pity in Coach's eyes it showed.

Screw my life. Screw it all the way to the wall.

"You saved Mr. Miłosz's life."

"Me-wash?" Huh. So that's how you said it.

"He has a minor concussion from hitting the ice. But that's all. He'll be fine."

"That's good. Really good."

"Mr. Kowalski didn't handle the shock of your...interference quite as gracefully. Still, better a panic attack than involuntary manslaughter charges, eh?" Coach smiled. It looked like he'd bit a hot pepper and couldn't swallow.

Was I supposed to apologize because the defenseman had lost his shit over one harmless spell? It wasn't like I'd conjured a fire-breathing dragon in front of him.

"Sorry?"

Coach shook his head once. "Don't be. I'd have had quite the mess on my hands without your quick thinking and reaction."

"Very quick reaction," the sensitive said. Even the lawyer-guy grunted in agreement.

Okay, whatever. Also, it made me wonder how fast most people threw magic. Anyone could have done what I did, right?

"In any case, while we appreciate your actions and your decision to use magic to save a player's life..."

"No," I said.

"...I will not allow deception in this club." He speared me with a look that was not approving at all. "You lied to us, Mr. Hazard. To this club, to your teammates, to this league."

"I didn't..." My throat closed up, and I swallowed hard. He was not wrong. I had lied. But not just to him, the team,

13

the league. I'd lied to everyone. To myself. "I'm unregistered." It came out like I'd borrowed someone else's voice. Someone broken.

"That explains why your background check came back clean. How long have you known?"

I couldn't speak. I opened my mouth, but couldn't find the words that would slow the freight train full of dynamite roaring down the track of my life.

"Whether this is the first time you've realized you're a wizard, or something you've been hiding for years, is beside the point." That was all coach. No nonsense. No backing down. No mercy.

"There is no room for you in this program."

My stomach knotted and I broke out in a cold sweat.

"Please." I don't know why I thought that one word, sort of whispered, would change his mind. Marked didn't play in the major league of any sport. Marked weren't allowed in the minors either. "I'll do anything."

Something in him shifted. He blew out a breath and wiped a palm over his face. "This isn't..." He tapped the end of his pen on his desk. "You have talent, Random."

It was the first time he'd ever used my first name like that. Friendly. Sympathetic. I wished he'd go back to using my last name like a coach instead.

"Maybe even great talent on the ice. I expect to see you do great things. But not here. Not in the NHL. If you want to play hockey, and as your ex-coach I hope you will continue, you have to do it in the league for your kind."

My kind. Not human kind.

Marked.

Freaks.

Hammer, meet nail. Coffin lid closed for good.

That was it.

I was done. Over.

He stood. I stood. We shook hands. He said something about contacting my agent to dissolve the contract. I told him I understood. Thanked him for his time. Thanked him for the opportunity.

Choked back the apologies, the begging, the pleas. If I was going out, I was going out with my head held high.

I absently wondered how my agent would take finding out I was a wizard. Knew he'd let me go too. There was no money in the league for my kind. No reason for him to keep me. There was no future for me. I was worthless.

In an instant, I was no longer a man, a hockey player, a center with the kind of ice-sense that had people saying I could one day stand with the greats. One day see my name on the Stanley Cup. One day make history.

I was less-than. I was other.

Marked.

Inferior.

There was nothing left for me to do but leave. Leave and try to make sense of what was left of my life.

THERE HAD BEEN A long call from my agent who broke up with me, a plane ride I couldn't remember, and then a car ride from the airport that had just about cleared out the remains of my bank account.

I was broke, broken, and wondering if I still had a home to return to.

I knocked on the bright blue door that looked like it had gotten a new coat of paint recently. It was only when I was standing there for a while that I wondered what time it was.

With the morning cloud cover—not that unusual for July in Portland, Oregon—it was barely light. So it must have been just after dawn.

Too early to unload my troubles on anyone.

But I didn't know where else to go. I turned and sat on the porch, leaning against the side of the house, numb, nauseous, and exhausted.

The slide and click of locks behind me broke into the quiet.

I could feel more than hear the door open.

"Random?"

I looked over my shoulder.

The man who had always seemed as tall as a tree in my childhood still stood four inches above my disappointing five-foot-ten. He was lean and neat as a librarian, his straw-brown hair cut short without even a flash of silver in it yet. He peered at me from his small wire-rimmed glasses, his navy blue bathrobe draped over a T-shirt and flannel pants.

"Hey, Mr. Spark. Sorry it's so early."

He nodded like it was perfectly normal to find me, unannounced, on his doorstep before the sun was up. It hadn't been all that unusual for me to wind up on his porch like a lost Frisbee when I was a kid. But I wasn't a kid anymore.

"Come on in. I don't know why you knocked. You still have a key don't you?"

Did I? Yeah, now that he mentioned it, my key ring was somewhere at the bottom of my duffel. "I just...it's been a long day. Long bad day."

He strolled to the kitchen. "Coffee to start?"

I followed him through the living room. "Thanks. Yeah. Okay. Is Duncan home?"

Mr. Spark was my best friend's dad. He'd been the closest thing I had to a father. Duncan, who had told me we were best friends when we met in first grade, was the closest thing I had to a brother.

"He's in his room. Want me to wake him?"

"No, it's early. I just..." I just wanted to know that something in my life was still normal. Like me being here in this house, a part of this family.

Mr. Spark worked at the counter, setting up the coffee pot and filling it with the roast he liked to grind himself. He didn't say anything. His quiet nature was one of the things I'd always liked about him. While Mrs. Spark might scold Duncan and me about leaving our gear all over the living room or for bleeding on her carpet while she simultaneously patched us up and shoved cookies in our faces, Mr. Spark was steady, quiet, and unflappable.

It made me wonder why I'd never told him I was marked. Broken. Less than human.

No, I knew. I hadn't wanted to disappoint him. Hadn't wanted to admit I was that badly flawed.

When the coffee stopped grumbling, he filled two mugs and handed me one with a spoon. He sat across from me at the old reclaimed barn door table, the raw sugar and little pitcher of real cream between us.

Duncan and I had carved our initials in the table legs when we were ten. Mrs. Spark had grounded us. Mr. Spark had complimented us on our penmanship.

"Are you okay?"

I stared at my black coffee, then added two heaping spoons of sugar and a lot of cream. He'd left me just enough room in the cup to make it all work.

He knew me. Had practically raised me. And I was about to tell him I'd been hiding something from him, lying to him all my life.

When someone unofficially adopted you, they couldn't just as easily decide to let you go, right?

"Random?"

"I got kicked off the team."

"Okay. Can you tell me why?"

He didn't demand, didn't instantly assume I'd done something wrong, nor that my privacy wasn't important. If I said I couldn't tell him why I'd been let go, he'd never ask again.

But I had a vague memory of my agent saying he'd make sure the press release was fair to me. I didn't know if that meant it was going to announce to the world that I was secretly a wizard or just that training camp hadn't turned out how I expected and I was no longer being considered by the Avalanche.

"I'm done. I'm out. I can't play anymore. Not in the NHL." The words were clipped and climbing as the panic started kicking in. As the realness of my life started kicking in.

I wanted to yell what I was, shout out my failure. Then never, never say it again.

"Just because one team didn't work out—"

"You don't understand." Panic made my words weird and manic. I was having a breakdown in the middle of the kitchen where my only birthday parties had ever been celebrated.

"Help me understand, Random. I'm listening."

"I'm…I'm n-nothing! I'm stupid. I can't play. I'll never p-play!"

His raised eyebrows and concern that etched lines at his mouth and eyes made me stop. Made me breathe.

I didn't remember standing away from the table. Didn't remember bending my knees, setting my shoulder forward, ready for the hit that would knock me off my skates.

Mr. Spark hadn't moved. He did now, though. He took a sip of his coffee then tipped his head to tell me to keep talking.

What was there left to say?

The truth.

"I'm marked." This came out soft, faint, dead.

I wanted to puke.

His expression didn't change, but his color did. He went flat white before color rushed back to his face.

"You…you're." He ran his fingers through his hair as he swallowed and swallowed.

"I'll go. I can just g-go."

"Random. Son. Sit down and give me a minute. Just. Drink your coffee. Let's both drink our coffee."

It was the *son* that did it. He was the only one who had ever called me that and meant it.

I dropped back into the chair and pulled my cup between my palms.

He lifted his cup, took a drink, his eyes focused at a middle distance.

I couldn't bear to see what he thought about me so I stared at the tablecloth. It was blue with little yellow daisies on it and only covered the middle of the table. I knew he had picked it out.

"First, you don't need to call me Mr. Spark, Random. I like it when you use my first name. Kit likes it too. So let's go back to that, okay?"

I nodded. I hadn't been sure he would still want me to call him Sean.

"Okay, good. Do you want to tell me what happened in Colorado?"

I shook my head.

"Did you shift during camp?"

"I'm not a shifter."

Silence stretched between the snap of the old wall clock's second hand.

"Random? Look at me."

It took everything I had to raise my eyes.

"I love you. Nothing has changed about that. Nothing will ever change that. We'll figure this out. Together."

Tears stung the edges of my eyes. He had told me he loved me ninety-six times. Even though I was twenty-two years old, I had hoarded those words each and every time he'd given them.

He had said them when I was seven and my mother signed over my guardianship to the Sparks. He had said them after he'd caught me sleeping on the hallway floor in front of their bedroom door, again, and I'd admitted it wasn't because it was more comfortable, it was because I was afraid they'd leave in the middle of the night without me. He had said it when I'd been drafted by the Avalanche.

Hearing it now changed everything. Settled everything. Put roots in my shattering world and held it tight.

"Okay?" he asked.

"Okay."

He reached over and patted my forearm.

"Good. So, then. Are you a sensitive?"

"No."

His mouth fell open with a soft, "huh." That was the only indication of how surprised he really was.

"So. Wizard?" he mused. "I don't suppose you have any spells that would keep the English Ivy from taking over my rose beds do you?"

I huffed out a laugh. "I don't know. Maybe?"

He smiled and refilled our mugs from the carafe on the table, then got up to toast a couple bagels. This was normal. My home was still normal. I belonged.

As the mountain of worry lifted off my chest I realized how tired I was.

"Why don't you take this in to Duncan?" He held out a plate of bagels. "I'm going to shower, then we'll go over the details of what happened in Colorado together. Should I expect a call from your agent?"

"I don't know. He said something about a press release. I can't remember."

He placed the plate into my hand. "I'll check into that so we know."

"Thanks. Thanks, Mr…thanks, Sean."

"Ran." He shook his head. "Of course."

I accepted the bagels and his help and walked to Duncan's room on autopilot.

I pushed the door and shuffled through the crumpled mounds of dirty clothes to the lump snoring under the blankets on the bed. I balanced the plate on top of the clutter on his dresser, then crawled onto the other side of his big king-size bed and yanked one of the blankets out of his death grip, wrapping it around me.

My back was toward him and I was fully clothed, hugged up to the edge of the bed. I still had on my shoes. I didn't care.

"Jerk," he mumbled, rolling away from me and hogging all the rest of the blankets.

"You missed me," I said.

I was already asleep before he had a chance to reply.

2

"CAN YOU READ my mind?" Duncan asked. "Quick, what am I thinking?"

"No. And about hockey."

"Whoa."

"You're always thinking about hockey."

"Not always."

"Was I right?"

A grin that reminded me of a dog with a stick spread over his face. "No."

"Liar."

"Can you tell when people are lying?"

I shrugged. "I don't know."

"Can you see the future? The lottery numbers? Can you tell who's going to win the Stanley Cup?"

"No. Yes. No."

His reddish eyebrows dipped down. I'd never really thought he looked much like his dad. He took more after his mom—reddish hair, freckles over pale skin, and a nose that had a bend in the middle of it. But he was tall like his dad. With a lot more muscle and wide shoulders that made him intimidating on the ice.

"Wait? Really? You know what the lottery numbers are going to be? Why haven't you said so? Oh, wait. That's right. You've been a lying jerk all your life." He didn't have to lean over the table much to punch me in the shoulder.

He did get his height from his dad—a disgustingly unfair six foot three.

I didn't bother dodging the hit, though I totally could have. The smooth plastic tables at Burgerville USA weren't that wide. But I wasn't about to risk spilling my marionberry milkshake if he decided to follow up the missed punch with a tackle.

It had happened before. More than once. In public.

He was a second-marked: Canidae shifter.

"Shut up," I said. "Who taught you to hit? A three-year-old?"

"You taught me to hit, idiot."

I had too. Duncan had always been bigger than me, nicer than me, more patient than me. He'd gotten teased in first grade for being a wolf shifter. After one too many dog jokes, I'd spent a week convincing him he should fight back, then all weekend teaching him how to land a punch.

We'd both had to wear long sleeved shirts to school for the next few days, because we'd taken the "who can hit the hardest" thing a little too gleefully.

"What did you think I was going to do, Ran? Hate you because we had something *more* in common?"

"I'm not a shifter."

"No, but you're marked. Like me." He shoved the rest of his burger into his mouth, chewed. "Didn't you ever want to tell anyone? Tell me? You could have told me."

The hurt in his voice hit me harder than his punches ever had. I stared at my purple milkshake and felt sick.

"I just wanted to play hockey."

The guitar riff of *Miserlou* piped through the place and Duncan tapped his thumb on the table to the beat.

"You can play hockey if you're marked. I do."

I picked up my straw wrapper and smashed it into a tighter ball. "Not pro."

"And that was worth it? A chance at the NHL was worth lying to…everyone?"

"It wasn't lying."

He snorted.

"I don't use magic. Well, only twice before. That's it. I thought as long as I didn't use it, I was still human, you know? Maybe if I got the chance to play in the NHL, to prove I was good, I'd tell people? Show them a marked can play the same as anyone else. Can play better."

Those clear hazel eyes stared at me, unrelenting, pinning me to my bones. He'd been doing that more now that we were in our twenties. It was so self-assured it was a little disconcerting from a guy who had figured out how to laugh two different colors of Kool-Aid out his nostrils.

It was a boss look, a coach look. Like he was top of the pile and you weren't. It wasn't mean, just...strong.

"You weren't ever going to say anything to anyone."

"You don't know that. I was going to say something. Maybe when I retired. Or...hell. Fine!" I tossed the little ball of paper into the puddle of mustard on my hamburger wrapper.

"I wanted to tell you. I would have told you. I would have."

"You've had a few thousand chances to do it. Why didn't you?"

"I hate what I am."

"And me?"

"What?"

"You hate me too? Hate all us freaks?" His voice was dead level now. Like he was used to hearing the answer to this. Maybe not used to hearing it from me, but like he knew what was coming.

Except he didn't.

"Don't be stupid, Duncan. You're not a freak. I don't hate you. I've never hated you. I don't care that you're marked. I've never cared about that."

"But you're too good for it? Too good to be infected like someone like me?"

"No." I stared at the fries I wasn't going to finish. "I'm not too good. I'm...crap for lying to my best friend for my entire life. To everyone for my entire life. So that's crap. I'm crap.

"I didn't want anyone to think I used magic to get what I wanted. To play. I'm not even something cool like a shifter. Or useful like a sensitive. Who wants a wizard in hockey? Fragile, skinny, breakable, useless wizards."

"You are not fragile," he practically growled. He flicked a finger at my burger basket. "But you are skinny. Eat your fries."

"Shut up, moose. Wizards only make good doctors and counselors and school teachers. Wizards only make good artists and musicians and cheerleaders."

"Cheerleaders?"

"Lucy Trapp in senior year?"

"Oh, yeah." He gave a dreamy sigh. "Yes. Wizards should always be cheerleaders."

"Wizards don't play sports. They're as non-physical as possible. They're walking magic dispensers that make weird shit happen, you know? Brainy nerds. But I just...I just want to play hockey."

"So you lied."

The music moved on to something slower and the milkshake felt like a rock in my gut. I was starting to think lunch was a terrible idea. Maybe coming home wasn't that great of an idea either.

Mr. and Mrs. Spark, I mean Sean and Kit, told me over and over that I was still welcome in their home. Kit had hugged me so hard with her rugby arms, I'd thought I'd bruise. They wanted me here, but I wasn't so sure about Duncan.

"Does your mom know?" He pushed my basket closer to me again.

I leaned back in the metal chair and shook my head. If she knew, she had never talked to me about it. Of course, she would have had to be around enough for us to actually have a full conversation. She'd checked out of my life as fast as she could. I hadn't seen her in four years. Hadn't talked to her in three.

Since I had been smaller than Duncan when we first met, he had shoved all his old hockey stuff at me and insisted I was going to play the game with him.

Sean, who had competed in short track speed skating, had agreed. He had taught me how to skate and signed me up right alongside Duncan for our first Mite league. Hockey became my everything. It was where I belonged. It was where I was challenged to be better than I was. It was my brotherhood and my family.

Until this year when I'd been called to the Avalanche's training camp. Then it had been my dream come true.

I'd had a shot at the NHL.

And I'd screwed it up.

"Does she?" Duncan repeated.

"I never told her. I don't do magic, so I don't think she knows."

"Giant wall of color solid enough to stop a puck sound familiar? Ran? Random? Dude. Stop staring at your food, it's weird."

I glanced back up at him. He was still mad at me, but there was something else in his eyes. Curiosity. Maybe something more.

"Okay, I did that magic," I admitted.

"And twice before."

"Yes."

"And you never told anyone."

"No."

"Not even my dad?"

"No."

"How did you?" He waved his hands around as if trying to shake the words out of the air. "How did you keep it a secret so long? There had to be a million times it would have been so easy to use it. A million times you could have used it for something awesome."

"I knew it would ruin my life." I tried to smile, but it sort of drooped off my lips into a frown. "And it did."

Duncan inhaled a breath so hard, his nostrils flared.

I got ready for the yelling.

He exhaled and choked on a laugh. "You look like the saddest bunny in sad bunny town."

"Saddest *what*?"

"Big blue eyes. Fluffy ears. Where's your fancy top hat house, sad bunny?"

"Screw you. My ears do not fluff. If anyone's ears fluff around here, it's yours."

His face broke into a grin that was all teeth. "That was a terrible comeback. C'mon. Let's hit the ice until we can't think straight."

"Now? You want to skate now? Weren't we busy telling me I suck?"

"Naw. You don't suck. You're just stupid sometimes. Plus, you got somewhere else to be? Some *bunny* waiting for you?"

That was the problem when one's life was over. One's calendar was pretty much open. "You're gonna pay for the bunny thing."

"Oh, I'm *so* scared."

"You will be once you're on the ice. I was an Avalanche."

He stood, popped three of my French fries in his mouth. "For what? Two seconds at a training camp? Then you just couldn't keep it in your pants, could you? All that magical power. You just had to save a guy's life. Seriously, Random. You saved a guy's life. That's worth something. That's worth everything, isn't it?"

It was. That was why I'd saved the guy.

"I hate you," I said.

"I hate you too, buddy. Honk-honk."

"Did you just quote the were-car episode of Futurama at me?"

"My gut says, maybe. Let's go hit something." He grinned some more, pushed my milkshake into my hand. When I stood up, he looped an arm around my neck.

Together, one guy too tall, one guy too short, he steered us out through the door and into the sunny day.

3

ONCE MY SKATES HIT the ice, the world and all my problems faded away. It was just me. No magic. No worries.

Just breathing, sweating, pushing. Speed and power and the puck on the end of my stick making me whole. Making me right.

Making me free.

Duncan had packed our gear before we left for lunch so we didn't have to rent anything. The skating center was scheduled for an hour open skate, and half a dozen hockey players of various ages took up a third of the ice. The rest of the rink was occupied by figure skaters.

It was a little crowded, a little run-down, but with Duncan at my left, and a net ahead of me, it was life, warmth, sanctuary.

We worked lazy drills, falling into familiar patterns. His slap shot had improved since I'd been gone for the last two months, but he was still crap at defending my moves. I could juke and dangle, slipping the puck between his skates, around his stick, and catching it half way across the ice before he even knew I was moving.

But passing a puck across the ice together? Oh, yeah. We were a thing of legend.

Backhand pass, saucer pass, drop pass, tape to tape, we always knew where the other person was on the ice.

I stopped by the boards for a bottle of water. As I drank, a soft whistling caught my ear. It was a low, moody melody, kind of slow and catchy.

I looked around for whoever had just given me an earworm and spotted a guy in the first row of the stands. He lounged in his seat, lanky legs stretched out in front of him. He wore cowboy boots and faded jeans with holes in them that looked like they'd been worn out from honest work, not as a fashion statement.

His hair was dark brownish, so was his close-cut beard. His eyes, even from this distance, were as pale and faded as his jeans, but instead of blue they were the lightest brown I'd ever seen. I thought he might be in his thirties.

He was watching Duncan and me. Only us, and when he caught my eye, he tipped his chin down once in greeting.

Then he started whistling that song again, absently, as if he didn't realize he was doing it.

His St. Louis Blues T-shirt hugged his flat stomach and showed off the muscles in his shoulders, chest and arms. He was fit and looked all kinds of comfortable here, as if this was his second home.

I might not be able to spot a shifter in a crowd, but I knew a hockey player when I saw one.

"You know him?" I asked when Duncan stopped next to me.

"Who?" Duncan downed half his water, then poured the rest over his face. I pushed back to avoid the sprinkler action as he shook.

"The whistler."

Duncan scanned the stands. Finally landed on the guy. "Looks familiar, doesn't he?" He sniffed the air like he could identify the whistler by scent.

And, yeah, maybe he could. Wolf shifters were like that. He tipped his head to one side.

"I've seen him before. Too old for WHL or ECHL. Could be AHL. Coach? Scout? Local?"

"Dunno. Hockey though," I said.

"Obviously. Why's he staring at us?"

"Like I care."

Maybe now that I'd used magic everyone could see it on me. Maybe I stuck out like a sore thumb. A wizard playing hockey.

That wasn't the kind of attention I wanted.

"Let's find out." Duncan powered off across the ice. Just like every other time in our lives, I followed right behind him.

The man saw us coming, but didn't move. Just watched with pale sand-colored eyes.

"Hey," Duncan said. "You got a problem with us?"

That was Duncan. Friendly and blunt and always straight to the throat of the matter.

Those eyes weighed us as if he were trying to fit all of our details into a very small box.

"Not a problem," he said.

I'd expected a cowboy drawl out of him, and I got it. I wasn't great at accents, but I thought maybe Kentucky, or Texas. I couldn't really tell the difference.

"You're the wizard, aren't you?"

Oh. Great. My screw-up was already big enough for someone to recognize me.

"Naw, man." Duncan played it cool. "You must be thinking of somebody else."

"Don't think so." The guy's gaze shifted to me. Intense, hard. "That was you I saw on the video clip. Avalanche training camp."

"There's a video?" I squeaked.

Duncan pushed in front of me, all shoulders and height and attitude. "You got a problem with him? You got a problem with me, buddy."

That startled me. Duncan wasn't the kind of guy who fell into fists at first sight. Ever.

"Whoa, hold on." I grabbed at his sleeve, yanked. "It's cool, Dunc. People are going to see...whatever they see."

I tried not to freak out. I knew there would be a record of what I'd done. The team filmed practices so they could go over the footage and talk to players about how to improve. I just didn't expect it to be released to the public.

"Are you a reporter?" I wished I still had an agent to handle this stuff.

"He doesn't have anything to say to you," Duncan snarled.

The guy smiled, but it was no more than a slight quirk of his mouth.

He thought this was funny?

"Easy, boys." His voice soothed and vibrated somewhere beneath my range of hearing. "I don't have a problem with either of you. I said that once. I meant that. This is good ice, a good day, and good conversation. Didn't mean to give you the wrong idea."

He stood and clomped over to stand in front of Duncan. He held out his hand like he was calming something that was about to bite.

His sleeve slipped up enough to show the edge of a tattoo. Black ink with a slash of red. His hand was steady, his voice calm, eyes on Duncan and only Duncan.

"My name's Hawthorn Graves. Folks call me Graves."

Duncan stared at his hand like he wasn't sure if he should shake it or hit it.

What was up with him?

I punched him in the shoulder. Duncan grunted. I pushed to one side so he wasn't blocking my view, his body between me and Graves like I needed protecting.

Duncan finally took Graves's hand and shook. "Duncan Spark. Call me anything you want."

Graves, nodded. "Nice to meet you, Duncan." He didn't seem dangerous. Just curious and relaxed.

Duncan settled, his shoulders losing that stiff angle, his chin tipping upward just the slightest amount, like he was going to bare his throat, though I didn't think he realized what he was doing.

"Random Hazard." I offered my hand.

Graves didn't so much as crack a smile at my stupid name, which either meant he'd already known it, or he didn't get the joke. "People call me Ran. I'm Hazard on the ice."

That got a smile out of him. "You've said that a time or two, haven't you?"

"Gotta embrace your weird, right?" I'd used that reply a million times, and it suddenly seemed hypocritical. "You play hockey?"

"I do. Got picked up by the Thunderheads late last season. Hope to put down roots here. Make my last stand. You like this facility better than the one south a ways?"

I nodded. "They're both good. That one's newer, but this one's closer to where we live, so we come here more."

"The Thunderheads practice here," Duncan added as if he wanted the guy to pay attention to him again.

"Sure." He said it like *shore*. "Just wondered which rink you liked best during public skate. Since you're local."

Duncan grinned like the guy had just told him he could eat all the extra fries.

"What's it like?" Duncan asked. "Playing for the Boomers?"

"It's good. Hard work. Coach Clay is...well he's odd, but he knows how to steer a team."

"I watch every Thunderheads game," Duncan said. "I don't remember you on the ice."

"Played three games total in March. Which is why I'm not sure they're going to pick me up this year."

Duncan had been sick for part of March, and also had forgotten to record some of his favorite shows. So it made sense that he'd missed a game or two.

"Well, good luck," I said. "They played really solid last year."

The Thunderheads were part of the Western Hybrid Hockey League, or WHHL, which everyone shortened to West Hell. In the early days the WHHL had been little more than an excuse for blood and guts and violence on the ice. The kind of violence that only shifters and retired goons could dish out.

West Hell was the freak league of hockey. Gladiatorial anything goes kind of hockey.

Except for the last five years. Things were slowly changing. West Hell was playing hockey more and bleeding less. Games were starting to look like games. Exciting. Fast. Skillful.

Though it was still ten times more violent than pro hockey.

"Well, I don't want to take up you boys' ice time. Nice meeting you both." He gave us a short nod and rambled down to the exit.

We watched him the entire way, Duncan with the head tip that I wasn't going to tell him made him look like a puppy.

"Think he played offense?" Duncan asked.

"I bet he's defense. Shifter?"

Duncan tipped his head the other way. I coughed to cover a laugh. "Yes? But."

I waited. He was quiet for a long time.

"But?"

"But something." He shook his head. "He's. I dunno. Something. Hey, time's almost up. I'm starving."

"You just ate, you bottomless hole."

"A single burger and fries. Two hours ago. Besides, the dinkies are here."

Squeaky little kid voices bounced off the rafters as a class that looked like a troop of girl scouts zipped out onto the ice in a flurry of pinks, purple, camo, and skulls.

"Let's get out of here before we accidentally squish one," he said.

We made our way to the lockers and Graves's words echoed around in my head. He was putting down roots. Making a stand. I wanted to put down roots too. Not in a city, but in a league.

I wanted my life to start. The one I'd worked for, the one I'd fought for.

But that was done now. Over.

It sucked to think all I had to look forward to now was hobby skating and pickup games. Stealing an hour of ice time between grade schoolers.

I didn't want to play pickup hockey.

The blood in me, the breath in me, my bones and brains, were all made to compete. To prove myself against my peers and betters.

I wanted to play hockey competitively. Hard. For keeps.

I wanted to make my stand.

Grow roots.

By the time we reached Duncan's car my mood had gone to shit.

The Chevy Vega groaned to life and Duncan babied it into gear, muttering as he did so. It was ancient and had been given to him when he was sixteen in lieu of payment for mowing an old lady's yard all summer.

He loved that old wreck.

The car, not the old lady.

"You owe me," he said as the car rattled forward an inch at a time.

"What are you talking about?"

"For lying to me. You owe me something in return."

I rubbed at the headache spreading behind my eyes. The early evening sky was a perfect bright blue, the temperature mild and breezy. Summer day all around while I was nothing but storm inside.

"Seriously, Ran."

"An apology isn't enough?"

"You didn't apologize."

"Oh."

Duncan stomped on the gas trying to gain some speed for the hills that were ahead of us. The Vega gave it a go, but the fastest it had ever gone was the short trip it had taken rolling off the assembly line.

"I'm sorry for lying to you."

"All these years."

"All these years," I added.

"And you owe me something for that."

"Fine. Okay, fine. I owe you for lying." I held tighter to the door handle to keep the door from popping open. The Vega shook like a washing machine full of bricks.

"Fine," he said.

The car topped out at forty miles an hour and was rattling so hard there were two roads ahead of us instead of one. Somehow Duncan could tell which lane was the right one to be in.

I clung to the frame of the window and reviewed my drop-and-roll technique in case the car flew apart.

"It was good, right?" he sort of shouted once we'd topped the hill.

My ears were ringing but at least the engine was quieter when it was coasting.

"What?"

"Today. On the ice. It was good being out there together. Like it used to be. You and me, the puck, the ice. Except I'm so much better than you now, of course."

I didn't know what he was getting at. Maybe he was trying to shake my bad mood and headache.

Duncan was ultrasensitive to the mood of his pack, and he'd adopted me as his pack early. He knew me better than anyone.

"You're, you know, not too bad for a big, clumsy, slow, stupid guy," I said.

He grinned and flipped me off. "I'm beautiful on the ice and you know it."

I snorted. "Sure you are, buddy. Like fine art. You gonna tell me what I owe you?"

His grin didn't fade, but he kept his eyes on the roads ahead and hit the gas. We went slower.

"Later," he said.

All right. He had the metaphorical ball in his mouth. I'd just have to wait until he dropped it.

"That Graves guy." He frowned.

"Yeah?"

"Something about him."

"You said that before."

"What did he look like to you?"

"I already told you. D-man. Southern. Texas, Kentucky maybe? I thought he was…I don't know, a reporter, but when we got closer, he seemed nice enough."

"Just enough?"

"I think he'd be intimidating on the ice. There's something sort of quiet about him. Like that one second between pushing the red button and *boom*."

"Yeah," Duncan said. "That. He's got *boom*."

"So do you, Donut. I thought you were going to give him a black eye."

"If he hassled you, I would have."

"Look at you. Alpha male all up in here. You're making me shiver."

He rolled his eyes. "You suck. We're no longer friends."

"You love me. Who else gives you extra fries?"

"I can get my own fries. You should eat more."

"I eat. If you're gonna give me shit for being a skinny wizard, I'm going to get out of this car right now, walk around to your door and punch you."

"I'm not stopping the car."

"The speed this thing goes, you wouldn't have to."

That got a laugh out of him.

Me too.

And just like that, my mood was better.

MR. SPARK KNEW HOW to make a mean lasagna. He put mushrooms in it and fresh garlic and so much cheese I salivated just thinking about it.

The amazing smell hit me in the face as soon as we opened the door. I groaned.

"Lasagna? Is that lasagna?"

Duncan flopped down on the couch and nodded. "And garlic on sourdough." Heightened sense of smell was another thing he got from his wolf side.

No one knew why magic infected people in different ways. The whole shifting thing had been a shock and a horror back in the day. Not that people were particularly comfortable or proud about it now.

Most shifters fell into two categories: Felidae shifters— all kinds of cats—and Canidae shifters—all kinds of dogs.

Science argued more people should shift into animals closer to human DNA, like chimpanzees and, I don't know, pigs or something.

But science hadn't unlocked the puzzle of magically infected DNA. They were still generating more questions than answers.

The majority of marked shifters went feline or canine. There were a few exceptions. An occasional bear or badger or warthog, but mostly it was cat or dog.

I dropped down on the couch next to Duncan. He messed with the remote, pulling up the hockey channel to see if there was any news.

He had crap timing. The clip—a cell phone video—of me casting a spell in the middle of the neutral zone scrolled across the screen. The video tracked the wall of magic, colors swirling and thick like paint pouring from the ceiling. Then all that paint, all that sound, shattered and disappeared.

I hadn't realized it had only stood there for four, maybe five seconds. In my head that wall of magic had lingered for hours.

Duncan was stiff. Silent. Didn't look over at me.

"You can ask," I said, not looking at him either.

"Is it always so beautiful?"

Okay, that was not what I thought he'd say.

"It's always colors."

"And music?"

"Yeah."

"Do you have to memorize spells and Latin, Mr. Potter?"

"I don't know. My owl got lost in the mail."

He chortled. "Nerd. So how does it work?"

"I just…think of what I need to happen and it happens."

"What about the other two times you used magic?"

"Does it matter?"

He turned and gave me that even, hard gaze. "It matters to me."

"Is this what I owe you for lying?"

"No."

I didn't have to tell him. But he was my best friend. Who else could I share this with?

"A bicyclist was almost hit by a car backing out of a driveway."

"When?"

"Fifth grade."

"Where were you?"

"Walking to school. Your dad took you to a dentist appointment that morning. So I walked."

"Okay. What happened?"

"The guy on the bike didn't see the car. I think the lady in the car couldn't see out of the windows. It was raining."

"And?"

"I wanted the car to stop. I wanted the bike to stop. I knew if I yelled they wouldn't stop. Wouldn't hear me."

I picked at the seam on the arm of the couch. It was a weird plaid color. Mr. Spark loved it. Mrs. Spark had been caught holding lit candles and gas cans too close to it on more than one occasion.

He waited for me to finish.

"I made the engine stop running. I made the bike tires stop spinning."

"With magic."

"With magic. It tangled in the tires, sounded like wind chimes caught in a storm. It flooded the engine and poured out of the hood, silver with oil rainbows. When it hit the ground it sounded like slapped cello strings."

"Did it work?"

"Yeah. They didn't see me. I ran and hid behind a bunch of garbage cans. I snapped the spells off as quickly as I could."

And got so sick I passed out for a half hour. Showed up to school late. I didn't tell him that part.

"Jesus, Ran. You saved his life. That makes two people you've saved."

I shrugged, picked at the stitches. They were strong and unfrayed even though I knew the Sparks had had this couch for years. Mrs. Spark said it was too ugly to die.

"Was the other time saving someone's life too?"

"Maybe? No. Not really. He stumbled off the trail. I just made sure there was something there to catch his foot, to push him back up from the cliff."

"Cliff?"

"When we hiked the falls in sophomore year."

"Who?"

"Brian Setter."

He was watching me. He narrowed his eyes. "You got sick. I remember that. You barfed all over your hiking boots. I sat with you on the trail for almost an hour until you could move. I thought you had the flu. Or were dehydrated."

"You gave me your water and let me eat your trail bar."

"Yeah. And it was one of the heavy ones. In case I shifted." He shook his head. "I cannot believe I didn't realize you had just used magic. I know the signs. I've *lived* the signs. Jesus."

"There was no reason for you to think it was me. And there weren't any sensitives close enough to notice the magic."

"Plus Gary Towns shifted and went running into the forest. They couldn't get him out of the tree. Hilarious."

I smiled. "That was funny. Didn't he get suspended for a month?"

"And kicked off the football team."

"He should have come down out of the tree the first time they asked him. Coach Ricker probably would have let him stay on the team."

High school sports were mixed. Integrated. But that's where the tolerance ended. After high school there were no mixed college games. No mixed pro.

"Are those the only times?"

"Yes." I put my hand over my heart. "You now know all of my secrets."

"Okay." He went back to watching the clips from various training camps.

"You going to tell me what I owe you?" I asked after we both sat silently through a report listing the ten best rookie plays of the day. No one from the Avalanche. I wasn't sure what I thought about that.

It should be me. I should be on the rookie highlight reel.

"Not yet," Duncan said.

"Dinner's going to be ready in an hour, boys." Mr. Spark, I mean, Sean leaned through the living room doorway. "Kit will be home about then. Maybe you could hit the showers?"

"Do we stink?" I lifted an arm, took a sniff.

Sean just raised one eyebrow. "In a word—yes. Clean up, come on out. Random, it's your turn to set the table."

Duncan lingered, but I got up and headed toward the bathroom he and I shared.

"Ran?"

"Yeah?"

"You did the right thing with magic. All those times. When it mattered, you did the amazing thing. I'm glad you did it, even if you hated it."

"Thanks, Donuts." I gave him back the serious nod he offered me, then turned to the shower.

I needed to wash off the sweat, the bad mood, and the lie. Because Duncan was wrong. I didn't hate using magic. Even though each time I'd used it I'd been terrified of it, I liked using magic. Liked how it made me feel.

Liked it too much.

DINNER WAS UTTERLY NORMAL and because of that, fantastic. Not for the first time in my life I crossed my fingers under the table and made a wish that this wouldn't be the last time I got to sit at this table with these people.

Mr. and Mrs. Spark kept the conversation going. About her job at the hospital, about his at the library. About Duncan and me bumming around today.

And then about Duncan's prospects.

"You're trying out where?" I'd heard Sean say it; I just couldn't believe Duncan hadn't brought it up.

"Portland's very own Thunderheads," Kit said. Her red hair was pulled back in a braid, which made the freckles on her high cheekbones and nose even brighter. She was wearing her after-work comfy outfit: yoga pants and an oversized, colorful T-shirt. "WHHL. Right here in our own backyard. It's exciting."

She was proud of him. I could hear it in her voice. I could see the pride in Sean's eyes too.

The Portland team was part of the long-neglected joke of a league that was finally trying to dig itself up out of blood sport level play. They played by NHL rules and regulations except for one thing: anyone could try out. And that included the marked.

There was always room for thugs and sinners in West Hell.

"I haven't made the team yet," Duncan said around a mouthful of garlic toast.

"But you're going to try out, right?" I asked. "Have you been invited? Why didn't you tell me? When is it?"

"He was invited to try out," Sean said. "We sent a video of his work to Coach Clay and got a letter back."

"Holy shit, Donut! That's awesome!" I punched him in the shoulder.

"Hell yeah, I'm awesome!" He was smiling so wide, he almost lost his bread.

"Gross," Kit scolded. "Manners, you heathens."

"I have tomorrow off." Sean scooped more salad on his plate and offered to do the same for his wife. "Thought I'd go with Duncan and watch. You should come with me, Random. Give him tips."

"Like he knows hockey better than me," Duncan scoffed.

"I think he's got this," I said. "He doesn't need me there."

"No!" Duncan looked panicked. "I didn't mean you can't be there. You're gonna be there. You *have* to be there. You're just not going to tell me what to do."

"Maybe I have plans for the day." I watched Duncan squirm. Why was he so nervous?

"*Do* you have plans?" Sean asked mildly.

Everyone knew I had nothing planned for...well, for pretty much the rest of my life. I needed to pick up a hobby just so I could say I was busy instead of telling the truth.

I didn't know if I could just go sit in the stands like a...like a bystander and watch Duncan make the hockey team. I mean, I wanted him to make it and I was happy for him, but hockey was still a big ole magical pain in my life right now.

"No," I said. "No plans."

"Well, then," Sean said like that was settled.

"Fine. Okay. I'll go with you."

"You will?" Duncan sounded relieved.

"To see my best friend make the bigs? Duh."

"Hey. Just because it's not the NHL." Duncan scowled.

"I didn't mean it like that. West Hell is big, Duncan. Especially for guys like you. Like...us."

The table went quiet. I shoved salad in my face and chewed. Sean cleared his throat. We still weren't quite used to me admitting my wizardliness.

"Well, then it's settled. Random will come with us in the morning."

"Are you going to make it, Mom?" Duncan asked.

"I've got shift until 2:00. I'll be there as soon as I can. Promise."

"Good. Okay. Good." Duncan went back to eating, but even from across the table, I could tell how happy he was.

4

THE THING I COULDN'T figure out was why I had to put on my skates. But if Duncan had been nervous last night, he was in full-out panic mode this morning.

If not for me and Mr. Spark making sure he ate, hydrated, and put on pants, he would have never made it to the arena on time.

Or clothed.

He wasn't freaked out enough that his eyes were doing that glowing-wolf thing, but the sweat covering his forehead was soaking through his Volcanoes baseball cap.

And then the weirdness started.

I had to put on my skates. I had to change into my gear.

Duncan refused to get on the ice unless I got on it with him.

"I wasn't invited," I said for the millionth time.

I was on the edge of the ice, right before the tryouts I was not going to try out, feeling stupid and conspicuous. "You seriously don't need me to hold your hand, Dunc. You're all grown up now." I wiped fake tears from under my eyes and sniffed. "My little boy."

He rolled his eyes.

"It doesn't matter if you were invited or not," he growled. "This is an open tryout, you dork. Anyone can be on the ice. You're going to be on the ice. You're not going to leave me alone on the ice. You can't, Ran. You're doing this. If I'm doing this, you're doing this. You have to."

"I'm not trying out for the Portland Thunderheads."

"Yes. You are." Suddenly Duncan's nerves and panic were gone, replaced by that steely resolve. The wolf I rarely saw him lose control over slipped through, eyes flashing an eerie green before they went back to their normal hazel. He locked his jaw in that way that meant he was in for the long fight. That he would do anything to win.

I hated that look.

"No, I'm not."

"You promised."

"When did I promise that I would try out for the Thunderheads?"

"I said you owed me something for lying and you agreed to give it to me. This is that something."

"Trying out for West Hell is not something someone does to apologize for a lie!"

"A lie they've been living their entire life? Since he and his best friend were in first grade, Random?"

I hated that tone too. It was the one that said he wasn't above fighting dirty.

"You can't make this kind of decision for my life." It wasn't much of an argument. He'd been making these kinds of decisions for my life since first grade. Well, when it came to hockey. He was the one who had insisted I try it. He had not been wrong about how much I would love it.

But I hadn't really thought about the WHHL. That had always been Duncan's dream. My dream was the NHL. This might be a good idea, but I wasn't ready for it, hadn't thought it through.

It was happening too fast.

"You have to try out. That's it. If they offer you a spot?" His eyes went a little hard and he lifted his hands palm up. "You can always turn it down and do that *other* thing you want to do with your life. Right? Oh, wait. There is no other thing."

I stood there, anger building like dry kindling in my chest, ready for a flame. He was being an ass. He was also not wrong. I wanted hockey and this was a way, maybe the only way left, to get it.

"Or," he said, wrapping one hand around the back of my neck and bending down so that our faces were even because he was stupidly tall. "You could impress the hell out of them, prove how good you really are, and be the first damn wizard to win the Broughton Cup and take home a hockey championship."

The kindling in my chest burst into an inferno of hope.

I wanted that. I wanted to fight hard and work hard and play hard. I wanted to be on a team and play hockey with everything I was.

I wanted to show the world, or at least the NHL, that a wizard wasn't less, wasn't flawed. Wasn't something other than human.

Those emotions hit me like a hard wind. Strong enough I had to breathe heavy to catch my breath.

Magic didn't push at me. Not often, but right here, with the possibility of hockey almost in my grasp, I could feel it, tempting, sweet, needy. Telling me I could make things happen. Telling me I could make things happen my way.

I was good at hiding magic, even better at denying it. I'd been doing it all my life.

Duncan raised his eyebrows in challenge. "Step up, Houdini. Show them what you got." He grinned and skated away from me.

My heart beat fast, faster and the rhythm pounded like a chant: *hock-ey, hock-ey, hock-ey.*

I could play. I could strive and fight and battle and win.

I could do it with Duncan at my side, just like he had always been.

This could be my team. My family.

All I had to do was outskate, and out-play every other person on the ice.

I glanced back at the stands, immediately zeroing in on Sean. Had he known about this? Would he approve?

He smiled and held up a sheet of paper and pen. The tryout forms. He tipped his head in question, for that moment looking so much like his son, I almost laughed.

I'd been set up. Ganged up on by the Sparks. I wouldn't be surprised if Kit was in on it too. It had probably been her idea to begin with.

They all wanted me to play. They knew how important it was to me.

And family always had each other's backs.

I nodded.

Sean gave me a thumbs up, then started filling out my paperwork.

I turned and took a full three minutes to watch the other players on the ice, my heart pounding with excitement.

And then I joined the fray.

5

COACH CLAY WAS LIGHT-haired, blue-eyed, and had the kind of sunshine intensity I'd expect from a surfer. Physically, I could see the retired forward in him. Fit, muscled, and tall. He'd played right wing through his college league, his skill ignored by the NHL because he was a Felidae shifter. Snow leopard.

Which meant he'd played in the WHHL when it had been nothing more than a freak league, filling the venues with promises of men turning into wild animals that got into blood-spilling, bone-breaking fights. Literally.

It did happen. Shifters had to fight to control the magic that wanted to shape their bodies. Stress made that control more slippery. So did anger, aggression, violence, competition. High emotion.

Contact sports triggered shifts on an almost regular basis.

Contact sports like hockey.

Ten years ago, the WHHL, and its sister leagues, the SHHL, EHHL, and NHHL, were mocked as staged theatrics instead of an actual sport. Rumors that the coaches and players were on the take and could be bought off to throw games were common. Most events never made it through all three periods, dissolving into fights that closed the venue down.

Allegations that players received money for not only shifting, but also causing life-threatening injuries hit the headlines every week.

Players had become famous for that sort of thing. Teams reveled in their bloody theatrics.

Basically, it had been a shit show.

But that started to change five years ago when a right winger named Clay, and an old defenseman named Beauchamp, somehow got enough money together along with a cake mogul/part-time politician named Franklin, to buy the Portland Thunderheads. The team had been on the brink of folding.

Clay had been thirty-five and Beauchamp had been fifty-five. Neither of them had been rich, but they'd pulled some favors from friends who had money and Franklin had pitched in the rest.

They put a lot of effort into cleaning up the team's image, requiring community service and charitable involvement from players. They kicked a lot of players off the roster, and only kept those who could not only hold their own physically, but who could also *play*.

It hadn't been a smooth transition. The WHHL's reputation still wasn't all that stellar. A lot of players hated and resented Coach Clay and Assistant Coach Beauchamp.

But they'd single-handedly turned the Thunderheads into a real team that played hard, old-school hockey by the rules and *won* despite the fights that still broke out on the ice.

That pretty much shamed the other teams in the league to step it up.

When the word got out that the team's roster was full of top-notch NHL-level marked hockey players, along with actual retired NHL players, the stands filled steadily. With the growing audience came money and advertising to keep the team going.

It hadn't taken long for other teams to decide they wanted a piece of that success. Except for a few holdouts, the other teams were following the Boomer's example: cleaning up, bringing in players with talent, and coaches and trainers who cared more about hockey than the freak show.

Five years of good, hard hockey was slowly pushing the league toward something that almost resembled a respectable competition.

It still wasn't enough to abolish the reputation from all the previous years, and there were still coaches and players who liked the league the old way, but it was a hell of a start toward something new. Something better.

Coach Clay and Assistant Coach Beauchamp might look like a surfer and an old leather daddy biker, but they were pretty much legends.

And that's why the open tryout was insane.

I put my head down and did the work, lost myself to the burn of excitement and determination and competition. I knew Duncan was going to make the team. They'd specifically invited him, which meant they'd seen him play. He'd been scouted, and that almost certainly meant he'd get picked.

If I had anything to say about it, I was going to make it too.

I didn't know how long Graves had been on the ice, but when we broke up into smaller teams, he was in front of me at the face-off.

I grinned. "Don't break a hip, old man."

"Blow me, Harry Potter."

What?

He was fast. And strong.

My stupid shock at his insult gave him the edge and he won the face-off. It should have made me angry, but he laughed, and I swore, grinning the entire time.

I loved this game. Even when I lost it.

Later, when Graves winged by, whistling that same haunting tune from the other day, I found myself humming it. Duncan was humming it too. I'd catch a few bars of it from other players, heard it whistled briefly by a goalie, caught it started and finished as it was passed between people, cut sharp by shortened breath, panted out in stuttered notes.

Those of us who caught that song seemed to fall into a smoother rhythm with the puck, with each other, as if there was something tying us together: a rhythm, a beat that pushed us, pulled us.

It wasn't magic.

There were half a dozen sensitives on the ice to keep an eye on the players. If someone was too fatigued or stressed, if they were on the brink of losing control and shifting, a sensitive would take them aside, give them a minute or two to compose themselves. Feed them, make them hydrate.

I assumed they were looking for magic used by wizards too, even though everyone knew wizards were too frail to play contact sports.

Most wizards.

If the song were magic, it would have been shut down pretty quickly by the sensitives. There were now rules for how magic could be used in a hockey game. Shifters were allowed to tap into their primal abilities, up to eye-change, which was the first part of a shifter that changed. If it went as far as step two: fangs and claws, the player was warned. If it happened twice in a game, the player got a two-minute stay in the penalty box. A full shift could take the player out for that game.

Of course, a full shift usually meant a fight too. And penalties for fights were the same as the NHL. Two-minutes for minor, bloodless skirmishes, more if refs thought things were getting out of hand.

Sensitives were easier to deal with since their main claim to magic was they could tell when it was going down and how hard.

So there wasn't much the refs could do to someone pointing a finger on the ice and saying another player was slipping hold on their animal self.

Wizards…well, that was virgin ground. I didn't think there were any rules in place. If Clay and Beauchamp brought me on, they would be setting new standards, which meant they'd have to come up with new rules.

My gut twisted. That was a lot of trouble to go through for a rookie center. Especially since the rules would have to be written and agreed upon by the entire HHL before start of the season which was only three months away.

Worry swamped me, pushing even that catchy tune out of my head. My rhythm faltered and I whiffed a couple easy shots.

Graves swung past me, eight low notes swinging upward to carry over the scrape and hiss of skates on the ice. Damn, for a big guy, he could handle the puck. That was the kind of defenseman I wanted to play with.

And if that hope was ever going to become a reality, I had to put in some sweat to make it happen.

Today was hockey. Today was proving I was good enough for this team. Today was standing out and fitting in. And I'd be damned if I was going to let this chance fall through my fingers.

6

THE WEEKEND WENT BY in a blur. Duncan and I were at the arena each day of tryouts, hitting every drill Coach Clay and Assistant Coach Beauchamp threw at us.

Of course there were about thirty other players out there working hard too. Some impressive talent.

"I would kill for a pizza," Duncan said as we hauled our exhausted bodies out of Sean's hybrid SUV.

"Already ordered." Sean remained behind the wheel, engine idling. "I'll go pick it up. You boys shower and pull out the plates."

"Mom going to be home for dinner?" Duncan asked.

"Not until late. She'll call on her break."

Duncan nodded and he and I dragged our gear into the house.

"Dibs," I said as I headed to the shower.

"Don't care." Duncan flopped on the couch face first and didn't move. "Even my brain is sore."

"That's 'cause it's so tiny and had to work so hard."

He raised a hand and flipped me off without looking at me. I chuckled.

The hot water felt so good I groaned and stood there for a solid five minutes before I even reached for the soap.

I didn't know if I was going to make the team. There were a lot of amazing players on the ice. Men and women, marked and unmarked. The coach would call each of us over the next few days to let us know if it was a yes or no. Rumors said they were looking for talent in both defense and offense, and weren't looking for goalies.

That meant I had a chance. Duncan had a chance too.

I'd tried to read Clay's sky-blue eyes as he calmly weighed and measured each player while he issued orders that sounded like suggestions but certainly were not. It was weird to have a coach who seemed so pleasant all the time.

Not like he was constantly all-out smiling, but like nothing really got under his skin. He seemed to be the kind of guy who would pat you on the back and buy you a beer if you were having a bad day.

Had he been watching me more than other players? Had he been disappointed in my speed? My hustle? My skills? Would I even know what disappointed looked like on his serene face?

Sometimes I caught him talking quietly to Beauchamp, both of them glancing at me.

That couldn't be good.

But the ice was full of players—rookies and pros, human and shifters. And one lowly wizard. He could have been staring at twenty other people. He might not have even noticed me.

I groaned and thunked my forehead on the tiles. That would be worse.

I got out of the shower, dried, and with the towel around my waist, slid into my room. I dragged on sweat pants and a T-shirt, then barefooted it to the living room.

I thought I'd been in the shower for hours but Duncan was still face down on the couch and hadn't moved.

I slapped the back of his head.

He grunted.

"Shower's open."

He grunted again.

I snorted and went into the kitchen to pull out plates and glasses.

My phone rang from somewhere in the gear I'd dumped in the living room.

"Your phone," Duncan muttered into the pillow.

"I know, dork." I finally found it and answered without looking at the number. "Hazard."

"Hello, Mr. Hazard, this is coach Clay."

I knew who it was from the first word out of his mouth. My heart started rattling like Duncan's car, and the honey-sweet taste of magic exploded across my tongue.

I took a deep breath, trying to settle my nerves.

"Hello, Coach."

This was it. This was where he'd tell me if I was good enough to be on the team. If I had a future or if my dreams had been for nothing.

"I wanted to catch you before you left the rink, but got detained. I know you might already be home, but I wonder if I can inconvenience you to return to the arena?"

That wasn't what I'd hoped he'd say. I'd hoped for something more on the lines of *welcome to the team*, or *we'd love to have you be a part of our roster.*

I didn't know why he wanted me at the arena, but so far he hadn't said I couldn't be a part of the team. I held on to that with everything I had.

"Sure, Coach. Anytime. When?" The words came out a little fast and probably a little louder than I intended, because Duncan finally turned his head and blinked blurrily at me.

Coach? he mouthed.

"Would now be possible?" Coach asked.

"Yes. Of course, yes. Not a problem. I'll be there in fifteen, twenty minutes."

"Good. And Mr. Hazard? No need to bring your skates."

7

DUNCAN RELINQUISHED THE KEYS to the Vega only after I'd wasted five full minutes arguing with him that he couldn't come with me.

"But why not?"

"Because Coach didn't ask you to come."

We'd repeated that refrain over a dozen times before I decided to change the tune.

"Look. If he's telling me I'm off the team, I don't want you to be there to see it. If he's telling me I'm on the team, you'll be the first person I call. But I don't think that's what this is about. I mean, he could have just said those things on the phone."

"So what do you think it's about?"

"Probably the magic thing at the Avalanche. Hiding...what I am? Lying."

That was the wrong thing to say because all it did was put Duncan's protective mode into overdrive.

"I'm going with you."

"No, Duncan, you're not."

"Where are we not going?" Sean strolled through the door and the heavenly scent of pizza whooshed in with him.

I hungrily eyed the two large boxes he balanced in his hands.

"Coach called him back to the arena. I'm going with him."

I shook my head and mouthed *no* behind Duncan's back.

Sean considered us. Then he addressed Duncan. "You haven't showered yet, have you son?"

"So?" Yeah, a little more wolf than necessary came out with that word. He was edgy, sharp. He needed to eat, pronto.

"You need a shower and you need food." Mr. Spark didn't sound upset but those words were brick walls that weren't budging. "I'll go with Random and make sure everything is okay."

"I don't need anyone to come with me."

"Yes, you do," Duncan said. He took a couple breaths then rubbed his hand over his hair making it stick up even worse. "Okay. Fine. Yes. Not going to save you pizza though."

"Like I'm leaving it all behind." I snagged one of the boxes out of Sean's hands and started toward the door. I already had a piece in my mouth before I'd gotten more than three steps away from the house.

Sean, used to living with a couple of bottomless hockey players, simply strolled to his car and unlocked it with the fob. I clambered in, balancing the closed pizza box, the last of my slice, and the door.

"What did the coach say?" he asked.

I swallowed and popped the glove box. Two bottles of sport drinks and a few heavy meal bars were tucked in there, just like always. I took the drink, and held it up, offering the other one to him.

"No thanks."

I cracked the lid, drank. "He wanted to talk to me before I left but we didn't connect. So he wants me to come in to talk to him now."

"Hmm."

I didn't say anything else. Neither did he. I took the opportunity of the short drive to polish off another slice of pizza and finish the drink.

Just like always, the food and drink made me feel better, more settled. That honey sweet taste of magic across my tongue was gone.

I could do this. I could face this music.

The front door of the arena was unlocked and we walked in. Coach met us in the lobby. "Mr. Hazard. And…Mr. Spark, I believe? Duncan's father?" Coach Clay held out his hand and we both shook it.

"That's right," Sean said. "I hope you don't mind me coming along."

Coach Clay slid me a look and whatever he saw on my face must have been permission. "Not at all. Come on back to the office."

We followed him down a hall and past several doors until we came to one door that was open. He stepped inside, motioning us forward.

"I'm sorry you had to make the trip back tonight. You live in town now, right?"

I noticed the slight emphasis on the "now." He knew about Colorado. Knew I'd left there fast and ran back to the only home I had.

"Yes, sir. I'm living with Mr. Spark and his family."

Coach nodded, then waved at the chairs on one side of the desk. We sat and he did too, the desk between us littered with papers, notebooks, folders, and various little stone statues of a round faced guy wearing a red hat. The little guy reminded me of statues I'd seen in the huge Asian grocery and gift store out in Beaverton.

"I've been keeping an eye on you, Hazard, for a few years now."

I wasn't sure if I should be happy or worried about that. The serene smile on his face told me nothing.

"It came as no surprise to me that the NHL called you up right out of juniors. You are a skilled player who will only improve in the coming years. Any team would be happy to have you."

"Th-thank you, sir." My heart was pounding hard. I knew there was a "but" attached to this conversation. And I had a feeling it would change my life.

Probably not for the better.

"I want you to tell me why you're trying out for the Thunderheads."

I had prepared for this, honestly I had. I'd spent years rehearsing an earnest speech just in case I was asked this question. And I had been asked it just recently when I was at the Avalanche's camp.

But instead of my carefully prepared speech, the truth came tumbling out of my mouth.

"My best friend made me do it because I'd lied to him all my life about being a wizard."

The silence in the room was *suffocating*. I tried not to squirm.

"So you don't want to be on the team?"

"No! I mean, yes. Yes, sir, I want to be on the team. So much." All that came out too fast, and I suddenly felt like a little kid asking Mr. Spark if it was okay if I slept over another night because my mom hadn't been home in three days.

In other words, I felt lame.

Blood washed hot beneath my skin as my embarrassment rose from my chest up to the tips of my ears.

"Talk to me about being a wizard, Random."

I slumped back in the chair and swallowed a couple times, getting up my courage.

"I don't know what I can tell you. I—I am a wizard. I've used magic three times."

"Three?" Coach sounded surprised.

I met his curious gaze.

"Yes, sir."

"Your entire life?"

I nodded.

"How have you...I know how difficult it is for wizards to resist the draw of magic. I know the...compulsion."

I waited for him to say something else. I wasn't sure where he was going with this. Out of all the marked, wizards were often seen as the most addicted to magic. It was why there was so much more magic training for them than the other marked.

"Three?" he asked again.

Was that a lot? Or maybe it wasn't very much. And yeah, magic got pushy. But I'd been shoving it down, out of the way, under my mental thumb for my entire life.

When I was younger I was convinced my life—or at least the parts that mattered: my friendship with Duncan, my place on the hockey team, my home with the Sparks—depended on me remaining normal, human, non-magical.

So that's what I'd done.

He glanced at Mr. Spark, who sighed. "Random just recently told us."

"Have you known him long?"

"He's been a close part of our family, our second son, really, since he was six."

"And you never suspected?"

He chuckled and it was warmth and home and safety. I hated how much it put me at ease—I was an adult here—but I couldn't deny how glad I was that Sean had come along.

"Not once," he said fondly. "And while that might reflect on his ability to be honest, I feel it speaks to some of his other great strengths: discipline and determination."

It felt weird to just sit there and let them discuss me like I was invisible. I was about to say something adult when Coach Clay spoke again.

"Why didn't you tell your family?"

It was a personal question, one I could tell him was too personal to answer. But his sky blue eyes were soft and encouraging, like he was pulling for me to come up with the right answer on the test.

I didn't know the right answer, so I went with the truth. "I wanted to play hockey. Real hockey." The blush caught fire again, but I pushed onward. "I thought the NHL was my only chance at that. So I decided to be normal. That meant never using magic."

I shrugged like it was no big deal not to use magic. But it had been hard. Not using magic had meant years of nightmares, headaches, and sleeplessness that had almost landed me in a cat scan once.

"When did you decide that?"

"I was seven?" Something about my tone was broken, childlike. I hated it.

Mr. Spark made a soft sound and then he cleared his throat. "Random. Ran. Look at me."

I did so.

"You *are* normal. You have always been normal. You just also happen to be a wizard. Using magic wouldn't have changed a single thing about how much we loved you when you were a child and it changes nothing now. Understand?"

I nodded, not trusting my voice, then glanced over at Coach. I suspected he didn't want to watch this little Hallmark moment unfold in his office.

Coach's eyes were still curious, still encouraging. I wasn't sure if I'd given him the right answer but he didn't look angry or disappointed.

"Why did you use magic at training camp?"

"I was pretty sure the guy was about to get his head knocked in. Even his helmet wouldn't have saved him from that swing. Kowalski has a hell of a shot."

"And so you threw up a wall of magic strong enough to stop a full impact."

I nodded. My mouth was too dry to say anything and the pizza in my stomach suddenly seemed like a bad idea. Was this going to happen at every tryout? Was it so weird for a wizard to have accidentally-on-purpose used magic to save a guy?

"You do understand that using magic in that way, a physical manifestation, is extremely unusual."

No, I did not know that. But then I didn't keep up with Magical Instachat or however people shared facts and tidbits like that.

Coach tried a different tactic. "I understand you didn't lose consciousness?"

"They gave me a sport drink. And a bar."

He waited. I thought he might be holding his breath. I was right. He let it out in a soft puff then leaned back in his chair. His gaze slid back to Sean.

"Water and a bar, and he's good to go," Coach said, picking up one of the little red-cap guys and turning the round body in his palm like a worry stone.

I didn't know why he was repeating what I'd just said.

"He's a hell of a player," Sean said. "He has grit and soft hands, and a keen ice sense, and speed. He's good-hearted all the way through. If you don't pick him up for your team, Mr. Clay, I assure you it will be a mistake. You aren't the only team in the WHHL who could benefit from a wizard on their ice."

Wow. And *what?* My brain couldn't quite catch up to him going to bat for me like that. Not that I should have been surprised. He had always been my biggest supporter. He was just usually a lot more quiet-librarian about it.

"That's good to hear," Coach Clay said. "I'd like to offer you a place on the Thunderheads, Mr. Hazard."

My heartbeat shot off the chart. "But?"

Coach Clay frowned. "But…I'd like to know if you'll accept the offer?"

Oh. *Oh!* There was no but. Not really. If I wanted it, I could have it. It wasn't the NHL, but it was hockey. Professional, competitive.

I could play.

All my muscles unlocked at the same time and I went a little light-headed.

I opened my mouth to accept. Instead, this fell out: "Are you sure?"

Sean sighed. "Random."

"It's going to mean extra work for you," I pushed on. "There aren't rules for wizards who want to play hockey. The league will have to approve how and if wizards can use magic on the ice. I don't know how long that will take. You might have to bench me for the whole season."

"There are already rules in place for wizards." He placed the little rock down and leaned his forearms on his desk. "We drew them up when we revised our approach to the league five years ago. The commission signed off on it. But since there haven't been any wizards playing, those rules have never been put into practice."

His mouth quirked at the corner. "You are a test case, Mr. Hazard, one I am very interested in. The league, the world, will be watching you. What you do will influence how wizards play hockey in the future. You should understand that before you decide to join the team.

"I am curious as to what it will mean to have a man with your powers on our team. But what the Thunderheads need more than anything you, as a wizard, can offer us is your hockey skills. We need our fourth line shored up. If you can give me your best as a hockey player, you can be a part of that. Can you do that, Mr. Hazard? Give me your best as a hockey player?"

"Yes, Coach. I can."

He smiled and pointed a finger at me. "Just keep saying that, and we'll get along fine."

"Yes, Coach." And this time, I couldn't hide my grin.

8

"HEY." DUNCAN SLAPPED MY arm and sat next to me on the front step of the house. It was sunny out. Hot, with just enough wind to keep the sweat off my face.

Down at the end of the block a kid stood next to a cooler. He had a handwritten sign that advertised HUCKLE-AID 50 CENTS. I was trying to decide if he was selling huckleberry lemonade or if huckle-aid was some kind of charity the cool kids were collecting for now.

"You still worried?"

I was. I didn't tell him that. "You'll get in," I said. I'd been saying it for a week now. I refused to believe that I'd be the one who made the Thunderheads and my best friend got left behind.

"I don't suppose seeing the future is in your wizardly bag of tricks?"

"No."

"It's been a week."

"I know. They haven't announced their final picks yet, Dunc. You're too good to pass up. They want you."

"But what if they pass me up? It's too late to try out for another team."

"You don't know that." I glanced over at him. "Why are you smiling?"

"Comfort me, Random." He batted his eyelashes. "Tell me I'm the best player ever to play. Tell me if I don't make the team you'll sob for days and beg the coach to let me in. Tell me you'll give up your place for me and start a protest movement with a sassy slogan and a viral video of sexy dancers. Tell me life is worth living. That I'll somehow go on."

He tossed his phone at me. I looked at the screen. Read the text there.

"You got in, didn't you? Did you get in? Is this real? Really from Coach Clay?"

"Text and a phone call. You are looking at the Thunderheads' newest, and best, left winger."

"Yes!" I grabbed him and patted his back, while he slapped at mine.

When we pulled apart, Duncan grinned like he was getting Christmas, his birthday, and the Stanley Cup all in one big cardboard box. "We are going to set the hockey world on fire, my brother."

"Damn right we are!"

"We must consume pizza! Victory pizza!" He stabbed a finger at me. "And you're buying."

I laughed and didn't even argue. Because getting the chance to be on the same team as my best friend felt like getting Christmas, my birthday, and the Stanley Cup all in one big cardboard box.

9

COACH TOLD ME THAT getting my magic tested was one of the requirements for a wizard who wanted to play hockey.

He'd given me a copy of the rules. There was no using magic during the game to alter or enhance any player, the ice, the equipment, the refs. Of course there was a lot more to it, but basically that's what the magic rules boiled down to.

Wizards couldn't use magic on the ice. The rules did say minor magic could be used to enhance the wizards themselves. It was a little fuzzy on what constituted minor magic, but since the marked all carried extra strength or speed or faster reflexes because of how magic infected them, the league thought it was only fair for wizards to have that advantage too.

The magic test was just to set my abilities in a category. Of which there were apparently many. They wanted to find out how I used magic so there would be no surprises.

Some wizards could mess with a person's thoughts or mind. They were pretty rare, but were seen as a possible complication to playing the game.

I wasn't one of those.

I didn't think.

So, yeah, I was hoping the testing would answer some of my own questions that had been buried for too long.

My knee shook as I bounced my foot. The walls of the small reception area were decorated with aggressively calm mountains, in-your-face ocean waves, belligerent nesting birds, and a grumpy little log cabin beneath autumn colored trees. I liked nature as much as the next guy, but those paintings were all "calm your shit down."

"Random Haz…" A dark-haired woman about my age with the prettiest green eyes I'd ever seen frowned at the screen in her hand.

"Hazard," I said. "Random Hazard." Great. I sounded like a James Bond villain.

Her gaze lifted to meet mine, and her mouth, no lipstick but oh so soft-looking, quirked at one corner. "Really?"

All the air knocked out of my lungs. She was beautiful. Heat washed down my chest to pool in my belly. My skin felt kind of tingly, like I wasn't getting enough air.

Those eyes. That smile. How was a guy supposed to act normal in front of all that?

"My parents thought they were hilarious."

That got more of a smile out of her, revealing straight white teeth and a dimple in her cheek. The wrinkle in her nose was adorable and made me want to rub my thumb over it to smooth it out.

I'd just met her, but I was already wondering when I could see her again. If she would want to see me again.

The loud thumping in my chest was a signal. Not a warning. It was recognition. Attraction.

"Well, if you'd just follow me, Random."

"Ran. Uh, you can call me that. My name. Short name. Ran."

Who had taken over my mouth and why were they so stupid?

"All right. Ran, I'm Genevieve, Doctor Phelps's assistant." She started down the narrow hall and I followed. "You can call me Gen."

Her perfume smelled like wildflowers and cinnamon, her hair was glossy and swung below her shoulders.

She was about my height, and I snuck a look at her feet to see if she was wearing heels. Black boots with buckles, and yep, at least an inch of heels. That meant she'd be a little shorter than me barefoot.

Good hugging height. Great hugging height. Not that we were at the hugging stage. We weren't even at the "hey, you want a cup of coffee?" stage.

"Just step right in here."

The room didn't have an exam table. Two office chairs and a desk took up one side, leaving the rest open except for some shelves and a projector screen against the far wall.

Small black cameras hung in the ceiling corners.

"On a scale of one to ten, ten being the best, how are you feeling today?" Genevieve asked.

"Maybe nine? Well, physically, ten."

Her eyebrow quirked up, stylus poised over the screen in her hand. "Why nine?"

"I'm a little nervous. I guess. So…that." I sat and wiped my sweaty palms on my jeans.

"You have nothing to worry about. It's just the standard tests. Any kindergartner can pass them. When was the last time you were tested?"

"Never."

She grinned. "Right. So when was the last time?"

"I've never been tested."

"Sure you have."

"Nope."

"Everyone gets tested."

"Not me."

Her gaze stilled on my face and I fell into the rich soft green of her eyes like I was finally coming home. Like I could breathe.

"Are you serious?"

I nodded.

"Not even as a kid? Or in middle school?"

Magic pushed extra hard during puberty. Middle school was that oh-so-awkward time of crazy hormones and weird hair in weird places. If you were a Canidae shifter you got to add fangs and claws and fur, plus crap coordination to that list.

Felidae shifters got the claws, fangs and fur, and migraines.

If you were a sensitive, it was all about being so distracted or jumpy people thought you were high or stoned or blind.

Being a wizard in middle school? For me it was the same as always: body aches, nightmares, and exhaustion that never went away.

"Never tested as a kid. Never tested in middle school."

"That's…unusual. But okay. All right." She jotted notes then put the tablet down on the table and pulled out a blood pressure cuff and finger clip.

I wanted to talk to her, to get to know her better. But her touch was professional and all business. It would be weird to flirt and would make the appointment awkward.

She released the pressure on the cuff and turned to me with a smile. And oh my God, that dimple and wrinkled nose.

I also might have been staring. A lot. Too much.

"So…you good here? Still nine/ten?"

"Still good."

"All right hang tight and Dr. Phelps will be right in."

"You don't want me to take my clothes off? For the doctor. Do I need to…" I waved at my shirt and jeans.

"No. Unless you can only use magic in the nude?"

She looked me up and down, checking me out.

"Yeah. No. That's not… I don't have to be naked."

"Too bad." She winked. Then she walked out of the room.

Holy shit. She was flirting. Maybe she was kind of into me? Or maybe she was just joking around.

I rubbed my face, so glad Duncan hadn't come along. He would have tortured me with that conversation for a year.

A polite knock tapped on the door and the doctor walked in.

He was tall, maybe six-three, skinny as a stick, and somewhere in his fifties or sixties. His gray hair was swept back and cut just beneath his ears and his wide, thin mouth turned down in the corners so it looked like his face had frozen in the middle of a hummed letter "M."

Really, with those chipped blue eyes, he reminded me of the *Love Actually* actor who played Davy Jones in that pirate movie.

He was also a wizard.

Yes, I could tell. The magic sort of rolled off him.

"Mr. Hazard? I am Doctor Phelps. I'll be handling your tests today. I understand you are a wizard."

"Yes, sir."

"And a…" he checked the screen in his hand "…hockey player?"

"Yes, sir."

Something shiny kindled in his eyes. "Oh. And you've never been tested. Is that correct?"

"Yes, sir."

He sat in the other chair and set the screen down. "I understand why your team wants you tested. But may I ask why you've never been curious as to the limits to your abilities?"

"I just… I've never used it. So it never really mattered to me."

"Did you suffer a magic-related trauma when you were a child? Perhaps saw a family member injured or killed due to magic?"

"No."

"Did you see a family member or friend use magic in a way that injured themselves or another person or otherwise frightened you?"

"No. Nobody in my family is a wizard. None of my friends are wizards. I just don't use magic."

Those sharp eyes seemed to puncture right into my brain.

"Was it a professional goal, then? Perhaps you wanted to play in the National Hockey League and knew a wizard wouldn't be allowed to play pro hockey?"

He leaned toward me conspiratorially. "I saw the clip on the sports channel. That was an impressive full-physical barrier you cast to save that young man's life."

"Thank you."

"What other types of spells have you cast?"

I filled him in on my impressive three magical jobs, one of which he already knew.

He blinked a couple times. "That's it?"

"I don't use magic." Having to repeat myself was getting old. Maybe I should just get it printed across my forehead.

"Today you will, Mr. Hazard." He glanced at his watch, then tapped the screen again. "We have exactly one hour, so we'd better move through this quickly. We'll assume you have the basics, since you handled the four F's and were able to find magic, filter it, focus it, and form it to your will.

"We will test how you use your mind and body to cast, and shape magic. We'll look at your endurance and control, your discipline and range."

"Range as in distance?"

"No, that's tested under strength. A wizard's range is his skill set, his natural tool box, if you will.

"Place an ice cube in a wizard's palm, and he can filter magic through many aspects of it. Ice is cold, he could make it snow. Ice is hard, he could create a physical force, ice is melting, he could create a fluid motion. Stack those aspects and magic could become many things. It is up to the wizard and his focus to decide what magic will create."

"What about music?" I asked.

"Can it be used to create a spell? Yes, of course. Have you?"

"No. I don't think so. You said a wizard can use an ice cube to make snow. Like a blizzard?"

His thin, wide mouth moved toward a smile. "No. A single ice cube wouldn't offer enough "frozen" aspect for a wizard to fuel a storm. A spell that large would take a great toll on the wizard's body and mind. Could even be deadly. Larger magics are built with many wizards casting small parts of a larger spell. There is always ample recovery time needed between magic use."

"How much recovery time is normal?"

"Hours. Days. Sometimes weeks, depending on the wizard and the magic."

Coach's comment about my quick recovery time made a little more sense.

"How long did it take you to recover from throwing the full-physical barrier?"

"A couple hours."

"Hours?"

"Well, I was sort of getting kicked out of the majors. That was, um…stressful? Yeah. Stressful. So I felt pretty sick for most of the night after that. But the weakness and stuff that hit me after the spell faded pretty quick after I ate and drank."

He narrowed his eyes. "Is that so?"

"Is this part of the test?" The sooner I could hold an ice cube and check off the magic boxes, the sooner I could leave.

"Not part of the test, but it is history, which your records are seriously lacking. Since our time is short, let's fill in your history at another appointment. I want you to do a small magic for me."

He opened the desk drawer and pulled out a box. He picked a rubber ball out of the box and placed it in my palm. "Spell from that. Nothing large. I just want to see how you cast."

A rubber ball. I rolled it in my hand. This was the first time I'd try to cast magic on purpose that wasn't to stop a life-or-death situation.

That alone made it weird. Like now that I had every possibility in front of me, I wasn't sure what to pick. What to do.

Something small like the ball. Something simple. I could focus on the bouncy aspect of the ball, or the smoothness, or the compactness of the rubber.

He wanted simple, so I went with the bounce.

I pulled on magic; that kindling in my chest behind my heart, flickered and caught fire. I drew it into my empty fist, forming a ball of magic about the same size as the one in my other hand.

Then I tossed the magic ball onto the floor. The magic ball swirled in candy colors that sang out like a calliope whistle as it bounced up to the ceiling, changed tone and color, zipped to the shelf along the wall, pealed out another soft note, then bounced along the floor, making happy, chuckling little toots as each bounce became shorter.

Finally, it rolled and stopped against the far wall, the colors pulsing and throwing off a little glow.

The doctor stared at it. Then he stared at me. "You used magic."

"You told me to use magic."

"I told you to tap into an aspect of the ball."

"I did. It bounced."

"You turned magic into a ball. You made magic bounce."

"Yes?" There was no way I had failed this test. That had to be the most straightforward aspect of a bouncy ball.

"How long can you maintain that spell?"

He had gone back to looking at the little ball, so I stared at it too. It didn't look all that impressive. It was just glowing and pulsing and giving off a slight humming C-chord.

"Well, it's small. So, for a while?"

"No, I mean, when will it fade?"

"They don't... I don't know."

"How long have you held a spell before it began to falter?"

"Not very long. I just sort of cut off the magic to make it go away."

"You cut..." He was quiet again, his mouth flattened. "Let me make a few notes. I want you to keep the magic ball going. Don't do anything else with it, just allow it to remain."

He scribbled furiously on the screen. "When you begin to feel fatigue, nausea, or pain, please tell me."

I waited. Thought about making the little ball roll or bounce, wondered if I could shift the sound to toot out *Twinkle Twinkle Little Star,* but he'd told me to just leave it there so I did.

"All right. Keeping the ball in the state it is in, I'd like you to cast another spell. Can you do that?" He drew a wool sock out of the box.

"I guess?" I gave him back the rubber ball, which he took, all the while staring at the magic ball.

"Want me to do anything that comes to mind?" I asked.

"Yes. Anything simple."

The wool was soft and warm.

"Can I have your wrist?"

He extended his left wrist.

It was easier this time now that I knew the concept of how to channel magic. I tapped into the warmth from the wool. I wanted to create a magic wrap around his wrist, like a bracelet of warmth and comfort and support.

Magic spun out from my fingers, weaving a wide band that rolled from the deepest brown, through greens, reds, orange and yellow. It looked like autumn and as it wove into existence, the

71

subtle sound of bamboo sticks clacking in a low breeze filled the air.

"What aspect of the wool did you choose, Mr. Hazard?" Dr. Phelps' voice had gone a little soft and funny. He couldn't seem to take his eyes off the band on his wrist.

"Warmth. Wool socks always remind me of cool weather. Autumn."

"And so the colors…and the sound. Autumn?"

"Yeah."

"Can you maintain this spell as well as the ball?"

"I think so." They were each a different thread extending out of me, magic pouring from that kindling behind my heart, outward. One thread was thin and rainbow colored, one wide and rust-orange.

"Where does the magic originate in your body?" he asked.

"You can't tell?"

"I believe it is in your chest. Is that correct?"

I tapped my heart. "Behind my heart."

"Can you feel it or sense it in some way?"

"It's like a pile of dry wood. When I pull on magic, it catches fire. There are strings, like lines of fire, or magic, pouring out of me."

"More than one line?"

"One for each spell."

"Very good. Very good." He added to his notes. "Now." He traded the sock for a small mirror. "What will you do with this, Mr. Hazard?"

I was starting to warm up to these little spells. I turned the mirror over in my hand and thought about what I could cast. Maybe something bigger? Maybe something that would actually impress the doctor?

What could I do with a mirror?

I drew magic through my body, pulling it past the lines sustaining the ball and the bracelet. I dragged on the magic harder, taking big gulping breaths of it, filling my lungs, filling my body.

Exhale.

The bloom of honey coated my tongue and I felt a little dizzy.

Time to get amazing on this shit.

I sent magic to fill my vision. To shape what I wanted it to become.

I dove into that, gave magic cut and arc and shape and form.

Bells filled the air, a sweet high chime offset by the deeper thrum of lower notes. The room seemed to fade. Walls became a forest covered in snow, trees made of mirrored bark, silver leaves shivering in an unfelt wind. The floor poured out like a frozen lake, mirroring a blue sky and dusky clouds where the ceiling had been.

The scent of campfire filtered through the pure, clean cold. My breath made small clouds in the air.

Then the scrape and scuffing of skates coming from far off grew louder. The skates cut ice in rhythm to my racing heartbeat and then...

...*and then*...

...*yes*...*then*...

Two hockey players made of silver, glass, mercury, mirror, pushed through the forest of trees, following an impossible river as they tapped a puck that was gold *gold*, like fire, gold like battle, gold like victory.

The players looked like Duncan and me, one tall and brawny, one short and skinny, both monochrome as winter's dreams, chasing after the win.

I laughed as the mirrored-Duncan hooked at the mirrored-me's skates, trying to trip me up, a move that never worked.

Mirrored-me pushed past him with a burst of speed, stretching out with his stick, sailing, flying, as if it were not skates that were carrying mirrored-me, but wings.

I could feel the cold, smell the sharp clean scent of snow in the breeze that shouldn't exist.

Dr. Phelps' and my reflection slid and shattered and warped across mirrored-me's face, arms, chest, and legs as he rushed past, magic and speed and cold fire, mirrored-Duncan on his heels.

The crack of a puck hitting a net filled the room. In the distance, a crowd cheered.

It was glorious. It was beautiful. It was a dream.

"Random," Dr. Phelps said quietly. "You can let it go. You can let it all go."

I was sweating, my heart pounding as if I had been skating drills. I shivered from the ice and snow in the room, panted as if I were the guy out there on the ice shooting the net.

But this was not real snow and ice. Not a real game. This was only magic. Nothing more than a mirror of my mind.

I mentally pictured scissors in my hand and made the snipping motion with my fingers.

The ice, the snow, the trees, lake, sky, and skaters, all disappeared. Dreams and hope swallowed by the sound of rain-drenched chimes.

The room was the room again. Lit by fluorescent light: just a desk, two chairs, Dr. Phelps and me. The space felt too small. Too bland. Too plain.

"This one too." Dr. Phelps held his wrist in front of my face.

I blinked sweat out of my eyes. I was thirsty and sick to my stomach and was going to barf if I didn't get some water.

I made the snip motion and the bracelet melted away with the sound of a plucked string. I shivered again as sweat slipped down between my shoulder blades. My hair was stuck to my forehead. It itched.

"Random? Do you need to lie down?"

"Uh…could I have some water?" My mouth was almost too dry to make the words, but Dr. Phelps understood because a bottle of water was in my hand almost instantly.

I drank it down. It went a long way to settling my stomach but I was so hungry, my gut was cramping.

Then there was a bar in my hands. I wolfed that down in three bites, sucking the last of the water to chase it.

Another water bottle appeared in my hand. I looked up and Genevieve gave me a small smile. "Feeling better yet?" she asked.

Dr. Phelps was taking my blood pressure. I must have missed a couple minutes.

I hated that. Losing track of things when I used magic.

"Did I pass out?"

Dr. Phelps shook his head. "You've remained conscious, just hyperfocused on food and water, which is to be expected." He pulled the stethoscope ends out of his ears and the blood pressure cuff deflated with a hiss. "How are you feeling?"

"Good. Fine. Better. Fine. Normal."

He flashed a light in my eyes. "Any pain?"

"Not much."

"Stomach? Head? Spine?"

"It's okay. Really." I wanted to push him away so I could get out of here fast. This was just a test, but I felt like I'd cracked myself open and shown him my gooey middle.

That scared the crap out of me.

"Did I p-pass?"

"What do you mean?"

"The test. D-did I pass? Am I strong enough or whatever enough to be on the team? Did I do it right? I could practice more. I'm good at practicing. I can do better."

"This was never about if you were strong enough, or good enough. This was simply to see what scope of magic your abilities might cover."

"Oh. Right. Okay. So that's...I'm...it's good?"

"You are...this has been—" He blew his breath out and sat back, big hands waving in the air. "A *very* impressive test. Very. Impressive. The ice scene? Was it a memory? Was it something you once did?"

"No. Not a lot of frozen lakes here in Oregon. But I always thought it would be...I don't know. Fun?"

"And so you cast that physical scene from your imagination and a scrap of mirror?"

"That's how it works, right? Use the aspect of a thing, like the cold reflection of a mirror, and make it another...thing?"

He stared at me for long enough I got worried and glanced at Genevieve. She shook her head slightly.

"What did I do wrong?"

"Nothing," the doctor said, still studying my face. "That was the most effortless and natural use of magic I've seen.

"You didn't use magic to enhance a thing—make a pen bounce like a ball, or make the stapler reflective like a mirror—no. No, you used, you *pulled* magic—color, sound—it was cold.

I could *smell* the snow and a campfire. I *felt* the ice on my cheeks." He shook his head.

"You pulled magic and turned *magic* into the thing you wanted. The wrap on my wrist, the ice, the snow, the *people*. They were real. Solid. I could hear the exhalation of their breath. I could feel their joy. It was…" He dropped his hands into his lap.

"I have never seen any wizard use all three aspects— physical, mental, emotional—so seamlessly. I have never seen a wizard shape magic—just magic itself—so cleverly. Most wizards enhance the world around them, but what you did. What *you* did, Mr. Hazard…" He sounded more composed, but still looked a little wild-eyed and hadn't finished most of his sentences.

"I passed?"

The laugh that came out of him was short and unexpected. He shook his head.

"Yes, Mr. Hazard, you passed. You rank *astoundingly* high in the standard categories. Your recovery rate is exemplary, your raw talent remarkable. I would strongly urge you to take further tests. A wizard of your abilities doesn't come along very often, and the more we understand what you can do, the better we will be able to support wizards with your skills in the future."

It was a nice speech, but all I really heard was "*yes, you passed.*"

"Okay, thanks." I stood. The doctor stood. I could feel every bone in his hand as we shook, his grip was warm and sure.

"Any time you want to come back, I would be happy to continue the tests. We could fit them in between your practices. I would gladly bend my schedule to fit your needs."

"Thank you. I'll think about it and let you know."

There was no way I was going to take more tests. Sitting here and throwing magic around made me nervous. A lifetime of hiding wasn't something I was going to kick in one day.

I started toward the door.

"Mr. Hazard?"

I turned back. He had an amused look on his face. "Would you please extinguish the ball?"

I glanced over at the far wall. The little magic ball was still there, still glowing and humming to itself.

Oops.

"Sure. Uh…thanks." I imagined scissors and this time I snipped the thin thread of magic that was feeding the spell with just my thoughts alone. I must have snipped a little hard because the ball sort of exploded with a honk and glitter splattered the wall in Technicolor.

Gen laughed, but quickly schooled her face into something more professional.

"I see," Dr. Phelps said. "I see. You… I see."

"So just follow the exits?" I didn't want to know what he saw. All I wanted was normal. And hockey.

Gen pointed with a clipboard. "Here, I'll show you out."

She stepped in front of me and I caught the hint of her perfume again. I wished I knew which flowers smelled like that because I wanted to buy bushels of them.

She stopped on the edge of the lobby. "We'll send the records to your coach and we'll send you a copy too. You should see them by tomorrow morning at the latest."

"Okay, thanks." I hesitated. I wanted to ask her out but maybe I was reading this wrong. Reading her wrong.

Say something. Ask her for coffee. Ask her for lunch. Ask her for her number. She says no, it's no big deal. Just ask if she wants to talk sometime.

"Okay, I've been second-guessing this since you walked into the waiting room. Um…if you like hockey I could maybe get you a ticket to a game?"

She stood with one hand on her hip, her eyes curved a bit with her smile. "I've never seen a game in my life."

"Right," I said, stepping back. "That's cool. I just thought I'd ask."

"But I'd like to."

I stopped in my retreat. "Yeah? It would be WHHL, which isn't the same as the NHL, but it's still good. Fast. Hard plays. Physical."

"I don't know what those letters mean, but it sounds like fun."

"Good. Great. When would you like to go? Like what's a good time?"

She gave me a considering look. "This is your cell number?" She tapped the screen in her hand.

"Yeah."

"I'll call you and let you know when I'm free."

Hell, yes!

"Perfect. Thanks. Talk to you soon, yeah?"

She gave me a tilted nod and waved me off. I turned and grinned my way to the car.

10

THE VIDEO CLIP WENT viral. It only took hours after that for reporters to start calling me. Calling Duncan, calling Mr. and Mrs. Spark.

I didn't answer them because I didn't know what to say. The video spoke for itself. There was a guy who was going to get hurt, and I stopped that from happening.

With magic.

My social media blew up. At first I tried to respond to some of the comments and questions, but then it got too angry, too weird.

There were a lot of wizards excited for what I was doing.

There were a lot of wizards angry about what I was doing.

Pro-West Hell. Anti-West Hell. Pro-sports. Anti-sports.

When it got too angry, I tried to bring people back to the game. To the team. My team.

Luckily, Betsy Miner, the Thunderheads' social liaison caught me at practice.

She was barely over five foot tall, had hair shaved short on one side and bangs that hung in her eyes. "Hazard, got a minute?"

"Sure." I wasn't in my skates yet, so I followed her down the corridor.

"We've been getting a lot of interest from different reporters about your time at the Avalanche."

"The magic vid?"

She nodded, the piercings lining the edge of her ear glittering. "I've seen your social media, and don't want to overstep, but if you'd like a little help handling this?"

"Yes. God, yes. Anything."

She grinned. "All right. Good. I'm thinking you can direct any interest in the Avalanche Miracle to me here at the Thunderheads and I'll handle those. Yeah?"

"Please."

"And I think you should give an interview."

"I don't really want—"

"I know it's been over two months since the Miracle."

I rolled my eyes at that name, which I had absolutely not given the video.

She waggled her triple barred eyebrows. "But now that you've been picked up by the Thunderheads, I think it's time to go on camera. Talk about what happened, talk about your goals for the year, and talk up the Thunderheads, thanking the team, owners, and coaching staff for taking a chance on you."

I inhaled, exhaled. "Would you write that down for me?"

"If you want me to. But I'll do you one better. Let's get together after practice today and I'll coach you through a few easy tricks for answering reporters, yeah? We can go over what you want to say and make sure it comes out how you want people to hear it."

"I might be in love with you."

She barked a laugh. "Yeah, naw. This is what I get paid for. See you after practice, Wiz."

I threw myself into practice with everything I had, just like every day. I wanted to prove that Coach Clay had made the right decision to give me this chance. I wanted to prove that magic wasn't what made me an amazing player.

Two solid months of drills had done a lot to bring the team together, but we were far from perfect. I got along okay with most of the players.

We had the multinational mix that you'd expect out of hockey, and multi-marked that you'd expect out of West Hell in particular. There were three women on the team, since West Hell was also co-ed. One of the women was our goalie Joelle

Thorn. She was a sensitive, and had immediately welcomed me to the team the first day I set foot on the ice.

Of course she hadn't let me score a goal on her in drills, but still: nice.

Our backup goalie was a guy from Chile named Tomas Endler. He was quiet, but it was hard to miss the adoration in his eyes every time he looked at Thorne.

Our captain was a very serious Swede and Felidae shifter named Laakkonen. We called him Lock and he called us on our shit.

My line, the fourth line, was made up of me at center, Duncan at left wing, Johan Jorgensen—or JJ as we called him— at right, and the mismatched D-men: Nazareth "Watts" Watson and the whistler: Graves.

We were starting to gel, starting to figure out how our playing styles fit together. We had better. Our first game was in a few weeks.

"Wiz!" JJ waved me over. "Stop daydreaming and start working."

Duncan zipped past me as he took his warm-up laps. "Yeah, *Wiz*. Quit daydreaming."

I groaned. I hated that nickname but the longer I was on the team, the more people used it. I really had to come up with a plan for them to just call me Hazard. I mean, that was catchy, right? Hazard on the ice?

Before I could politely tell them to shut up and call me by my actual name, Coach blew the whistle and it was time to quit daydreaming and start working.

"DON'T WORRY, RANDOM," I muttered. "It's just going to be a small gathering, yeah? We practiced all the answers, yeah? I'll be right there with you, yeah?"

Duncan snorted, but didn't stop lobbing the handball against the corridor wall. "Who said that? Betsy?"

"She said it would be small, Dunc. *Small.*"

"You are such a whiner."

"You're not the one going out there to give an interview in front of thirty cameras."

"I'll do it if you want me to." He caught the ball one last time and leaned away from the wall. "Seriously, Ran, if this is too much, I'll do it."

"You can't do it. You weren't there when it happened. You didn't throw magic around at an NHL training camp."

"I didn't make a miracle spell?"

"Oh, screw you."

Duncan grinned and bounced the ball on the floor. "You're going to do fine. They just want to hear you be humble and nice and all those other disgusting things you are. They just want a little look at the first wizard to ever play hockey. You don't have to be anything you're not, dude. Not anymore."

And dammit. He was right. Going out there in front of the cameras was a way of telling everyone who I was. Not who they had decided I should be.

"Hazard." Betsy rounded the corner and gave me a smile that should have been worn by a shark. A very short shark. "What are you doing pouting back here? They're ready for you."

"I'm not pouting."

"Are you ready for them? This doesn't have to happen today." She had closed the distance between us and I knew that if I told her I couldn't do it, if I told her we needed to call this off, she'd do it, no judgment, no foul.

But I wanted this done.

"Ready."

"All right. Follow me out. Duncan, you can come as far as the sidelines. I'll show you where to stand." She paused and gave me an up/down glance. "Hockey players sure do look nice in suits."

"Whoa, Betsy," Duncan said, "no hitting on him. What would your girlfriend say?"

"How about a threesome?"

Duncan laughed and I blushed so hard, the roots of my hair were on fire.

But then we were walking, and I was thinking about a threesome with a miniature shark and trying to imagine what her girlfriend looked like. Betsy guided me behind the table set up for the cameras and the interview began.

The lights were blindingly bright. So many cameras: both what I'd seen on news channels and also just cell phones. Several microphones and recorders were arranged on the table.

There was also an envelope in the center of the table with my name on it. I rested my palms over it and gave the world a smile.

"So. Anything interesting happen in hockey lately?"

The reporters chuckled, and I got ready to give my very brief statement, and answer their rapid fire, endless questions.

I DIDN'T REMEMBER A single word of the press conference. Not a single question, not a single answer. But the lights, the dryness of my mouth, the sweat pouring off me, pooling under my palms and soaking the envelope—that, I remembered.

When Betsy came out and thanked the press for coming, she motioned me to my feet, and waved me toward the exit. I didn't remember walking out of the room.

"Here," Duncan said. "Drink." He pressed a bottle in my hand and I took several gulps before I even registered that it was water.

A few gulps later, and I saw that I was in the trainer's room next to our changing room.

Betsy was there. "You did great, Hazard. You're a press conference dream. Those dimples, that easy smile. They were eating out of the palm of your hand."

"Yeah?" I asked.

"Yeah. Solid work and a good job. I'll let you know if you need to do anything else. But in the meantime, just play hockey and try not to worry about all this, yeah?"

"Thanks, Betsy," I said as she walked out. She waved her hand above her head and never looked back.

"Wow," Duncan said. "She's something, isn't she? Like a tiny Tsunami."

I nodded as I finished off the water.

"Was it okay?" I asked.

"It was actually what she said. You looked relaxed up there. And your answers were good. She's a miracle worker. You're a star, baby!" He did jazz hands for no reason I could fathom.

"Let's just go home and ignore the news, okay?" I said.

"Oh, I think we need to go home and watch every clip. See if they got *those dimples* and *that smile*." He fluttered his eyelashes and I threw the empty water bottle at his head.

He ducked because we'd been brothers for a long time. I stuffed the envelope in my jacket pocket and shoved Duncan toward the door.

Outside, a man stepped away from the overhang and approached us.

"Random Hazard?"

I turned. "Yes?"

The guy was familiar, but it took me a second to place him. He had been standing in the back of the room, behind the cameras during the press conference. He wore slacks and a button down under a light jacket. Built on the thin side, his face was sallow and bony with a puckered scar on one cheek, his dark hair styled and combed back.

"Shit," Duncan whispered.

"Mr. Hazard, my name is Don Nowak. I coach the Tacoma Tide."

He didn't offer his hand, so neither did I.

"Nice to meet you, sir," I said.

Duncan was stiff next to me in that way that said he sensed danger. Of course he had done the same when we first met Graves. Graves had turned out to be a decent guy, a solid defenseman, and a linemate.

Still, it was a little weird to have the coach from a different team, from our *rival* team, introducing himself to me.

"I just wanted to put my eyes on you," he said. "First wizard in the league. That's a hell of a burden to bear, Mr. Hazard."

"Yes, sir."

"It's a hell of a publicity stunt too. Get the eyes of the WHHL and NHL staring right at you. Put your name out there. Make yourself special. You've certainly used it to your advantage, blocking that shot. If I were a less charitable man, I'd say that was planned."

I clenched my fists and settled into a stance that could take a punch. Or land one.

"It was not planned. Not in any way."

"Well, you lied your way into the NHL, Mr. Hazard. You expect me to believe anything else you say?"

Duncan growled. It was low, but there was no way Nowak missed that warning.

"You don't know me, Mr. Nowak. I don't expect you to think about me at all."

For a split second, his face flashed with fury and I knew he was going to strike. But just as quickly, the anger was gone, locked down with a cruel smile.

"What I know is that this league doesn't have a place for you, Hazard. Not for your magic, not for your weaknesses. You will fail."

"You will." He nodded. "No question about that. Clay has always been a little soft in the head when it comes to hockey smarts. And this *stunt*."

He gritted his teeth. "This inclusive, every kid plays, get your participation prize *bullshit* will not stand in this league. We play hard hockey. This is a blood sport not fucking afternoon tea. Clay is out of his mind. Because good press or not, magic fucking spells or not, you, Hazard. *You* are going to drag this team down so far they won't see a win for decades."

Duncan started forward and I grabbed the back of his shirt and held on. The last thing we needed was him punching out a coach.

A thousand furious comebacks rolled through my brain. But Betsy had spent hours coaching me on how to handle heated barbs and attacks.

"I disagree. But I guess we'll find out. See you on the ice, Mr. Nowak."

I pulled with all my weight and dragged Duncan away with me, toward his broken-down Chevy Vega.

He was too angry to drive. Too close to losing control of the beast within him to even speak. I forced him into the passenger seat and put all my focus on getting the car to start, and getting us the hell out of there.

"YOU COMING OUT WITH us tonight, Hazard?" Nazareth "Watts" Watson, was a third-year defenseman and a tiger shifter. He held the league record in penalty minutes for fighting two years in a row, which he was ridiculously proud of.

Coach had paired him up with Graves. It was like watching oil and water wrestle: Graves's easy-going, slow-whistling, hard-as-hell hitting attitude colliding with Watts's win-or-die, fire-and-fight, skull-busting drive.

I wasn't sure pairing them up would work, but Watts seemed to be calming down a little when he was out there on the ice with Graves. Seemed to be playing better, smarter. Who knew? Maybe he'd even score a goal someday.

"Nope." I rubbed the towel over my hair, threw it into the pile and shrugged into my T-shirt. "Gonna go home. Sleep. Big game tomorrow, remember?"

The game was against the Tacoma Tide. I wanted to pull the win away from Nowak so hard, I could taste it.

"Naw, you gotta come out with us," Watts insisted. "We're going to Downpour. There's live music and shit."

"And cheap beer," Johan "JJ" Jorgensen, played right wing on the fourth line. He was a sensitive and had incredible ice intuition out there—like he always knew where the puck was going to be and made sure he got to it.

He put his hand out dramatically and wavered a bit on his feet. "I can feel it. Your ancestors are talking to me. What's that, Uncle Owen? You want Random to go to Downpour? You want him to drink a beeeer?"

"Sorry, Uncle Owen. Still no."

"You should listen to the sensitive," Duncan said.

"Yes," JJ agreed. "You should all listen to the sensitive. The sensitive wants free beer."

Duncan threw his towel at him, then came over and wrapped his arm around my neck. "It's Friday, first game of the season is tomorrow. We need to celebrate!"

"After," I wheezed, slapping at Duncan's beefy arm. "We celebrate after we win."

"A toast to our impending victory!" Duncan crowed.

"Graves," I pleaded. "Make them stop."

Graves finished tying his shoes. "Naw. It's tradition. One beer and a pile of nachos before the first game. Just like all the Thunderheads before us."

"You weren't here for the first of last year. You don't know tradition."

"I know when I'm about to start one."

Watts gave him a high five. "Word, Grave Digger."

Joelle "Josky" Thorn, our goalie, strolled into the locker room. She had already showered and changed in the women's showers.

"What's up, boyos? Are we drinking or what?"

"See," Duncan said. "Even Josky wants to go out."

"Hell, yes. Josky wants to dance." She gave a little hip shimmy.

Half the team moaned and I heard several "not again" and "this year too?" and "kill me."

Tomas Endler ducked his head, but kept his eyes on Josky. Yeah, the backup goalie had it bad for her.

"Yes, again." She swung a finger at the entire room. "Each and every year. You don't want to bring a season of bad luck on me. You get your asses the hell to Downpour and be prepared to drink cheap beer and dance right outta your cheap shoes. All of you. With me."

She zipped up her hoodie and gave us one more glare. "Downpour. Last one buys the nachos."

There was a mad scramble of hockey players shoving feet into shoes, grabbing duffels, and hauling to get out of the locker room. I would have just left them to it, but Duncan still had his arm around my neck. He hustled me out the door in front of him.

"Go, go, go!" He pushed us into a jog through the rain, the hoots and shouts of our teammates echoing around the parking lot.

I ducked into the passenger seat and Duncan shoved both of our duffels into the back before landing behind the wheel.

"She's got weird superstitions," I grumbled

"She's a goalie." Duncan said that like it explained everything.

And it did.

"C'mon, baby," he coaxed the car. "Start up. Start up for me. Daddy wants some free nachos."

"We're never gonna beat them there."

"Oh, we'll beat them." He turned the key again and the Vega wheezed to life.

I think it might have even topped twenty-five as we raced to the bar.

11

DOWNPOUR WAS A ROADHOUSE-meets-garage sale kind of place. This being Portland, they carried some amazing local craft beers and put one on sale each day. They stocked a line of cheaper beer too.

For a dive, it was comfortable, and served decent sandwiches and live music.

We were not the last ones to get there, a fact that shocked me. Nachos were on Graves, who sauntered in long after the last of us had arrived, and held up his credit card to a rousing cheer.

He'd done it on purpose. We all knew that. He was tied as the oldest member on the team, but unlike our other senior, Bucky, there was something about Graves that made most of us look to him as a mentor of sorts.

That might have been because he was the most experienced in the league out of all of us. He'd played in the Eastern Hybrid Hockey League where there'd been one death a year, done a stint in the Southern Hybrid Hockey League where the injuries were legendary, before finally ending up here out west, where it was a bone-breaking blood sport.

He hadn't shied from the fights and physicality of the sport, but still, there were very few clips of him actually shifting. The two Duncan and I had been able to find were blurry and grainy. You couldn't even make out quite what he'd shifted into.

He was better known as someone who could keep his cool even while he was pounding a rival into the boards or unconsciousness.

He'd taken the role of old experienced guy pretty handily, and answered all our questions about teams and people he'd played with. I'd seen our captain, Laakkonen, go to him a couple times for advice on plays.

Hell, even Coach asked his opinion now and then.

So while Graves was a nice guy who seemed easy to get to know, he was also the only person who hadn't admitted what kind of marked he was. Watts had snuck a look at the records to find out.

"He's a wolf," Watson said as he elbowed down at the table next to me. "That's what they have him down as anyhow."

Duncan and Josky sat across from us. There wasn't a table big enough for the whole team—all of whom had come despite their grumbling. Josky kept a headcount as they dragged through the door, ticking off each person with an approving lift of her chin. We'd had to split up into three groups at smaller tables.

"Who? Graves?" Duncan asked.

"Saw it listed. Canis lupus et al. So why doesn't he talk about it? Are all you wolves secretive about that stuff?"

Duncan snorted. "All us wolves aren't the same person, you dolt."

"Just thought it might be behavior specific to you cute widdle puppies."

"Bite me, Stripes."

Watson grinned and took a drink of beer. He wiped the foam off his lips with his middle finger. "It's not like he's the only wolf on the team," he went on. "So why hide it? I thought y'all were pack animals. Or maybe it's just that he doesn't want to be associated with you, puppy-butt."

Duncan punched him in the shoulder. Hard.

"Keep it up, cat-ass. I'll tell Coach the only reason you start so many fights is you're winded and can't skate end to end without heaving."

Watson laughed and leaned back in his chair to tell one of the other guys that Duncan was a puppy narc.

From there the conversation turned to hockey, like it always did.

"Tell us about the Tacoma Tide." Duncan pointed a tortilla chip at Josky and Watson. "I've seen the tapes, but you've played them. What should we know?"

Josky scooped a hunk of pepper off the pile and crunched down on a chip. "Their coach is a real ass. Hates our team. I think he's got history with Coach Clay."

"Like nobody else in this league got history with Clay." Watson reached across the table to steal her chips, which she handily blocked by slapping his hand.

Goalie.

"What kind of history?" I hadn't told Coach Clay or anyone else about Coach Nowak catching up with us the other day. It didn't seem like anything more than talk to try and get into my head. It would be nice to know why he thought he had a chance at that.

"Coach played a lot of teams back in the day, like Graves," Josky said. "He knows a lot of people. He was up for the coaching job in Tacoma before Nowak swooped in and pushed him out of the running. They used to be teammates. Some say they were pretty tight."

"How tight?" Duncan asked. "Like, personal? Intimate?"

Josky shrugged. "Coach is pretty private. Rumors say friends. Not more than, but still, friends."

I'd heard rumors that Coach was gay, but that didn't really matter in this league. West Hell wasn't exactly hugs and rainbows, but there had been a few out players and staff and no one cared one way or the other.

Officially, sexual orientation wasn't something a player could get canned for. Unofficially, most players just wanted to play hockey and didn't care.

The conflicts usually came from between the different marked and the unmarked. Or what country someone was from. Or what kind of music they liked. Or who they had voted for in the last election.

"No soap opera forbidden lost love? Too bad," Duncan said.

Josky threw a chip at him. He tried to catch it in his mouth and almost knocked over his drink. "Nowak is a dick," she said. "Coach could do way better."

"You know Nowak's a dick, how?" I asked.

"One, I'm a sensitive. Two, I got eyes, Wiz. So Coach goes from losing the coaching position at the Tide, a team that always ranks higher than us."

"Jerks," Watson piped up.

"Jerks," Josky agreed, "and takes over the Thunderheads, right? Buys the whole team with Assistant Coach Beauchamp and the cake guy, Franklin. Starts making changes, turning the team into hockey players, *good* hockey players. Makes waves that starts changing the league. Made it better for us, but not so good for some people."

Watson tapped his fingers on the table. "Whole lotta money made on shifter fights. Whole lotta money made on thrown games. Not so much anymore."

"You fight," Duncan said.

"Not for money. I fight for my team." He slapped his hand over his heart a couple times.

"Was Coach Nowak making those kinds of bets? Throwing games?" I asked.

Josky sniffed. "I don't know. But whatever his problem is, we are on his shit list, his team's shit list, and their fans' shit list." She took a moment to consider that, and I knew she was replaying time on the ice with them. "Their captain is kind of a tool too."

"Hey," Watts said, "you tell me if Steele so much as breathes too hard on you and I will break his face down the middle."

"Down boy," Josky said. "Keep the fight on the ice."

"Oh, trust me, I will. Fourth-marked to fourth-marked."

"Tabor Steele's a centerman, right?" I asked.

Josky nodded. "And a panther. He's strong and has fast reflexes. Always goes for the garbage goals. Stupid sneaky wraparound attack."

"Hey," Watson said, "don't profile us. Just because he's a cat doesn't mean he's sneaky."

"He's sneaky because he's Steele." Josky flicked an olive at his head, which he made a bite for and caught. Show off.

Watts grinned. "Reflexes like a cat! But yeah, Steele sucks. Good thing we've got Wiz here on our side. Anybody who can keep magic a secret for all their lives can out-sneak Tabor Steele."

Wiz. There was the nickname I didn't want to stick.

"How about we use Ran?" I suggested.

"What?" Watson asked.

Duncan just snorted. "Like you got any say over what we're gonna call you."

"You *already* call me Ran," I pointed out.

"And that matters why?"

"Because it's my name. My well-established, most-of-my-life nickname that you have always called me."

"That was before I knew you were a wizard, Wiz."

"All right!" Watts high-fived Duncan.

I scowled into my soda. "I hate you all."

Duncan laughed. "What? Did you want us to call you, Gandalf?"

"No." *Yes. Maybe.*

I shoved chips in my mouth, ignoring them.

Over on the other side of the room, the band had settled in on the raised stage and was warming up.

I took a deep breath and just sat, content to be exactly where I was. I liked being a part of a team. I liked being a part of *this* team.

Going out and blowing off some steam—in moderation—before the game had been a pretty good idea.

But I couldn't wait for tomorrow.

The first notes of music vibrated through the bar and people closest to the stage whistled and clapped.

They kicked into a song that was part rock, part grungy-folk. It was good. I finished my nachos, drank my Coke and mentally recited the drills we'd just practiced.

"Time to dance!" Josky declared. "Dance with me, Donuts!"

She grabbed Duncan's arm and dragged him laughing off toward the stage. A small crowd of dancers pulled together, jumping and swaying.

Watts tipped his chin at me.

"Gonna make my rounds. See ya, Wiz."

I really had to get ahead of that nickname. Before I could say anything, he was off, prowling through the crowd and flashing a smile at any lady who caught his eye.

"You Hazard?"

I glanced over at the three guys striding up to me. The leader was about my age, light-haired and dark-eyed. He was over six feet tall, bulky in the shoulders, solid and fit everywhere else. A real All-American football type. He looked familiar, but I couldn't quite place him.

"Yes?"

"You're nothing but a fake and a liar. You lied to get into the NHL, and you lied to get into the WHHL." He planted one hand on the table top and loomed over me.

"You must be a fan," I drawled.

"I'm going to fucking pull you apart and pick my teeth with your bones."

Holy shit. This guy was hardcore asshole.

I was so not impressed.

One thing that came with being shorter than just about everyone else on every team I'd ever played on or against was I didn't back down from shitheads no matter what size they were.

"Pick your teeth with my bones? Seriously? That is some bargain bin bullshit."

He showed me his teeth, which were sharp and elongating. His dark eyes bloomed with amber and his pupils narrowed to cat-slits.

Terrific. A shifter.

One of his buddies grabbed his arm. "Come on, Steele. Don't do this here. Keep it on the ice."

Well, well, well. Tabor Steele, captain of the Tide. I'd never met the dude, but he sure hated me.

Neat.

"Maybe you should listen to your friends." I didn't make any quick moves, but I wasn't afraid. I'd dealt with pissed off shifters before. I'd grown up with one.

The other guy next to him rolled his eyes like he was used to Steele catting out, and was so done with it.

"Dude," the first guy said. "I'm hungry and want beer. Deal with your shit."

Those cat eyes zeroed in on me. His hand was now clawed, pressing so hard into the table as he clenched his fist, he left gouges in the wood. He was panting a little.

"You don't belong in this sport, *wizard*." He spat that last word. With all the extra teeth in his mouth it came out a little garbled, which was funny, but now was probably not the time to laugh.

If I were the kind of guy who could be intimidated, I'd be looking for a way out of this. But I was a hockey player.

I leaned toward him and got up in his face.

"Kiss my magic ass, Steele."

He snarled, a deep, chest-wrenching, bestial sound.

Well, shit. This was going down. I had never used magic to defend myself. I'd taken my beatings just like any other guy. It had been worth it not to reveal that I was a wizard.

I knew how to take a punch and how to throw one. And I knew when I was in a shitty position to do either.

Shifting took maybe five seconds tops. But orienting to the animal mind, senses, and body could take at least another five seconds.

I had maybe ten seconds lead time if I ran. Staying here was just asking for pain.

Or I could use magic to save myself.

That thought, one I'd spent a lifetime squashing, floated through the back of my brain with a tempting, tingly kind of spin. I could use magic.

Would that be so wrong?

"The moment you step on the ice," he snarled, "I'll be coming for you. And I will take you out."

I was impressed he could enunciate all those words past his fangs.

But instead of making the smart move by leaving, I made a kissy face at him.

He growled.

Oh. Shit.

"We have a problem here, boys?" Graves's voice, behind me with that easy Texas roll, rumbled over the music.

I didn't look away from Steele. Cats, big cats, often attacked when their prey turned its back.

"No problem." Teammate guy number one tugged on Steele's arm again, then looked up and over my shoulder.

At Graves.

Then something really weird happened. The guy pulled his hand off Steele and he took a startled step back. "We don't want any trouble."

He tipped his chin up, exposing part of his neck, his gaze sliding to the side, then to the floor.

That was full submission posture. Which told me two things: one, the guy was a wolf shifter and two, he instantly deferred to Graves as an alpha.

Interesting. Almost interesting enough for me to turn around so I could get a look at Graves for myself. But seeing as Steele in front of me was still part cat—the fang and claw part—I didn't do so much as blink.

"Then you can leave," Graves said. "You too."

The other guy either wasn't a shifter or wasn't a wolf because he didn't bare his neck. But he did give Graves a long look, then nodded. "He's just…it's been a long day, and he's a little intense before a game."

"Are you saying I need to make him leave?" Graves's voice was low, a rumble. There was something big behind it. The quiet before the *boom*.

That got Steele's attention. He blinked and his eyes slid more brown, less feline gold. He straightened and squared off toward Graves.

No. Nope. No.

I did not need Graves fighting my fights. I didn't need anyone fighting my fights. It didn't matter that Graves was a D-man and his job description pretty much meant that he was all about defending his teammates, me included. We were not on the ice.

I could handle my own problems. On or off the ice.

I pushed the chair back so I could stand between the two of them. Graves was still at my back and placed a heavy hand on my shoulder, holding me there.

"Mr. Steele," he said over me. "You seem to take umbrage to my friend, Hazard here. That doesn't sit right with me. If you have a problem with him, you have a problem with me. I'd be happy to step outside right here, right now, and settle that."

"Hold on," I said. "Wait."

Steele slid his jaw back and forth, teeth elongating and shortening as he tried to control—or not control—the cat. His eyes slitted down, narrow and mean.

"Listen." I was addressing Graves, but since I couldn't turn around, I was still looking at Steele. "This doesn't have to be a thing. You don't like me? Fine. We've got a game tomorrow. Let the scoreboard settle it. We can just walk away from this. We can both walk away."

Silence.

"Right, Graves?" I craned a look back at him.

I guess I expected him to look different somehow. From the way the other guys had quickly backed down I thought he'd Hulked out or something.

Nope. Same Graves. Although even regular Graves was just a calm second away from *boom*. There was always something tight about him. Something dangerous right beneath the surface.

It wasn't his wolf. Or at least I didn't think so. I'd seen Duncan angry, seen him lose control of his wolf more than once. He had never looked like he knew how to dismantle a man, joint by joint, and would take pleasure in doing so.

"Happy to walk away," Graves said. "I'd be even happier to see you walk away. Now."

Steele scowled at me then at Graves. His teeth were more human shaped, his eyes a hot brown. He'd gotten control of the shift. But just because he didn't look like an angry cat didn't mean he wasn't still an angry man.

"You're garbage, Hazard," he said. "You won't last. They'll have to scrape you off the ice and send you home in a bucket."

He stormed away, shoulders square, movements fluid, a predator in motion.

"When did you spit in his shoes?" Graves asked. "That man in no way cares for you."

"I've never met him before. But his coach doesn't like me either."

"How do you know that?"

"He told me."

Graves stared after Steele then scratched under his jaw. That trigger edge, that calm before the storm was hidden away until it was almost unnoticeable.

Almost.

"You've played in the league," I said.

"That's right."

"Do you know his story?"

Graves shook his head. "I've heard rumors. Locker-room conversations with players who have played with him. His father's a piece of work. Mom died five years ago. He changed then. And not for the better."

"How did she die?" Something that felt a lot like sympathy twisted in my stomach. I knew what it was like to lose a parent—well, to be missing one. I'd never really met my father, but I could guess at how much worse his absence would be if I had known him. If I had loved him.

"Accident."

"What kind?"

"Car, I think? Never heard for sure." His voice was tight. There was more he wasn't saying, more I suspected he knew. But the music, which had swung down into a smoother sort of grind, stopped and the crowd clapped and cheered.

That seemed to shake Graves out of whatever thoughts he'd been lost in. It also shook Duncan and Josky out of the crowd.

"Your turn," Josky said, grabbing my hand. "There is dancing to be done and I already wore that one out." She jabbed a thumb toward Duncan.

He grinned at her and waggled his eyebrows. With her in two-inch heels, they were eye-to-eye. "Give me five minutes and I'll be ready to go again."

"That's what all the boys say." She slapped his chest and yanked me after her.

"I don't dance."

"Don't care. This is for luck."

"I don't know what to do."

"Still don't care. You a Thunderhead, Hazard? Because no Thunder backs down from a challenge."

I snorted. "So?"

"So this is a challenge." She pulled me again, using my momentum to slingshot herself backward and me forward. "Dance!"

The movement was hard enough I stumbled, throwing my arms backward.

I caught myself on something hard. A person carrying something wooden, like a signboard, or a table.

"Jesus," the person—a woman—said.

Hands fell against my upper back and shoved me onto my feet.

I spun on my heel to apologize to whomever I'd been shoved into.

"Sorry—" The words died.

I'd run into a woman. A woman wearing a guitar slung over her shoulder. A woman who was the lead singer of the band. A woman wearing torn black jeans and a black T-shirt that skimmed just high enough above her waistband to show an inch of soft, bare skin.

A woman who I'd met, though she'd been wearing scrubs then.

"Genevieve?" I sputtered. "Sorry. Sorry I hit you. God, sorry. Are you okay?"

Her eyes, which were not just green, but that amazing yellow-leafy green of spring, were lined with black, making them huge. I couldn't look away.

She shook her head, her expression flickering with confusion, then maybe something close to laughter.

"I—" I began again.

But the drummer was counting, the crowd, which I could suddenly hear again, was chanting and then the music started and everything moved around me.

I might have danced with Josky. I might have even danced with some of the other Thunderheads. I had a vague awareness of the guys around me, sometimes shoving at my shoulder or patting my back. Might have muttered goodnight as they leaned in close enough to say they were leaving, land a palm-slap, a fist bump.

But what I remember is standing there, still a little too close to the stage, utterly enraptured by the woman singing. I was caught by the spell of Genevieve's voice, Genevieve's guitar. Caught by the spell of her.

"…looking ridiculous," Duncan yelled in my ear. "Or would you rather walk home?"

"What?" I turned. He had a grin and good timing. The music ended on a lilting rise, while the drummer rolled through to the end, and then the entire place erupted in applause.

Genevieve thanked the crowd, waved with one hand, the bracelets on her arm jingling and flashing with dull metal glints.

"How many beers did you drink?" Duncan asked. "You've been standing there like an idiot for almost an hour. It's time to go home."

Yeah, I still couldn't take my eyes off her.

Genevieve moved backward from the edge of the stage and her gaze met mine again. She smiled, showing that dimple and nose crinkle. Her breath was coming a little fast, and her face was shiny from the raw energy and joy of performance, her hair messy and curling around her face to stick to the sweat on her forehead.

She was the most beautiful person I'd ever seen.

I lifted a hand, then pressed it over my heart.

"Lame," Duncan laughed.

She waved back and made a pinky-thumb phone at her ear. I hoped that meant she was going to call me.

Her drummer and the other guitarist were both sending suspicious looks my way, but when she said something to them, they nodded and went back to ignoring me.

"So not lame," I said. "I got the sweetest moves."

Duncan shoved me with his shoulder. "Let's get out of here, Sweet Moves." He slung his arm across the back of my neck.

That wouldn't be a bad nickname: Sweet Moves. Yeah, I could do that.

I took one last look around the place. Didn't see anyone from the team except Graves and Josky over in the corner of the room. He faced her, one hand in hers, the other on the middle of her back. Her hand was on his shoulder. She was just an inch shorter than him. Their elbows bent and Josky's head dipped so she could watch her feet. Graves was talking, counting out the beat of whatever dance he was trying to teach her.

Waltz? Foxtrot? Box step? I wasn't even sure those were things, but thought I'd heard Mr. Spark groan about them when he and Mrs. Spark had taken a couple dance classes when I was in middle school.

Josky laughed, then slapped Graves on the arm. They stopped, switched hands so hers was on his upper back and his was on her shoulder. Then Josky started counting and Graves was following her lead, whistling a low tune to the rhythm of their steps.

It was sweet. Nice. One of those things that made me happy I'd come back. Come home.

Graves's eyes tipped up, his gaze searching then finding Duncan and me. He nodded briefly, and I nodded back.

I wasn't sure what we'd just said to each other in that exchange, but it felt like camaraderie. It felt like an understanding that we were in this together. That he had my back.

That we were a team

"Did Josky dance with every one?" I asked.

Duncan nodded. "Graves was the last holdout. Looks like she pinned him down. You know what that means, buddy?" Duncan shoved the door open, walking backward in front of me in the cold autumn air. I shivered at the difference in temperatures. It was roasting in Downpour, but early October chill had bitten down hard and held on.

"What does it mean?"

"It means we're gonna win!" Duncan shouted.

A couple people in the parking lot looked our way then looked away again.

I chuckled. "Good," I said, making finger guns at him. "'Cause that's all I know how to do."

12

TWO O'CLOCK IN THE morning, an alarm was ringing. I brought my phone up to my bleary gaze. Not an alarm. A text.

How'd u like the band?

I rubbed at my face, read it again. It had to be Genevieve. I propped up enough my thumbs were free.

All da love! Couldn't u tell by how long I stared & drooled?
You looked like u were into it. Are u stalking me?
???
Never seen u there before.
Was out w/team. Game 2morrow. It's a good-luck thing.
Hockey, right?

Yep. I hesitated, then took the plunge. *Want2 come2 a game? Tomorrow or????*

No reply.

It will be fun.
I can get u free tix.
Tomorrow is 1st game. Grudge match. Should be a good one.

A text finally chirped.

What time?
Is that a yes 4 tomorrow?
Yes.
Yes!!! 7:00. Ticket at the front under your name. Will need your last name. Oh, do u want extra for friend…or date?

I deleted, rewrote, deleted.

"Fuck it." I wrote it one more time then hit send. I chewed on my thumbnail and sighed. She probably had a boyfriend. I thunked the back of my head against the wall. Of course she had a boyfriend. I'd just met her and couldn't stop thinking about her. Someone else was sure to have noticed her before me. She was in a rock band. It was impossible not to see her.

Brooks. Two. :)

Before I could reply:

1 for me & 1 for friend. Which team r u on?

Portland Thunderheads.

How will I know which one is u?

My name will be written across my back.

Right. Ha. I knew that.

My # is 42.

Like life, the universe & everything?

No. Hockey is life, the universe & everything.

Lol. See you tmrw! Good luck!

Thx. Goodnight, G.

Night, R.

I reread the text until the screen went dark. I was pretty sure I had a goofy smile on my face.

This was a win. It might even be a sign. Tomorrow, my first game with my new team in my new league was going to be amazing.

13

IT WAS NOT AMAZING.

It was hell.

The Tide hit the ice with speed that made our team look like we had sandpaper on our skates and rocks on our backs.

In the first two minutes, we botched a pass. The Tide used that to out-muscle us in a scrum against the boards and their forward, a guy named Catcher, got a lucky bounce off the irons. The puck ricocheted over Josky's left shoulder and into the net.

Score: 1-0 Tide.

Things went downhill from there.

The crowd worked hard to push us up. Chanting, cheering, groaning at each missed opportunity, but we could not seem to catch our rhythm.

First games are always a little shaky. Especially if the team brought in a lot of new players. The Thunderheads picked up three new players this year. Me, Duncan, and Graves, and a lot of the other lines had been mixed up.

But we were playing like we'd never met each other, much less practiced together for weeks.

End of the second period we were down four-zip.

Coach was not pleased.

He walked into the locker room, a clipboard in his hand, his tie loosened. Assistant Coach Beauchamp lumbered in behind him and leaned up against a wall. The trainer, a quiet guy named Leon made his way between players checking to make sure there weren't any injuries that needed to be dealt with.

We hunched on the benches in front of our lockers, breathing hard and gulping down sport drinks and bars.

I was between the second line defensemen, Trotier and Tetreault, "T1" and "T2" the "Terminators" They were roommates and one of them, T2, was going to Portland University for a degree in marine biology.

Duncan sat in the corner next to Josky. Graves was opposite me, right next to Watts and JJ.

"Now that everyone has gotten their nerves over with, let's win this game," Coach Clay said. "Put in the hustle. Prove you want this. First home game on our ice. Stop trying to be fancy. Just shoot the puck at the net every time. Every chance. Get in there and fight for it."

He didn't yell, didn't even sound angry. But there was something sharp in his words, like a fire building. Like he was not going to let us let him down.

He paced, just three steps one way and three steps back, all of them uncannily silent.

Snow leopard shifter.

"Josky, did you get your dances?"

"Yes, Coach." She wiped the towel over her face and took a swig of water, spraying some of it down the back of her neck.

"Then this is not bad luck." Three steps, turn. Three steps.

"This is not a lack of skill. Not a lack of training. You put in the sweat. You put in the bruises and blood. The Tide want to tear us down, put us on our knees. In our home. In our territory."

He stopped moving, faced all of us. "Don't let them define who we are. What we are. Push back. Hard."

Our captain, Lock, first line left wing, stood and addressed us. "Just like in practice," he said in with that lilting Swedish accent. "We play our game, just like we always do. Play our pace, not theirs. They chase us. They fight for our puck. We out think them." He tapped a finger at his temple, then pointed that finger out to the side, toward the rink. "Our game. Our ice. Our crowd. Let's give 'em hell, boys."

The team clapped and shouted as we surged to our feet. Lock fist-bumped, slapped helmets, slapped shoulders of each player who walked out of the room and down the corridor past him. I fell in at the back of the line.

Coach Clay stopped me. "Your head in the game, Hazard?"

"I'm good."

His eyes, blue as old ice were sharp and hard. There was so much cat in that gaze that I held perfectly still, holding my breath.

But his pupils didn't slit, his teeth didn't elongate. His cat might be pushing to escape his bones, but his control was more than up to the task. It was a moment, though. A chance for me to see how much this game meant to him. How much this team meant to him.

"We don't need flashy. Solid work gets this done. You can skate circles around every one of the players on the Tide. So do that. I want you to get in there and shake them up. Get the puck. Put it in the net. We're not going out on a zero. Understand, wizard?"

I nodded. My heart was already beating too hard. He'd noticed how nervous I'd been all night. I'd made some dumb plays, misread the ice and players in a way that made me feel like I should be busted back to Juniors.

There were a lot of eyes out there—press, critics, haters—watching me.

Everyone wanted to see the first wizard in history to play hockey.

Most everyone wanted to see him fail.

Wizards were not expected to be physically strong. Wizards were not chosen for sport. So there were some people out there who really wanted me to win too.

It was a lot to put on a first game. It was a lot to expect from me, and my new team.

The crowd, the press, the critics, the haters all hoped I'd lose it again. Hoped I'd use magic.

And that was hard to swallow. Knowing it was that fascination with magic that packed the stands. Just like the shifter fights on the ice had packed these stadiums for years.

We were the side show, the freaks. And I was the main attraction today.

There was no changing that. What I could do, what I could prove, was that I was here because I could play damn good hockey.

14

FIRST FORTY SECONDS INTO the third, JJ sunk the puck. I whooped when the red light went off and joined Duncan and Watts in the pile on top of JJ, smacking his helmet for luck.

"That's how we do it, boys," he panted.

"Fuck yes!" Watts crowed. "Finally!"

The Tide doubled down on their defensive game, every hit was harder than the last.

My bruises had bruises.

We were all playing harder, faster, that goal doing everything to light our fire.

Josky was amazing in net. Solid, fast, and damned near acrobatic. She stopped everything they threw at her. We did everything we could to make sure she didn't have to.

Ten minutes in, we got two goals almost back to back with a little bait-and-switch behind the net.

Eight minutes left, the game was within one point.

The crowd hadn't stopped roaring since our back-to-back goals. All of us on the bench pounded our sticks on the ground or against the boards to make noise.

Another scoreless minute went by, and then it was the fourth line's shift again. I hit the ice hard, pushing to get in position for the puck. Graves took the faceoff against one of their forwards, dug hard for it and shucked the puck toward the corner.

Duncan was waiting, but so was one of their D-men. There was a scuffle, a couple shoves, elbow shots, grunts and growls, then the puck broke free. I was ahead of it, in good position to take it down the boards, one of their wingers right on me.

I scooped it up and made a break for the crease.

I never saw the other guy coming. One second I was pounding toward the net, the next I was hit from behind. My head slammed into the boards, pinned by an arm across the back of it. My knees buckled and my vision went black with pain. I lost my grip on my stick.

"Wizard trash," the voice snarled.

It happened fast. So fast, I almost couldn't register the reality of it.

Slick hot blood poured down my throat, the heat of it covered my face. I blinked and blinked trying to clear my vision.

Holy shit. I'd been hit before but this was a pile drive and illegal as hell. I swear my spine was busted, my lungs crushed.

I pushed to my knees, heard the shrill warble of a whistle, and after that, booing from the crowd.

Then there were hands on me.

"Shit, Ran, you okay?" Duncan panted, his hands pressing around my wrists, halting my movements.

"Who?" I grit out.

"Who else? Steele."

Leon, our trainer, was there, his voice low and calm. "Just let me take a look at your eyes, Random. Hold still."

He angled my head and I grit my teeth against the vertigo as the arena sloshed to one side.

"Might be a light concussion," he said. "Let's get you on the bench. Can you stand?"

"Yes. Yeah." I worked on getting my feet under me while Duncan and Leon hauled me up. Leon put a steadying arm around my ribs, and draped my arm over his shoulders.

"Just to the bench and we'll see how you're doing."

To my surprise, both my legs worked fine and other than a headache and a ringing in my ears I couldn't seem to shake, I didn't have any problems skating over to the bench.

A scattering of applause accompanied me, and like the sweetest music I'd ever heard, the ref called out Steele, earning him five minutes in the penalty box.

Asshole deserved it.

The crowd cheered for that, which made me smile, and then the game was on, harder, faster, my D-man, Watts, making it clear that breaking my brain against the boards didn't happen without retribution.

I sat on the bench and glared at Steele.

Steele glowered at me from the opposite side of the arena, his hatred palpable.

Both teams were tired and frustrated, and it showed. We couldn't knock the puck in the net even with the one-man advantage, and they couldn't get past our goalie.

Then, suddenly, there was a different tension in the air. I'd say electricity, but it was more like lightning looking for a place to strike, a storm pulsing and pulsing, waiting for a chance to break.

"Oh, shit," Leon, behind me, said.

I glanced at him. His eyes were wide, focused on the players on the ice. "He's gonna shift."

Okay, then. Apparently our trainer was a sensitive.

Coach, who I thought was too wrapped up in the game to hear Leon's soft voice over the noise asked, "One of ours?"

"Other team. I think their center. Lundqvist."

My gaze riveted to the play. The center was against the boards. Duncan was up against him, fighting for the puck.

I could hear the swearing from here, because Duncan had a mouth on him and loved to give players hell.

Then I heard the snarl.

It was a loud screeching growl of a big cat. Duncan heard it. He was there, crowding up against the guy. He must know Lundqvist was about to shift.

But instead of stepping back, Duncan stole the puck.

Lundqvist lost his shit.

He surged after Duncan. Swung his stick from behind and smashed Duncan's face. Duncan staggered, fell to his ass. Then he pushed back up to his feet and threw his gloves off, ready to fight.

The linesmen and refs were blowing whistles like traffic cops in a highway pile up, racing toward the players. The crowd roared and cheered, their hunger, their energy feeding the scene, feeding the impending fight.

Duncan was running his mouth, that gritty smile on his face that even made me want to take a shot at him.

My heart swelled with pride for him. Idiot.

I wondered if his parents were watching. Knew they were somewhere out there in the audience.

Lundqvist lost control of his magic. His big body twisted, bulked and stretched as he roared and yelled himself into the shape of a cat. A big cat. Lion.

His jersey and undergear all lay in shredded heaps on the ice, his skates twisted and broken from the force of his shift. His head was low, muzzle curled back to reveal huge teeth.

Duncan was breathing hard, his hands in fists, his grin now more of a grimace as he grappled with control to keep his own shift from taking over.

That was the thing with second-marked and fourth-marked. When one shifted, it often triggered the shift in others.

"C'mon, Duncan," I whispered. "C'mon, brother. Easy. Easy."

There was so much noise, so much chaos in the arena, I knew he couldn't hear me.

Still, he glanced up, his gaze a little wild as he searched me out. When he found me, our gazes locked and something in him settled.

Then he laughed, his whole body relaxing as he gave me two big thumbs up and that cocky grin.

I huffed out a laugh of my own. Just like all the years of hockey we'd played, and every damn fight Duncan had started. He loved pushing the other guy until he lost it.

To Duncan the fight wasn't won when the last hit landed, it was won before the first fist flew.

"Hell, yes!" I yelled. "You got this, Spark!"

That was when everything went crapbaskets.

Lundqvist lunged at Duncan. Duncan braced just in time to get under Lundqvist's shoulder and lift. Man vs. lion usually had one outcome: dead man. But wolf shifter vs. lion was a different playing field.

Duncan's wolf was so close to the surface, his reflexes were heightened, as were his senses and all those hard, conditioned muscles. He shoved with a grunt, lifting Lundqvist up so the huge teeth and head were pushed away. Shifter or not, a lion did not have good purchase on ice. Not as good as a conditioned hockey player still wearing his skates.

I'd seen Duncan do this before. We'd played mixed leagues when we were in high school, where shifts were almost a daily occurrence. So we all knew the best ways to deal with a shifter and come out of it with our hands and limbs intact.

Not that this wasn't dangerous. It was very dangerous. But if Duncan shifted into his wolf, he'd lose his calm. The beast would take over, all instinct and anger.

And then it would be a bloodbath.

For a minute I thought this was going to work out. The refs were there, ready with the short, low-voltage prod rods that looked like billy clubs.

When we were twelve, Duncan and I had stolen a prod rod out of our coach's office and tried it on each other. Even the lowest setting had knocked us on our asses. Duncan wanted me to try it on him when he was in wolf form.

I wouldn't do it, but he talked one of our teammates into it. The prod rod had surprised a yelp out of Duncan's wolf, and he sat back so fast on his haunches, it was comical. Then he sneezed and shook his head for two minutes straight.

Duncan had later told me it hadn't hurt that much, but it had shut down all his senses in a flash. Like a hard hit of smelling salts if the smelling salts were made of lightning and acetone.

One of the refs jabbed the prod in Lundqvist's flank. The lion snarled and shifted his weight off of Duncan's shoulders, turning in midair to land on all fours facing the ref.

Duncan got out of range, skating backward and keeping his eye on Lundqvist.

The refs signaled Lundqvist to sit and then lay down. He did so after a single, unhappy snarl. I thought that everything was going to be okay. But I hadn't been paying attention to the rest of the ice.

"Shit!" one of the T's beside me said. He hooked a leg over the wall and was on the ice, dropping his gloves, before I could register what was happening.

"He we go," Leon said.

Coach hissed a sigh, his hand coming up to wipe at the scowl on his mouth.

Because the ice was not calm. The players were not waiting for the refs and trainers to sort this problem out.

Over the cheering and whistling fervor of the crowd rose snarls and yowls. Three, no, four players on the Tide had lost control and were in various stages of shift. Two wolves, one coyote, and screw me to hell, the other was a tiger.

Shit.

I threw my leg over the board. Coach yelled at me and the rest of the team to stay on the bench, stay off the ice. But Duncan was out there. My team was out there. I wasn't going to let them face this alone.

The klaxon wail of a disaster siren rang out over the loud speakers and then a voice boomed through the arena.

"All players will take a knee. Immediately."

The voice carried power and authority. It had some kind of magic, might even be a wizard who could channel magic through his voice. Or maybe he was one of the fifth-marked—people who were changed by magic in random, unexpected ways.

All the shifters, all the sensitives immediately dropped to their knees, one hand on their hockey sticks, one on the ice. It was the required position for players losing control of magic. Everyone was breathing hard, chests rising and falling in ragged puffs.

I was still moving, though I should be on my knees. But I wasn't going to stop until I was in front of Duncan.

The thick honey of magic in the air was so strong, it felt like I was skating through a candy factory. The sweat on my body, the ice, the air, was heavy and hot with magic.

I breathed it in, let it fill me with that softly drunken ease, with that needful ache.

But I would not use it.

Not unless I had to.

A hand shot out, shoved my shoulder hard, the ref's voice calm in my ear. "Take a knee, son, we'll get this sorted. Just take the ice."

I knew he had the prod rod on him, I could smell the acrid snap of it. I didn't think he'd use it on me, but then again, maybe he would. By the rules, the refs had full say on when it was used and on whom.

Magic swelled in me, pressed. It would be so easy to use it. To drain the power pack in the rod. To throw a shield so electricity couldn't touch me. To bind the ref's hands, his skates with magic, strong as steel cables.

But I did none of those things. Instead, I fell to my knees, one hand on my hockey stick, the other on the ice. I had made it far enough across the ice that Duncan was just a few short strides away. If anything happened, I could reach him. I could save him.

Duncan was watching the shifters, but as soon as I hit the ice, he glanced over at me. He was still grinning. He mouthed, "Fuck, yes!"

I rolled my eyes and tried to scowl at him, because this was not the way we were going to win games.

He was completely immune to my displeasure. He smiled, his eyes bright and hopeful. Happy. Just so damned annoyingly happy.

I grinned despite myself.

What would I do without him? I didn't even want to imagine it.

The regular announcer was telling the crowd to calm down, keep their seats, be respectful while the refs took care of the players on the ice.

Eventually, the audience quieted.

That was either because they were trying to help the linesmen, refs, and trainers surrounding the shifters, or because they were hoping for a fight.

Someone on the ice growled, the sound half-man, half-beast and a low, expectant murmur rolled through the arena.

Who was I kidding? The crowd wanted a fight. A shifter fight. It was what they had paid for. This was the West Hell, Freak league, blood sport. This wasn't hockey. Not real hockey.

That knowledge hit my gut hard and suddenly all the adrenalin of the game came crashing down into disappointment.

This wasn't the life I wanted. This wasn't the league I wanted. This wasn't even the game I wanted.

But it was the only place that would take me.

The official sensitive skated out onto the ice and made her way through the kneeling players. She dropped her hand on Watson's shoulder and he shook his head.

She said something to him quietly and he tipped his chin toward one of the Tide's defensemen.

I knew what she'd asked him. Was he about to shift? Did he need to get control of the beast inside him? Was he at that dangerous point of exhaustion? Was he the one who had growled?

She skated by everyone else, and then over to the player he had pointed out. That man, who was one of the guys in the bar with Steele, nodded.

She indicated that he stand, and he did so. He was escorted off the ice between two trainers.

That left the four players who had already shifted.

The trainers spoke to them in even tones, soothing while the mind of the beast and the mind of the man tried to get in sync. This was the most dangerous part of shifting, really. If anyone made any threatening moves while a person was still in full animal brain, they would be seen as a threat and attacked.

I held my breath.

The lion lifted his head and sneezed.

Someone in the audience tittered, and a bunch of little kids laughed.

The lion yawned, his ears twitching forward, tail wrapped lazily around his paws. And while it looked like Lundqvist had his animal self under control, the same could not be said for the rest of his teammates.

The wolves were pacing, heads low and shoulders up. The coyote stood, stock still, nose in the air, big pointed ears perked up as if he were waiting for the signal to fight or retreat.

The wolves, at least, should have an alpha. Someone on the team who made them feel secured, grounded. But from the way they were acting, they were not pack mates, they were all lone. That was very, very dangerous.

I worried about them. But the tiger? Yeah, that was an even bigger problem.

The tiger paced with a sinuous slinking motion, eyes burning with fiery hatred, teeth bared as he yowled. The officials had sectioned him away from his teammates, corralling him toward the corner of the arena against the boards. Close enough to one of the exits off the ice that I knew that removing him from the rink was their ultimate goal.

But the tiger, a D-man we'd been hassling like hell because he'd sunk one of their four points, was agitated enough his teammates were getting worked up. His stress and anger poured into the spaces between us, through that strange connection all of us marked shared whether we liked it or not.

It was magic, and it moved like rivers, oceans, storms through us all.

A low, screeching started deep in his massive chest.

Marked players on the ice squirmed and cursed softly. We were breathing harder, deeper, trying to hold back the magic that wanted to drown us.

Magic that sucked the air out of our lungs before we could fill them.

I'd been under magic's pressure all of my life. But this was more, thicker, stronger. Concentrated by the crowd who were a mix of normals and marked, heightened by the players' emotions, the edge of violence, the heady competition we threw ourselves into with every second we played this game.

I locked my jaw, curled my hands into fists, bowed my head and breathed, breathed, breathed.

A soft whistle, just a short fall of familiar notes. I heard them through the low murmur of the crowd, the drone of the announcer, the growl and snap of the shifted.

Hearing those notes made my shoulders drop. My breath released in a whoosh like a band around my lungs had been cut away.

That song was mine. Ours.

We all knew Graves was whistling, soft halting notes tying us together so much better than magic. His calm, his steady presence filled that song, reminding me of practices, of hard work, good days on the ice and our team, that had slowly become something more than a collection of individuals.

Even with my head bowed, I could feel my teammates settle.

The press of magic eased and with that, I could better see my surroundings.

The wolves had been settled by the trainers and refs, and willingly trotted off the ice. The coyote, their fast D-man, Nadreau, got it in his head that running around the edge of the ice a couple times and making the refs chase him would be funny.

The audience enjoyed it and cheered him on. It helped change the mood of the place until even the tiger settled down and sat, tail wrapping around his huge paws as he watched the spectacle.

It took a full three minutes and one Zamboni, because apparently coyotes didn't like the big lumbering vehicles, before the coyote finally got maneuvered back toward the exit and off the ice.

The crowd clapped and cheered, and the Zamboni driver stood and waved before driving off through a different exit.

After all that attention given to the coyote, the tiger showed his indifference to being ignored and turned his back on the crowd, the ice, his team, and the game. He walked out the exit with regal disdain, the lion following.

Crisis averted.

Music played a peppy beat to get the crowd back in the hockey mood, while the remaining players on the ice stood and moved into place for the face-off.

The Tide were five players down, which meant they were going to have to cover those shifts with the players on the bench.

Duncan got thrown in the penalty box, two minutes for inciting a shift. He almost got five for arguing with the ref about it.

Coach called the ref over and insisted it was Lundqvist who had hit Duncan first, but the refs refused to budge on it. So Duncan skated over to the box.

Yes, he was still smiling.

He loved the game that hard.

That meant we were playing one man down until he was out of the box. And while that shouldn't be too much trouble, the shift had broken our rhythm all to hell. We couldn't seem to pull it back together, not even our veteran players who had a couple seasons playing together, and should be used to this shit.

The other team didn't rise up to their previous speed or skill either. But they were still strong enough and skilled enough to deny us the one goal we needed to tie the game.

We hustled. Both teams hustled. But there was no digging out of this hole.

Our audience was already streaming out of the arena before the last buzzer sounded.

First game of the season, and we had lost, wizard or no.

15

"WE MADE THEM BREAK," Duncan said over the rush of the shower.

"What, by letting them win?" I asked. "Yeah, Donuts. Real hardship we put them through."

Watts, who was walking out of the shower, snorted.

"Naw," Duncan said. "None of us lost it and shifted."

JJ, who was rubbing soap out of his hair, leaned to one side, his eyes still closed. "That doesn't mean anything. Coach Nowak keeps them on edge. Makes them work hard drills before a game, underfeeds them, so they're tired, edgy, and hungry. He likes it when the beast bleeds into a man. Says it makes his players more powerful."

Wow. Well, that explained some things. Also, it reinforced my belief that their coach was an ass.

"Okay," Duncan allowed, "but that's normal for them, right? I mean, it's fucked up, but that's all a part of playing on the Tide. Tonight five of their players lost their cookies."

"Cookies?" I finished tying my shoes and sat back on the bench, rubbing a towel over my hair.

"You know: magic. They shifted. And Nadreau ran the refs around the rink like an idiot. You know what that means?"

"We lost?"

"We won."

I knew that tone of voice. It was never not annoying.

I sighed. "So, about math. When one number is littler than the other..."

He flipped me off. "We know how to push them. We know they unravel in the third. We know they're already close to a breakdown by then."

"Except Steele," JJ said, rubbing at a huge bruise spreading across his ribs. He'd been on Steele all game and had taken shot after shot from him.

"Yeah, so he's the type who thrives on pain," Duncan said. "With a coach like that, he's probably always a blink away from catting out. Doesn't matter. We know what pushes them out there."

"Playing hockey?" I said. "I don't see how we can use that against them, especially since they *won*."

"Not hockey," Duncan said with the other tone of voice I didn't like—the smug one. "Insults."

It was quiet in the locker room. Just me, Duncan, and JJ were left. Well, and probably a trainer or two. I was still revved up. Even though I'd taken a lot of hits including the one that had rattled my brain, and spent the last of the game on the bench, the push, the pulse, the adrenalin of the game still coursed through me.

Like Genevieve, I'd be up for a couple hours now that I'd poured all my energy into this performance. I hadn't seen her in the stands, didn't know if she'd come.

Maybe she stayed home and hadn't seen how badly we'd lost.

"Are you listening to me, Ran?"

"Yes, Duncan," I lied.

"I called him a sellout. Told him he was a freak league old school hack and liked it that way because going animal was the only way he'd ever win. Drifting and shifting."

I frowned, trying to remember where this conversation was going. "Who? Lundqvist?"

"Yep. I spent most the night calling him names. He was dishing it back. But as soon as I told him he was just a little puppet boy for Nowak's freak fights, and asked him how much his coach paid him to throw the game, he lost his shit."

"Your mouth is going to get you killed, you dummy."

"What?" he said over the sound of the water.

I didn't bother repeating myself. This wasn't out of the norm for Duncan. He liked to think there was a secret way to make an opponent lose his temper and lose focus on the game.

I'd told him the secret was for him to show his face. The resulting anger would just happen naturally.

I raised my voice. "I don't think driving the other teams crazy is smart or safe, Donut."

He turned off the water. A second later he walked out, a towel slung around his hips. "Like smart or safe have anything to do with winning hockey."

He pulled off his towel and tried to snap me with it. But he'd been doing that for years. I caught it before it hit me and tugged.

"Maybe it should be," I said. "Smart and safe."

He threw me a weird look over his shoulder. "What has gotten into you? We play harder than the other team we win. That's it."

"Smart and safe aren't against the rules."

"Sure. But you have to take risks. Push every button. Every advantage."

He pulled on sweats and a T-shirt. Shoved stuff into his duffel.

I stood, shrugging my bag over one shoulder. It wasn't until we were walking toward the door that he spoke again.

"What's different?" he asked bumping my shoulder with his.

"What?" I asked.

"You're usually the one making crazy moves, taking the risks. You like to try everything, on the ice. Even the dangerous things. It's what got you noticed by the NHL, because you pulled off those dangerous things and made them look amazing. What was different about tonight?"

My first reaction was to laugh at him.

But, yeah, this was different.

I'd never pictured myself here. All my life, since I was seven, I'd imagined I'd be in the NHL. Years and years of winning and losing and working hard to make myself into something I could be proud of.

Something *someone* could be proud of.

And at the same time, I was making myself into something I wasn't.

Normal. Non-magic.

So just being here, in this league, felt like I'd fallen into the wrong life.

It also felt fragile. This was the last place I could play hockey, the only league that would take me. If I screwed it up here, there would be no place left for me to go.

And without hockey, I would be nothing. No one.

There had never been a wizard on the ice before. But after me, if I didn't completely screw it up, there might be wizards in the future. Some little boy or girl right now might be looking up to me and imagining that they could have the life they wanted, not just the one everyone expected them to have.

But my biggest problem was that I both ached to and was terrified of using my magic on the ice.

Oh, there were rules to follow. No affecting the ice, equipment, or other players.

But just like Coach Nowak drove his team hard to keep them on edge so that the strength of magic bolstered their physical abilities, I too could use magic.

On myself.

I could make myself faster, stronger. Even though I had very little practice with magic, I knew I could do amazing things with it.

There was a hunger in me, chewing its way out. A hunger I'd pushed away my entire life. I wanted to feed that hunger with magic.

A cold wash shivered over my skin. Just thinking about using magic whenever I wanted, for whatever I wanted, made me squirm with need.

And that scared the hell out of me.

"Did I break your brain?" Duncan asked. "'Cause I think I broke your brain. You okay there, Ran?"

"Yeah." If okay included staring straight into the eyes of what might be an addiction.

"So what was different about this game?" Duncan could be accused of being many things: too friendly, too sincere, too easy going, too spontaneous. But he could not be accused of being passive. When he took hold of something, he didn't let it go.

We had made our way down the corridor and were aiming toward the exit nearest where Duncan had parked.

It was dark outside, the sky mottled with clouds. It would probably rain soon.

"It's a lot of things, I guess."

"You are killing me here with the vague answers."

"Seeing the shifts in the third…" The images of all the magic-infected people dropping to their knees while the normals shouted and cheered from the stands, rolled through my mind.

"You've seen guys shift before." Duncan's tone was calm.

"I'm still getting used to being here. To belonging here."

"Here as in Portland? Or the team?"

"Portland's my home. I'll always belong here. But the team…" I just left that hanging.

"You belong." Said with authority he should not possess. "Coach wouldn't have picked you if he didn't want you."

"I'm not complaining."

He slid a look at me. "Right."

"Okay, so I'm complaining. But that doesn't mean I'm unhappy. I'm just trying to figure out how the hell to do this."

"Play hockey? Well, see, that's easy. You take your little stick and hit the flat rubber disk into a net."

"My stick is not little." I laughed.

"That's what they all say, brother."

We pushed out onto the bricked courtyard in front of the Veterans Memorial Coliseum, where a few people lingered in the hazy light from street lamps. Traffic was thick, but moving pretty well out of the parking garages and onto streets.

"Hazard! Hey!"

I knew that voice: Genevieve.

She sat on the curved brick median that framed the courtyard like a wave. A woman about her age with bright white hair sat next to her. I recognized her as the other guitarist in her band.

I lifted my hand.

"Still lame," Duncan muttered.

"Shut up."

Genevieve stood, dusted the back of her jeans, then sort of hopped down the steps and walked toward me, her friend following.

"Hey," she said when we were close enough not to yell.

"Hi. Sorry I'm a loser."

Her eyes went wide.

"I mean the game. That I lost. That we lost. The, you know, that the game sucked."

"Are you kidding me?" Her face lit up with that smile. "It was amazing! You didn't tell me hockey was so fun, and so fast, and so *bang, pow*! Why didn't anyone tell me hockey was such a rock-n-roll contact sport? Like roller derby with sticks and walls to slam into."

Uh, it was nothing like roller derby.

"Maybe you're hanging out with the wrong people?" Duncan suggested. Then he stuck his hand out. "Duncan Spark."

She shook his hand and I realized she looked surprised that he was standing next to me.

Her eyes had been on me, and me alone. Like she hadn't noticed anyone with me.

That sent a warm tingly vibration down my spine. I liked that she was looking at me. Seeing me.

"Genevieve Brooks," she said. "And this is my friend, Pippa Li."

"Hey." Duncan shook her hand too, and when she smiled, it made her dark brown eyes spark.

"Hey," she said. "So you're on the team too?"

"Yep. I'm the handsome one."

I smacked him.

"I saw you out there," Genevieve said. "You two played at the same time. What does that make you?"

"Linemates," I said, hoping her attention would turn back to me. It did. Warmth bloomed from my chest, pushing lower and higher. "Fourth line."

She shook her head and grinned. "I have no idea what that means, but it sounds important and cool? Is your head okay?"

I rubbed at my forehead. She was full of energy, animated, excited. The side of her I'd seen at the doctor's office was smart and composed, the singer side of her was passionate and focused. And hockey Genevieve? Well, she looked like she needed rocks tied around her feet to keep her on the ground.

"It's good. No big deal."

"Yeah, my man Haz is tough as nails. Little love tap like that wouldn't put him down," Duncan said as he slung an arm across my shoulders.

I rolled my eyes and Genevieve's dimples pressed little shadows on either side of her mouth. I wanted to step closer to her to erase the space between us. Then I wanted to tip her head up, because she was still an inch or two shorter than me, even in those rocker boots of hers. I would rub my thumb right there, at the edge of her lips, tracing the indents of her smile. And then I'd follow my thumb with my mouth.

"Concussion?" she asked, snapping me out of my little fantasy. "That's nothing to mess with. Especially with wizards." There was Work Genevieve, that serious tone that sounded like she'd drive me to the emergency room if I didn't make it clear that I was not brain-bruised.

"Trainer looked at me. Says I'm clear. No concussion. I have a headache, but took a couple pain pills. Did I pass the test, doctor?"

She leaned a little closer, her eyes darting back and forth as she stared at first one of my eyes then the other. Close enough I could smell her perfume—wildflowers that I suddenly couldn't get enough of—and could feel her breath, a puff of warmth in the cool night air.

I liked this. Everything in me liked this. And it seemed like I should make a move. Maybe touch her, or say something. Ask her on a date. But I was struck still again. Unable to move or look away from the light that was Genevieve Brooks.

"You don't appear to be compromised," she said softly. As if this were a very private moment between just the two of us.

"Funny," I said. "I feel a little dizzy." My hand lifted almost of its own accord. I brushed away the stray strands of her dark, heavy hair that had swung forward and caught at the edge of her mouth.

My fingertips skimmed the curve of her cheek, my gaze locked with hers. Her lips parted slightly as I tucked the strands of silky hair behind her ear.

She leaned toward me, just an inch.

I leaned toward her. Just an inch.

Her friend reached out and grabbed her hand. "So, it's been great to meet you. Thanks for the game. We gotta get out of here, Gen. It's really late." Pippa glared at me.

Genevieve blinked and whatever had been building between us was gone.

I wanted it back, wanted to make that tenuous connection strong. But instead, I let my hand drop, took a step back.

"I gotta—" She sort of waved toward her friend.

"Yeah," I said. "Me too."

"Thanks for the tickets. It was really fun. Really."

"Anytime. Just let me know. I'll get you tickets again, no problem."

"Okay. Thanks." She was already walking away, but still looking at me instead of where she should be going. "Maybe I'll call?"

"Yes. That'd be great. Anytime."

"Good. Great."

"Night," I called. They were almost to the sidewalk now.

"Night," she yelled. "Sorry you're a loser!"

I grinned and she grinned and I didn't feel like a loser at all.

"So," Duncan said as we just stood there and watched them walk away. "She's hot. So's her friend."

I shoulder checked him and started moving. "She's smart too. Works at the place where I took my test."

"What place?"

Oh. I hadn't told him about that.

"Coach sent me to a place to test my m-magic ability."

"Did they test your ability to say it without stuttering?" He was annoyed. I didn't blame him. "Or about keeping secrets *again* from your best friend?"

"It wasn't a secret."

He shot me a look that could have left a bruise.

"I wasn't hiding it from you."

"Bullshit."

"Okay. I was. But only because I didn't want you worrying. When you worry your dad always knows. And then he would have wanted to fix whatever was wrong and there wouldn't have been anything wrong other than I had to go, um, get my, you know *abilities* rated on a chart of one to ten and it felt weird to do it in front of you."

"They don't strip you naked, Ran. And even if they did, it's not like I haven't seen your junk. Like, for years."

How did I explain to him that it wasn't physical nakedness that bothered me. "Not...it's not a body thing with wizards. It's a...brain thing, I guess. I didn't want to do something weird or dumb in front of you."

"You're always weird and dumb."

We crossed the street to the parking structure where Duncan had left his ancient car.

"Not with magic. And that's...it's something I don't even know about myself. I'm twenty-two years old and don't know what I can do with magic. I mean, what if I'd gotten there and had been unable to do it?"

He smoothly raised one eyebrow, which always made me jealous because whenever I tried to do that, I looked like a constipated clown.

"You are not a magic virgin. You've done it before. Three whole times, buddy."

"But not on demand. Not when there was nothing at stake, no life-or-death circumstances. What if I couldn't do the test right? What if my magic only worked when I thought someone was about to die?"

He shook his head. "For a hockey player, you sure do overthink things. I blame your mother."

Yeah, well, he might be right about that. Being abandoned as a child made me hyper-cautious of some things; usually things that dealt with my self-worth.

"So?" he asked.

"So?"

"The test. The one you didn't want to tell me about. The one you didn't *trust* me to know about? How did you score?"

I thought back on what the doctor had said. *Something something something* exemplary. *Something something something* remarkable.

"Good. High score, I think. He wasn't really talking in full sentences after the test."

Duncan whistled low. "Nice. Maybe he was stunned by your brilliance?"

I shrugged, shifting the weight of the duffel on my shoulder. "Or easily impressed."

Duncan snorted and then stopped moving, his chin lifting as he sniffed the air.

I stopped too. Didn't ask him what was wrong. When a wolf shifter goes all wolfy it's best to let them listen, let them smell, let them interpret the world through the beast inside them.

When we were nine, he'd crawled into bed with me in the middle of the night, whining. Seconds later there had been a very small earthquake; a low hum and slight vibration that left no damage. Duncan had felt it like a volcano blast.

So this could be trouble, or he could have caught the scent of a particularly good pizza joint and was hungry.

With Duncan, it could go either way. Since we were post-game and I was starving, I was hoping for the pizza joint.

"Ran." Duncan eased his duffel off his shoulder. "You need to get in the car." He tossed the keys at me, which I caught.

"What?"

He tugged his shirt off, and was already toeing his way out of his shoes. He was also staring toward the darkened side of the parking garage, at a stairwell that led to the street and the upper levels of the garage.

"Get in the car," he said. "Lock the doors."

He was no longer the joking, friendly Duncan. This was all protector, warrior, wolf.

"You gonna shift?" That was a stupid thing to say because of course Duncan was going to shift. He had already shucked out of his sweats and boxers and crouched down on the balls of his feet completely naked and unashamed, one hand propped in front of him by the fingertips. He looked like a sprinter setting up against the starting blocks.

"Don't," I said. A shift this close to the outlay of physical exertion he'd used in the game could be dangerous. Especially without a heavy meal in his belly.

Shifting on low resources meant less control over the beast and a longer recovery time when he changed back to his man form.

The last thing I wanted was to try and tackle Duncan in wolf form. He wouldn't hurt me, but with only magic and the mind of the wolf fueling his body, he probably wouldn't listen to me.

"Get in the car with me," I said. "Whatever is out there, we'll drive and get the hell away from it. Cars are faster than wolves. Even your car." *Maybe.*

It was too late. He exhaled a stuttering breath and his body flexed and flowed as magic rolled across it like invisible hands over wet clay. Shaping, forming. Stretching and smashing.

The air filled with that lightning-strike sensation, heavier than electricity and sweet across my tongue. Magic gushed.

"Shit," I whispered.

Duncan was full wolf and beautiful. His thick fur was a mottled mix of sandy brown and gray. All four of his feet were covered in fur white as new snow, something I used to tease him about mercilessly when we were little.

He crouched, ears flicking backward, tight against his skull. He wasn't growling yet, wasn't showing teeth.

There was a furious negotiation going on in that head, in that body. The outcome would either be a wild wolf loose in the middle of a grease-stained parking garage, or man in wolf form loose in the middle of a grease-stained parking garage.

I was so focused on Duncan—waiting for the proof that he had the upper hand on his wolf—that I didn't notice the movement against the far wall.

But Duncan did. He growled, low and guttural.

Shivers ran up my arms and the back of my neck.

Growls answered him. Cat sounds.

It could be anyone. The world was full of shifters. There was no reason for me to think the cats—three of them—pacing our way were members of the Tide.

But that lead cat? The black panther? The way he moved between the mountain lion on his left and the leopard on his right was familiar.

It reminded me of how Steele moved, those eyes just the way he stared at me.

"Duncan, you need to get out of here. We need to get out of here."

Duncan was not listening to me. He bared a row of impressive teeth and growled loud enough it reverberated in my chest.

The cats paused, tails flicking back and forth, heads lowering so that their shoulder blades stuck up on either side of their spines. They snarled, that haywire broken string sound of big cats on the hunt.

Duncan shifted his weight, not moving yet, but about to. About to move in front of me, to protect me.

I didn't need protecting. If those cats jumped at me, I could do...

...magic. Throw a wall maybe, or a cage. Stop them with a spell.

The smart move would be to get in the car. A defensible position. Throw magic from there.

But that would leave Duncan out here. Alone. One against three.

Yeah, that wasn't going to happen.

"Damn it. You all couldn't just leave it on the ice." I griped as I dropped my duffel to the ground. "I know it's you, Steele. And I don't know you two, but I will as soon as this is over. So you might as well knock it off and leave us alone."

Duncan growled at me, trying to tell me to get in the damn car.

Nope. No.

I could take care of myself. Even without being a wizard there were things I could do to make sure the cats didn't pounce on me. Call 911. Use mace on them (not that I had mace, but if I did, I could totally use it.) And if I were the kind of guy who used mace, I might also be the kind of guy who carried a gun and rubber bullets, which were perfectly legal for citizens to use on shifters.

But I wasn't going to call the cops on a couple of thickheaded hockey players with a grudge.

"You won the damn game. What do you have to be mad about?"

The cats yowled and slid a few steps closer, overhead lights pulsing across their muscles like water over stones.

"Stop." I ordered, like a cop with a gun. "Back away now. If you don't knock this crap off, and go the hell home, so help me, you'll regret getting in my face."

I heard movement around us. Footsteps, some slow, some faster. I heard that fake camera-click of phones and someone was narrating quietly. Random people who were witnessing this, filming.

Great. Just what I needed. Another video.

I'd managed to duck out of the after-game interviews today. Lock had fended off the curiosity about the first game the team had played with a wizard teammate.

The first game we'd lost.

I could imagine the headlines.

WIZARD LOSES GAME THEN LOSES COOL

WIZARD CONJURES PAYBACK FOR GAME INJURY

WIZARDS AREN'T TOUGH ENOUGH TO PLAY HOCKEY

Steele snarled again, all teeth and fang and bristled fur.

Duncan snapped a ragged bark.

"Enough!"

My voice echoed off the wedges and slabs of concrete surrounding us. That one word carried power. Magic.

Sweet honey filled my mouth and poured down my throat. I swallowed magic, letting it fill me until I was something more than just Random. Until I was everything more than Random. Until I was magic, wild as the shifters around me.

The cats didn't pause. I hadn't expected them too.

Everything around me seemed to slow, slow, slow. Reality tightened down screw twist by screw twist.

Even my heartbeat calmed.

The cats fanned out. One mountain lion angled to get around behind us, the leopard flanked Duncan. The panther headed straight at me, eyes hatefully bright.

I knew Duncan would throw himself in front of me, fight Steele for me.

I knew what kind of injuries shifters could inflict upon each other. I'd been there when Duncan had been in bed for days at a time recovering from those injuries.

That was not going to happen here.

I drew upon magic. And it *sang*.

I needed to shut them down. Shock them into knocking this shit off.

So I threw that emotion, that *need* to end this situation, to fix this situation without bloodshed, into the magic.

Magic responded with two things: rubber balls and catnip.

And I mean loads of both.

Bright, cheery rubber balls fell out of the air like a confetti explosion, ricocheting and squeaking and pinging like some weird rubbery pinball game with extra squeakage.

Meanwhile the catnip drifted through the air like a frickin' sandstorm, so thick, I couldn't see three feet in front of me through the stink of green. I slapped my hand over my nose and mouth to breathe.

Okay, so maybe I shouldn't have given magic quite that much leeway.

I mean, where did it come up with this stuff?

People in the garage cursed and yelped. And then, they laughed.

As rubber balls bounced and squeaked and the tornado of catnip piled into thick, drifty hills, men and women laughed.

The cats looked stunned. They sniffed the air and opened their mouths in yawns. The mountain lion batted at the green falling from the sky and rubbed big paws over his face. The leopard dropped onto his back and rolled in it.

Only the cat in the middle, the panther with dark burning eyes, was still on his feet. Finally, even he sat. The lines of anger had been eased out of his muscles. He wasn't in "kill" mode, but he wasn't wriggling around like a dork on the floor in magical catnip either.

Duncan still stood next to me. His tail lifted and curled toward his back, both of his ears flicked up into sharp peaks. His mouth was open in what looked like a wide smile, tongue hanging out. His head moved in tiny jerks as he tracked the bouncing balls with eager eyes.

He whined. He'd always loved balls.

"They're all yours, buddy," I said. "You can play with them."

Duncan woofed once at the cats. Roll-on-the-floor stretched and wiggled. Face-rubber flopped down and twisted from side to side. Hatey cat ignored them, him, and me.

Duncan shifted his foot. It landed on a bright yellow ball that squealed.

Duncan's tail wagged furiously. He jumped back and leaned his head down at the same time, grabbing the ball in his jaws and chewing the ever-living squeak out of the thing.

I laughed. I'd never done something like this. Made a magic thing that made someone so happy. And seeing Duncan trying to get three balls in his mouth while batting at six more at his feet made me feel great.

Also dizzy. This was a lot of magic to pull upon, to draw through me, to cast out of me. My chest ached with the burn of it, my vision getting a little weird and dark at the edges. But I was feeling floaty too. And floaty was good.

But already I was starting to pant like I was jogging up a mountain. What was going to happen when I cut the spell and the catnip ran out?

Would it be all "thanks for the nip, now I'm going to claw your head off"?

I was in no shape to run out of here. Not even to the car. The darkness at the edges of the world rushed in toward me like shifting sand.

Headlines:

WIZARD FOUND DEAD IN PARKING GARAGE

HOCKEY WIZ KILLED BY STONED CATS

WE TOLD YOU WIZARDS WEREN'T TOUGH ENOUGH TO PLAY HOCKEY

I couldn't throw another big spell. This much magic was a lot more than what I'd done for my test. And I was fatigued from the game. If I cut the spell now, I'd be lucky not to blackout.

Crap.

"You can break the spell now, Hazard." A voice to my right. Calm. Deep.

Graves's voice.

I swallowed, my throat and mouth so dry, my tongue got stuck and my throat clicked. Breathing was impossible. I was covered in sweat, and that sweat was dripping to sting my eyes.

"Random." Graves again. So steady and sure. His words like an arm under my shoulders, like a body shooting down the ice at the same speed, each step rhythm-in-rhythm. Like a whistle that made me a part of something bigger than me. A part of something more.

"Let go of the spell."

There were still three cats just a few yards away from us.

But Graves evened the odds. Made it three against three. And he was my defenseman. Fourth line lucky. I could trust him.

"Yes," he said. "You can trust me. I've got you."

Oh. I must have said that out loud.

"Break it." This time it was an order.

I imagined scissors, lifted my hand, made the cutty motion with my index and middle finger.

The wide ribbons of magic pouring out of me snapped. An explosion of glass breaking filled the world, and behind that, voices of angels sang.

Magic melted upward, all the colors, all the textures of shiny and bouncy and green and wind and happy and joy, lifted. Up from the oil stained concrete, up the gray pillars, up the stony rafters that hung like squared off whale ribs against the ceiling.

Up, the magic traveled, softening, spreading to gather against the ceiling in swaths of sunset colors splattered over blue skies. Sunset colors that rolled like a storm chasing a horizon then faded, faded, faded.

"Drink."

I took the water bottle pressed against my palm, lifted it to my mouth with a shaking hand. Felt another hand steady the bottle, drank until it was gone.

Noticed heat across my back, around my ribs: Graves's arm.

"Eat."

The water bottle was gone. A bar in my hand was being steered toward my mouth. I did as I was told and ate it in four bites, each time I swallowed easier than the last.

I was still a little dizzy. If I moved my head too quickly, the headache growing there was gonna slosh over to one side and tip me and the world that way. So I didn't move quickly.

But hey. I was still on my feet.

Score one for the wizard.

"T-they," I tried, all raw and rucked up.

"I saw, Hazard. I saw it all."

I was so relieved I didn't have to explain what had just happened that I shut up and took the second bottle of water he handed me. Held it on my own this time.

Where was he getting these things?

"I don't w-want problem."

"There's no problem." Graves didn't move, didn't remove his arm from around me either. Even though I felt weak, I thought I should be able to stand on my own without his shoulder set to take some of my weight. I just didn't have the energy to do it yet.

Duncan, having no balls to distract him and no cats attacking me, was now leaning against my left side. Still in wolf form. Propping me up, all fur and strength and loyalty.

"It's time for you to return to your team, boys," Graves said.

I frowned, because I was with my team, wasn't I? Here between him and Duncan.

"Not you, Hazard." His voice had a layer of exasperation to it.

Oh. Right. He was talking to the shifters. Steele and cat buddies.

I focused on them again.

They were on their feet, looking a little stoned.

"You'll need water and food when you shift back," Graves went on, like everyone in the world didn't know this very basic fact about shifting. "I don't have enough here with me, but I'm sure your coach and trainers do. So you can go on now. Good game."

The total weirdness of him acting like this was something hockey players did all the time—play a game, go outside, show how much magic they could throw around at each other—hit me.

Why would he act like this was normal?

"Problem here?" That was a new voice. A stranger's voice. I turned toward it. Thought maybe we all did. Well, except Graves, who still hadn't looked away from the cats.

Two police officers were walking our way.

"No problem." I pulled away from Graves a little too quickly. I overbalanced and Graves's arm shot out and caught me by my sleeve.

"We're hockey players. All of us," I said, setting my weight over my feet more evenly and bending my knees, like I was expecting to be on ice. "These three are on the Tacoma Tide." I pointed at the cats. "We're on the Portland Thunderheads. We just played a game. Going home now. Uh…you know. Friendly rivals."

"We got reports that there was an altercation. Wizard throwing dangerous magic. Would that be you, sir?"

My heart started beating too fast and the rush of blood under my skin was hot and painful. I knew there were laws about what a wizard could and couldn't do in a public place. I knew it was a law to keep people safe, and I was all for safety.

I didn't know if what I had done counted as safe or not.

"I…yes. No. I mean, yes, I'm a w-wizard. But n-no dangerous magic."

Apparently my skills of persuasion were not as strong as I'd hoped.

The taller officer closed the distance toward us. He was at least Duncan's height—Duncan the human, not Duncan the wolf. He had all the normal looking police officer stuff on his uniform. But he had some extra gear too. Like a metal stick with a wire loop at one end that looked like an even stronger version of the refs' prod rods and a short, big-barreled gun at his hip for tranquillizer darts that worked on shifters and, I could assume, on wizards.

His partner, a guy only a little shorter and wider than him, was similarly outfitted.

More people had gathered, phones at the ready.

I didn't know how the word had gotten out so quickly.

"Can you step away from the wolf, sir?"

Could I? Maybe?

I gave it a go, and was glad when my knees held.

I was less glad when Duncan growled.

"Stop, Duncan. I'm not being arrested." I hoped that was true.

"I need to see your ID," the cop said.

"My wallet's in my duffel." I pointed to where it sat near Duncan and Duncan's duffel.

"Officers," Graves said. "I am happy to give a statement. There was no dangerous magic here."

"Did you see the spell?"

Graves took his eyes off the cats for the first time. The cats hadn't moved, which surprised me, because it was a smart choice. The way they'd snuck into this place to do...whatever it was they had planned to do...led me to believe "smart" wasn't on their playlist tonight.

"Yes, sir, I saw it. I'm sure many of these people with their phones recorded the spell too."

"I'd like you to tell me what you saw."

Graves smiled, a slash of white that did amazing things to lighten his face and send lines arcing out from the edges of his eyes. "I walked over here when Mr. Hazard and Mr. Spark were headed to their car. Three hockey players in shifted form walked calmly this way and then Mr. Hazard cast a spell."

I wouldn't say the cats were calm, exactly. Graves was downplaying that a bit.

"What was the nature of the spell?"

"Friendly."

The cop didn't even blink an eye at how vague Graves was being. "And can you describe this *friendly* spell?"

"He made catnip fall out of the sky. And rubber balls for the wolf."

Duncan's tail wagged.

That, apparently, was not what the officer had expected to hear.

"The illusion of…uh, catnip and balls?" I could tell he was trying to deal with this as if it were a serious kind of magic instead of the weird, stupid, and frankly silly spell I'd actually cast.

Embarrassment did a slow burn across my face. I didn't know which was worse: being exposed as a wizard, or being exposed as a wizard who cast a spell of *toys* for full-grown adult shifters.

The other officer snorted. He wore the blazing red band around his arm and chest to declare him a shifter. From his build, I guessed he was a cat.

"Can I help you, officers?" New voice. New problem.

Really? Like I needed more people showing up? And Coach Clay of all people?

This was not the sort of attention he wanted brought to the team. He had done everything in his power to distance the WHHL from the wild, bloody, freak league everyone thought it was. And here we were, shifters and wizards facing off in a public place.

Like we couldn't leave a game without making a big mess of things.

"I'm Elliott Clay, coach of the Portland Thunderheads. Is there a problem here?"

Coach had the stride and voice that managed to convey authority without being condescending.

I was acutely aware of Graves studying Clay like he was the most interesting thing in the world. Not in a player-coach kind of way. More like a personal kind of way.

Huh. I pushed the suspicions to the back of my brain because I was not thinking clearly after that spell. Also, their personal life was none of my business.

The second officer, the shifter, turned toward Coach. "Are these three people on your team?"

Clay glanced over at us. I wasn't sure if he'd ever seen Duncan shifted, but that didn't matter. He immediately answered. "Yes, they're my players."

"And those three?"

"They are members of the visiting team, the Tacoma Tide. Would you like me to contact their coach?"

"Yes. You do that."

The cats flinched, ears flicking back before popping forward. Steele, still in panther form, had his mouth open and was breathing a little hard.

If I didn't know better, I'd say that was fear.

Well, if he was worried about his coach finding out he was running around the city in cat form, he shouldn't have done it.

Coach pulled out his phone and tapped something on the screen. He waited a second and tapped an answer.

"I've contacted their coach. Someone will be here soon."

And that worked better to subdue the cats than Duncan's aggression, my magic, or Graves's reasoning.

The cats lay down and lowered their heads, waiting.

"If you don't have any other questions here, officer," Clay continued, "my players would like to go on their way. We have early practice in the morning."

We do? That was news to me.

"Five a.m.," he continued. "And we'll be doing strenuous drills."

Ouch. That meant we were gonna get a bag skate. Even Duncan winced.

"So I need them to go home and get some sleep." He might have said that for the officers' benefit, but I had a feeling it was also a direct order.

The officers nodded. "We'll need your contact information and the names of your players. Numbers where we can reach them."

"I'd be happy to supply that."

"You can leave," the non-shifter cop said. "But Mr. Hazard, was it?"

I swallowed and nodded.

"Keep the public displays of magic limited to pre-approved areas inside city limits."

"I will. Sir." I'd even look them up.

I waited to see if Coach Clay had something else to say, but he was talking with the other cop.

Graves reached over and pulled on the shoulder of my shirt. "Move it, Hazard."

I moved it. Followed along behind him like a brainless zombie.

Or like a guy who had just pulled on a lot of magic right after a physically demanding game of hockey and who still hadn't had dinner yet.

Duncan trotted behind us, silent as he moved except for the slightest click of his claws on the concrete.

I belatedly noticed Graves had slung both of our duffels over his shoulders. Right after that, I noticed we were walking away from Duncan's car.

"We're back there." I pointed over my shoulder.

Graves didn't slow. "You think you can drive?"

"I know how to drive."

"After you've thrown that much magic?"

"I'm fine."

He gave me a look.

"I am." I probably would have argued harder, but I was exhausted and hungry and magic was still pushing through me, fluxing like ocean waves rising and falling, looking for a way out of me, or a way into me past my control. Magic burned away at my body; I knew it was burning my fat and muscle. If I didn't eat, if I didn't take some time for recovery, it would keep on burning until it was gnawing on my bones.

There was a reason wizards were known for being strong of mind, and weak of body.

Magic ate us up, bite by bite.

Unless we fought for our body's health. Unless we were very careful to keep ourselves well.

Shifters had a price to pay too. Canidae lost all coordination when they shifted back to human form. If they didn't eat, they could end up seizing. Felidae suffered from crippling headaches that could become brain bleeds.

The only advantage to being a second-marked and fourth-marked was that carrying a beast just under the skin made a shifter stronger physically, which meant higher healing capabilities.

But that ten seconds after a shift—both ways—was a huge fight between the human mind and the animal mind.

If the human lost, the animal gained control. The feral animal.

And the longer a person remained in shifter form, the more of a chance the animal would smother the human mind. Smother and kill.

Duncan had been a wolf for about twenty minutes now. I knew he was good for up to three hours at least. Different shifters had different endurance, but when pushed beyond that, the animal always won.

Because magic always won.

"Burgers or Mexican?" Graves asked.

My stomach growled. Duncan whined.

We were down at the end of the parking garage where Graves's big black Chevy truck was parked.

Of course he drove a big truck.

He unlocked the doors and threw our duffels into the back of the bed. "Get in."

Duncan jumped in and settled on the bench seat in the back of the cab. Since it didn't look like I was going to be able to argue him out of this, and I sure as hell didn't have the energy to walk all the way across the garage to Duncan's car, I got into the passenger's seat, buckled the belt and leaned my head against the window.

"So?" Graves asked as he started the engine.

"I didn't start it. We didn't start it. I don't know why Steele and those other assholes were there. I don't know why they were stalking us."

Graves put the truck into gear, backed out of the parking space and followed the arrows painted on the overheads toward the exit.

"I told the police I was there and saw it," he said once we'd made it to street level. "I wasn't lying, Hazard."

Oh. Okay.

"So?" he said again.

For the life of me I had no idea what he was asking.

"So?" I asked back.

"Burgers or Mexican?"

I chuffed a short laugh and Duncan yipped. "Burgers," I said. "The bigger the better."

Duncan yipped again.

I closed my eyes and worked on not falling asleep to the hum of the truck's engine and the happy thump of Duncan's tail.

16

THE BURGERS WERE HUGE. Four meat patties, four buns, about half a pound of bacon, and a pile of onion rings topping them off. Graves opted for the drive-thru and parked behind the game store next door so we could all eat.

Just because Graves hadn't shifted into his wolf form—if that was his marked form—didn't mean he wasn't hungry. He had skated hard tonight too and the Tide had played a brutal and aggressive game.

Duncan chowed down in the back seat and I lost track of time while I worshiped the fast food heaven spread out on the white paper bag before me.

We didn't talk. I didn't want to talk. But after the food was gone, I was pretty sure Graves would want to talk. Maybe lecture.

To my surprise he just wiped his hands with a couple napkins, wadded them up and threw them in the takeout bag, which he tossed between us. I reached back for Duncan's papers, then added those and mine to the bag.

"What's your address?"

Oh. So maybe there wouldn't be a talk. I let out a relieved breath and I told him our address.

I had a bunch of questions running through my head about tonight, about him being there like he was waiting for us, about why the cats responded to his dominance: he was a wolf, right? Still, I didn't ask any of them.

I told myself I was too tired.

But mostly I was just raw from being exposed. Now more people knew I used magic. People with cameras, social media accounts, police officers. People who had called more people who had come to see the disaster.

The disaster of a wizard who just wanted to be a hockey player. There was, however, one question on my mind I wanted an answer to.

"What is the song?"

Graves glanced over at me as he navigated the narrow streets. "What song?"

"You whistle it all the time."

"I whistle a lot of songs."

"No, it's the same one. You whistle it when we're on the ice. All the time. It gets stuck in my head."

I hummed the beginning of it, and Graves winced.

"Just something I heard. And liked."

"Right. I get that. What is it?"

"It's a Decemberists song."

"Nice. Which one?"

"'The Shankill Butchers.'"

"That's. That's dark, Graves."

"Sometimes it suits the mood."

He gave me a measuring look, and I had no idea how to respond to that. If I remembered the lyrics to the song right, it was a warning about a group of butchers drinking a lot of whiskey, polishing their knives and cleavers and then heading into town on a wicked wind to kill people.

That's the mood he was in when he played hockey? That was the song that came to mind when we were digging out of a losing streak?

"Damn, Graves." I held out a hand for a fist bump.

"Don't read that much into it, kid. There are a lot of songs that get stuck in my head."

I waggled my fist. "Still, damn."

He sighed and gave me a bump. "This it?"

He had pulled up in front of our house. I was tired from the game, angry we'd lost (just because I was a good loser didn't mean I wasn't disappointed in our play) but also excited to play the Tide again so we could take away a win.

Add to that the echoes of magic chiming half-heard songs in my head, which now included crazed butchers, and I was crazy-beat.

"So, thanks," I said before I opened the door. "For the ride, the food, and for showing up in the garage. I swear I didn't do anything to piss off Steele. I didn't know he was there until Duncan was going all wolf."

Duncan growled softly.

"Yeah, yeah," I said. "Big fierce protector. Like I couldn't handle it."

He stuck his cold, wet nose in my ear, which he knew I hated.

"Gross." I jerked away and wiped at the side of my face. I pushed on the door handle.

"Hazard."

I paused, one foot on the edge of the open door.

Graves's desert-colored eyes almost glowed in the low light. Shadow from the street lights carved his face into edges and I wondered what beast lived beneath that human mask he had on.

"I don't want you leaving games without me. Steele isn't the only player in the league who has problems with wizards."

"Thanks but no thanks, Graves. I don't need you to hold my hand while I cross the street. I can take care of myself. With or without magic. Plus, I already have one wolf who follows me everywhere I go."

Duncan growled an affirmative.

Graves tried to out-stare me, but I grew up with a wolf who tried that for like a year straight. Never worked. Maybe because I'm a wizard and immune to the alpha stare, or maybe because I knew how to ignore what people told me to do.

It was even easier than ignoring what magic told me to do.

"See you tomorrow," I said. "Early skate. Lucky us."

Graves exhaled quickly enough his nostrils widened. Then he shifted his shoulders and lifted his head. A small smile tipped his lips and it was all human.

"Does a man good to remember he's part of a team," he said with a little extra drawl in it.

"Which means?"

"Humor me, Hazard. I've been in this league longer than you've had big boy skates. Don't leave the gates without me."

I rolled my eyes and shrugged. "Fine. If you're around we'll walk out together. I'm not holding my breath, though."

I shoved out of the truck, and stood aside so Duncan could jump out. He paused, stared back through the door at Graves who was staring at him too.

I don't know what those two said to each other, or even if they did. But Duncan's ears twitched, then he turned, stuck his freakishly cold and disgustingly wet nose into my palm.

"Jesus, Duncan. Personal boundaries."

He blew snot on my hand, which I tried to wipe in his stupid fur as he bounded off toward the house.

The front door opened and Mr. Spark stood there in his bathrobe, pajama pants, and glasses. It wasn't until I was on the front step and walking through the door that I realized Graves had waited until I was in the house before he finally drove away.

What? He was going to drive every person on the team home now? I snorted at that idea, then realized he wouldn't have to drive anyone else home. Only wizards were weak enough to need bodyguards.

Great.

17

THE ENVELOPE WAS BENT, crumpled, and looked like it had been wet at one time. I picked it up off of my closet floor and read the front. Just my name, printed out.

It took me a minute, but I finally remembered where I'd seen it. That night at the press conference. It had been on the table, waiting for me.

I had totally forgotten about it.

I changed into sweats and a T-shirt—no one was getting anything fancier out of me at four o'clock in the damn morning—then sat on the edge of the bed and tore open the envelope.

One page with text that said: THIS LEAGUE TAKES OUT THE TRASH. YOU DON'T BELONG HERE, WIZARD. GET THE HELL OUT BEFORE YOU END UP—

And beneath that was a photo of a stuffed doll with a wizard's hat on its head. Cute, except the doll was beheaded, naked, and the chest was torn up so that all the stuffing puffed out of it like squeezed mayonnaise.

I sat there staring at it while a weird numbness spread over me. This was a threat. Or a promise. And the last person who had called me trash, "wizard trash," was Steele.

He'd tried to attack me in the garage too. And he'd nearly given me a concussion.

It occurred to me that this was something I could use against him to make him stop harassing me. Something I could take to the police if things got out of hand.

Or it was just one guy with a grudge who was stupid enough to think one threatening arts and crafts project would keep me out of hockey.

I folded it back along the creases, wrestled it back into the envelope, then tossed it into the top drawer of my nightstand.

This had happened before the game, before the garage. Now that we'd played, I figured we'd work out our differences on the ice. He didn't have to like me. I sure as hell didn't like him. But I wasn't going anywhere.

I had a game to play.

By the time I made it down to breakfast, I knew the standoff in the garage was all over social media. It was all over the morning news. I couldn't bring myself to actually look at the video. Didn't want to see myself standing there in the middle of a stupid catnip and rubber ball tornado.

What had I been thinking?

At least the magic I'd thrown back at the Avalanche's camp had been flashy and kind of cool.

Rubber squeaky balls and cat weed. Seriously?

The newscasters smiled about it, but they also seemed kind of amazed.

Probably amazed at what a stupid waste of magic it was.

Duncan hadn't said much, except for the big grin he gave me over the breakfast table, and the comment: "That magic. That *magic*, dude."

I shook my head at him, then ate enough eggs and oatmeal to make me want to go back to bed.

We didn't argue when Mr. Spark—Sean—offered to drive us in to practice.

Early skate was me, Duncan, Graves, JJ and Watts, who did not look happy about the early call, and Coach Clay. I'd expected to have to skate 'til I puked, but for whatever reason, Coach didn't even have us change into our full gear. We hit the ice in sweats and skates, and ran through drills.

He was running them with us too, a constant, calm voice that held confidence instead of anger. He wanted us to get this, to get into step with each other, to develop a better sense of how we worked together on the ice.

Since we all played fourth line, I figured it was about time we nailed this down.

I pushed everything else away, the magic, the letter, the video—well, videos—and focused on making every action good, clean, precise.

By the time the rest of the team showed up for practice, I was loose, relaxed, and ready to play.

I opened my locker to change into my gear. Dozens of bouncy balls fell out and *boinged* around the room. All the boys in the changing room laughed.

"Well, I guess we know who has more balls than anyone else in the room." I grinned even though I felt sick to my stomach. As far as pranks went, this was harmless. Funny too.

"Nice moves last night, Wiz." Watts slapped me on the back. There was that nickname again. "Maybe next time you can make it rain mice or something really flashy."

"Like I'd want mice falling on my head." I pushed a few more bouncy balls out of the way. "Or anything flashy."

"You...you do know that magic you did was flashy?" Watts asked. "No? Then what the hell would you call it?"

"Wasteful." This was from our captain.

"It was not wasteful," Duncan said, quick to my defense. "It was awesome. Those cats went crazy for the nip and man...all those balls."

I sat on the bench, Duncan next to me. He was grinning and bright-eyed and absolutely unapologetically happy. That kind of energy, that kind of happiness was sort of contagious.

I felt my shoulders lower, my breathing even out. I ducked my head and fiddled with the laces on my skates, intent on gearing up and ignoring everything else.

Still, I could see our first line centerman, Upshaw, out of the corner of my eye. He was smiling back at Duncan just as wide.

"Balls," Upshaw said with a chin tip.

"Balls," Duncan agreed.

Wolves.

"Were they solid?" Upshaw asked as he shrugged into his jersey. "They looked solid."

"Totally," Duncan said. "They had *chew.*"

Upshaw's grin got bigger and now he was staring at me.

"Wiz can make anything with magic," Duncan said. "Make it real, man. Like *real* real. It's freaking amazing."

I opened my mouth to protest. Duncan had only been there once when I used magic. He didn't know that much about it.

Of course, I didn't know that much about it either.

"Really?" This was from T1: Troiter.

"Really," Duncan said. "He can do anything."

"That's the problem," Lock said.

"You doubt me?" Duncan laughed.

"Not you." Lock's gaze shifted to me. "You think you can do anything you want with magic? That's how it is with you? All under your control like that? Easy?"

The room went quiet. Everyone waiting for me to answer the team captain.

"No," I said evenly. "It's not easy. I don't—I haven't trained for it. All I know how to do, to control, is how I play hockey."

Someone snorted and made some derisive comment about how well I'd done that last night too. But Lock ignored them.

"I don't need magic on the ice. Not without training. Control," Lock said. "You don't know how to handle magic, you stay off the ice. Got that? No different than second- or fourth-marked staying off the ice when they lose control. They do what's right for the team. You do what's right for the team, and what's right for it isn't sloppy magic."

My face flushed hot, but I locked my teeth together. There was no reason for me to get angry at him talking to me like I was a child. Like I was stupid and didn't know the rules. This was his ship to steer. I was just here to row.

"You won't have to worry about it," I said. "The less I use magic, the happier I'll be."

Lock didn't seem convinced. "As far as I can see, you being a wizard won't do shit to help our game. So either hit the ice like a player who almost made the pros, or take your game somewhere else, Hazard."

Duncan moved, unconsciously leaning his shoulder toward me, facing down Lock. That man would stand between me and a firing squad if he got the chance.

"I'm here to play," I repeated.

"Good. Show me that out there. Live up to your hype." He slammed his locker shut and stormed out of the room.

Graves had told me there were other players who didn't like wizards. I hadn't thought one of those players would be the captain of my own team.

He'd never indicated that he didn't like me being a wizard in practice.

But we'd lost last night. And then I'd been caught on video playing around with magic. Yeah, I could see how it looked like I was just showboating. Using hockey to draw attention to myself, to the magic I could use.

That wasn't the attention our team needed. We wanted to be seen because we were winners. The novelty of a wizard on the team didn't mean jack if we couldn't put the W on the board.

I think Duncan said something to try to break the tension in the room. I didn't think it worked.

All I wanted to do was run drills, do them hard, ignore Lock, and get the hell out of here.

But just my luck, Coach paired me off against Lock.

Because of course he did.

Lock didn't act like there was any tension between us, but I could feel it in the set of his shoulders, in the anger that iced up his eyes. We didn't talk, which suited me fine.

He hated me. That was now perfectly clear.

I didn't know why I hadn't seen it before. But now that I did, it threw me. Threw me off my game. I lost every face-off, I missed every pass, I blew every drill.

My head wasn't in the game. Worse, I'd let Lock get in my head. His doubt. His anger. His judgment.

He didn't think I belonged here.

I wanted to prove him wrong, but every time I got near him, I choked.

It was so bad, Josky leaned back on the net, which I was totally not hiding behind, and reached for her water. "You okay, Wiz?"

"Don't call me that." It came out a little sharp. I hated that nickname.

"Crap day, huh? Well, get it out of your system now. I don't want you stinking the bus up tonight with your mood."

Coach blew a whistle and she went back to her place in the net, skating back and forth twice before scuffing the ice with her left skate and settling into position.

"Hazard," Coach Clay yelled. "Here."

Shit. I pushed out onto the ice and took my place behind the line of players.

He explained the shooting drill, and I heard him. Repeated it over and over in my head. Watched the guys execute it in front of me. Hoped I wasn't going to have to do it with Lock.

Turned out I was paired up with Duncan and JJ.

I managed to get through the drill without making a complete fool out of myself, but I was rough, sloppy.

And I couldn't blame it on the late night magic or yesterday's loss. I couldn't even blame it on Lock. This was all me. All my problem, all in my head.

After drills, Coach Clay and assistant Coach Beauchamp reminded us that we'd be leaving at three o'clock sharp to make the trip south to Redding, California.

Assistant Coach Beauchamp went over the list of what we needed to pack, what he and the trainers would make sure was packed, and where to meet the bus.

"Yesterday was yesterday," Coach Clay said in that soft voice that hid steel behind a smile. "We learn, we grow stronger, smarter, and we move forward. That's what I expect out of you. Learn, and move on. Let's go forward and get our first win."

He glanced at all of us, but I was pretty sure he stared at me the longest.

18

WHEN'S THE NEXT GAME?

I'd been reading Genevieve's text on my phone for probably three full minutes. Part of me wanted to lie and tell her some fake date. She'd already watched us lose. And I was pretty sure she'd seen what I was now referring to as my *stupidous magicus* in the parking garage.

At least she hadn't been at practice to watch me fail there too.

I should answer her, but all I could read from that text was *when are you going to fail again?*

Duncan dropped down in the seat next to me. I'd pretended to sleep, then had actually fallen asleep, only waking up when we stopped for dinner at some diner that handled a busload of hockey players like we were old, uninteresting news.

He'd stopped by my seat when we'd gotten back on the bus, but Watts had called him back to where he was sitting, and after hesitating over me while I mashed up my coat to make a pillow against the window and totally ignored him, he moved on.

I heard them laugh over some game they were playing on their phones, and closed my eyes.

But the rumble of the engine and the rocking of the bus over the twisting road kept me awake. Plus, I was getting a crick in my neck.

I sat up and stretched as best as I could and stared at the darkness beyond the window.

This was our first road game. We were playing against the Redding Rumblers, a team that was fast and inventive. They were the kind of team I loved to play. Their speed the kind of thing I liked to match. Liked to best. But the way I'd been playing, I was worried I'd be able to keep up out there.

Someone lurched forward then dropped down in the seat next to me. I expected it to be Duncan or maybe Graves, both of whom had positioned themselves behind me on the bus so they could keep an eye on me, but it was the D-man, Tetreault.

"Here." He tossed me a can of Coke, and was already opening his own before I could tell him I wasn't thirsty.

The Coke was cold. Okay, I actually was a little thirsty.

"Thanks."

"You still mad at Lock?"

"Who said I was mad at him?"

"I was there, my friend. I saw your face."

There was no use denying it. And sometimes the truth was what worked best in a team dynamic, even if it wasn't a comfortable truth.

"Yeah, I was mad." I shrugged and swigged the Coke.

"He's not a bad guy," Tetreault said as if we were suddenly chat buddies. "You're new to the team, and sometimes it takes him awhile to warm up to new guys."

"Two months of training isn't enough time to get to know me?"

"Not the wizard part of you." He frowned like he couldn't believe we were having this conversation. "None of us know that part of you, Hazard. You've never once shown us. Never once slipped."

"No magic on the ice, remember?"

He *snicked* air through his teeth. "We're all magic out there, Hazard. We're all on the ice. And if you think we don't tap into it, don't use it? Then you haven't been paying attention."

I wished Tetreault would go away, go study his biology textbook or whatever it was he'd brought in his overstuffed book bag.

"Okay," I said. "That's fair. But what you other marked do has like, a range of acceptable. Shift enough to help with stamina, breathing, speed, strength? Okay by the rules. Tune into the magic and whatever else it is sensitives do? Okay by the rules. But pull magic out of the air? That's going to get me thrown out of the game."

He turned the Coke can around in his fingers, pressing the metal just hard enough to make a crinkled paper sound.

"You're thinking about it like it's some kind of outside force you can control. Magic isn't like that. Magic is a part of us, Hazard. It's a part of you like blood and oxygen. Without it, you're not alive. So you can try not to use it, but it's there. Always there. In your skin, in your sweat, in your muscles. It leaves fingerprints on everything you do. Everything and everyone you touch.

"If you focus on something, if you really want something, magic is going to concentrate on that want. For me, it means I've got a little leopard in everything I do. That's a part of me. Nothing I need to fight. Nothing I need to keep off the ice."

"I'm not...I'm not that way. Magic isn't a part of me like that. It's just something I do."

He stared down the length of the bus for a minute, then turned so he could face me. "That's not true, Random. You might think it is, but it's not."

"You're not a wizard, Danny." Two could play at the first-name game.

"No, but my twin sister is. She tells me everything." His face scrunched. "I mean *everything*. Say what you want, but trying to keep magic off the ice isn't going to happen. Magic isn't *a* part of you, Hazard. It's *every* part of you."

"Well, every part of me wants to play hockey. Every part of me wants the team to win. Lock was right. I can't let magic get in the way of how I play hockey."

"You are so not listening. Look, you're a wizard. Magic is in your body *and* in your brain. It's in your dreams, in your subconscious, in your mind. It's in your hockey play too. And that's a good thing. It can give you an edge. Just like the magic in all the shifters out there gives them an edge. Don't hold it back. Don't try to ignore it. You'll screw up more if you're fighting it out there."

"I can't. If I don't have control." I shook my head. "It could be so, so dangerous."

"So what are you going to do? Fight it? Fight yourself?"

"I'm going to make the smart plays. I'm going to focus on hockey. And if my magic pushes too hard, I'm going to take myself off the damn ice."

"All right," he said like he didn't believe me and didn't think I believed myself either. "Good you have a plan." He tipped back his soda and drank. "Maybe Lock will ease off a little."

I didn't think that would be enough. A goal or two might do more for Lock's opinion of me. "Do you know why he hates wizards?"

T2 stared at me and there was more cat in his eyes than I'd seen before. I held his gaze because I grew up with a wolf and I knew what looking away would do.

"That's something you should ask him, don't you think?"

"Not really."

He blinked, breaking the tension, his cat once again hidden. "You're smarter than you look, Hazard." He grinned.

Just like that, we were teammates again. Hockey players. The heavy conversation was done.

Thank God.

I waited for him to leave, but he just settled into the seat and pulled his phone and ear buds out of his hoodie pocket. I went back to staring out the window at the nothing that was occasionally broken up by distant lights. Houses, or more likely warehouses and farms out this far away from any big city.

"Steele and Lock used to be friends," Tetreault said.

A chill rolled down my back. "What?"

"Long time ago. They came from the same town. Moose Jaw. Played together. Nowak was his coach for a couple years."

I didn't know what to say to that. "Sorry?" I tried.

"Yep. Coach Nowak is a prick. Everyone knows that. Some people say he's dirty. Throws games." He shrugged. Hockey was full of rumors like that. Especially this league.

"Did you ever play for him?"

"Played against his team for five years. That's as close as I want to know him. Or Steele."

"But…" I didn't know how to say it.

"Lock was Steele's friend. Yeah. I don't get it either. It's a *was* though. They don't speak to each other anymore."

I thought back on the game. Tried to remember if I'd seen Lock and Steele interacting while on the ice.

I didn't think they had been more friendly or hostile than anyone else.

"Never could figure out what they had in common," he said. "Besides hockey, I mean."

Hatred of wizards? I thought, but didn't say.

Tetreault put his ear buds in place and thumbed his way through his music selections. He tapped one and then reached down and rummaged in his book bag. The thick hardback he thumped open made me glad I wasn't trying to make my way through college.

I didn't know how he did it, juggling practices, games, and classes. I had enough trouble just trying to play hockey without screwing up the rest of my life.

But at least he knew where he was going with his life.

My plan, my big plan of getting into the NHL, was gone. And if I couldn't cut it in West Hell, then what?

We finally pulled into the cheap motel in Redding, California, just off of the highway.

Duncan waited for me to get my duffel and gear bag out of the bottom of the bus before he walked with me to the room we were sharing.

"Are you going to pout the whole trip?" he asked.

"Maybe."

He snickered and shoved the door open. The room was orange: curtains, two double beds, walls. Not fancy, but clean. I tossed my bags on the floor by the bed close to the window.

"Lock doesn't know you, Ran," Duncan said as he threw his hoodie on the chair and kicked his shoes in two directions.

"It's fine." I toed off my shoes and stowed them under the desk.

Duncan sighed. "Seriously. He's just worried about the team. Not you."

"Yeah, that's what I got out of him telling me that he didn't want a wizard on the team."

"Like he has any say in it, right?"

"Yeah," I grumbled.

"You're here because coach picked you, not because Lock likes you."

"I know." And I did. Duncan was right. I had earned my place on the team. But if I didn't keep the magic under control, I'd earn my place right off it.

"Want the shower?" he asked.

"I'll shower in the morning." I crawled under the covers, tired all over.

Duncan hesitated, like he wanted to say something more, then grabbed his shower kit and walked into the bathroom.

I lay there in the darkened room, listening to the hiss and splat of water running in the shower. The shoving match in the room connected to ours was probably the two T's fighting over who got the better bed. There was the crash of something like a lamp or heavy book falling, a full half-minute of silence, and then laughter.

I pounded on the wall above the headboard. They pounded back.

More laughter.

Duncan started singing, the same song he always sang in the shower: Duran Duran's "Hungry Like The Wolf."

I groaned, but smiled. I was surrounded by too many happy people.

I reached over the bed and dug my phone out of my jean pocket. Genevieve's message was still there, unanswered.

When's the next game?

I stared at it, trying to decide if I should tell her.

Duncan shuffled out of the bathroom and fell into bed. He tossed one way, then the other and then back. He'd been doing that since he was seven and I'd had my first sleepover at his house. It was before my mom had signed my life and care over to the Sparks.

"Hey, Ran?" he asked after he was quiet for a moment.

"Yeah?"

"Screw Lock. Don't listen to him."

"Don't listen to the captain. Great advice, Donuts."

A pillow walloped me in the face. "Don't listen to the guy who doesn't understand you. When he's calling the shots on the ice, fine. Otherwise? Screw Lock. Ran? Did you hear me? Ran? Random?"

I knew he'd bug me until I answered. If there was nothing else I was sure about in this world, I was sure I belonged to Duncan and his parents and that they knew me, knew the real me, even if I'd been hiding a big part of myself from them for years.

"If I say yes, will you shut up and go to sleep?"

He snorted. He did the side-to-side toss thing again and messed with how many pillows were under his head, adding, subtracting, folding, adding, and subtracting until he was back with the original two he'd started with.

He'd been doing that since he was seven too.

He fell asleep almost instantly and started snoring.

I stayed awake, staring at my phone.

By the time I finally fell asleep, I still hadn't answered her text.

19

THE REDDING RUMBLERS LIVED up to their names but not in the way I expected.

They were loud, shouting and whistling and slapping sticks constantly at each other on the ice. The insults flew fast and furious, and not always to the opposing team. They harassed each other just as often as they heckled us.

And they laughed. Laughed when they blocked a goal, laughed when they won a face-off, laughed when they earned penalty minutes.

Big, boisterous, noisy and just so frickin' *happy* it was impossible not to have a good time. I thought Duncan had died and gone to heaven.

Not to say that the game wasn't physical. It was. They were a fast team, felt like the entire bench was filled with guys who had wings on their heels.

All that laughing, all that name calling, all the good-natured swearing rubbed off on us.

I was grinning as often as I was grunting, chirping back insults that sounded more like happy invitations for them to do impossible things with their anatomy.

We played hard, worked together as a team better, making less errors, and reading the ice and play like we knew what we were doing. Our lines finally fell into rhythm players clicking like we'd been doing this for years.

I wasn't the strongest on the team by a long shot. I missed several obvious passes and the three clear shots I had at a rebound went nowhere. I was a little slow to react. My focus was all over the place.

Or maybe I was focusing too hard. I kept hearing Lock in my head telling me to keep magic off the ice, as if even me being there, breathing, reacting, giving everything I had, wasn't good enough. As if everything about me was tainted with magic.

Overthinking was deadly in any sport and twice as bad in a game as fast as hockey.

The Rumblers might have been good, (and they were) but they also brought out the best in the Thunderheads, present company excluded.

They brought out the fight, the scrabble, the last-second push, the risk and impossible shots that made hockey more than a game.

It made me proud of my team. Made me hungry for the more than just a glimpse of what we could be. Because right there on the ice in Northern California, I saw my team accelerate and rise.

They were good. They were amazing.

They were better than me.

My performance had been clumsy, slow, confused.

Coach wasn't happy with me either. He benched me for the entire third period.

We scored two more goals and still lost by one.

Down six to five. But a losing team hadn't skated off the ice with that big of a grin on their faces in a long time.

The energy, the sheer joy of hockey that the Rumblers radiated, was contagious. All of us felt it.

"Cheerful fucking rat bastards," Watson proclaimed as he peeled out of his gear and started toward the shower. "Love to hate 'em!"

"I'd love them better if they lost." Graves wiped a towel over his head and shrugged into a T-shirt.

"We're going out, right?" Duncan said. "C'mon, there has to be a good place around here we can eat. Get a beer. Hassle the Bumblers."

"That name's not going to stick, Donuts," JJ said.

"Not if I'm the only one using it, it won't."

JJ glanced over at Lock who was getting dressed, his back to the rest of the team. "Usually we just go to a Burger Thing and hit the road."

Duncan turned his pleading gaze to me, and I shrugged. Who was I to tell the team what to do? Also, who was I to ask the captain if we could go somewhere nice because my best friend was having a post-game happygasm?

I think he read that in my expression.

Duncan sniffed and turned those puppy dog eyes on Graves.

Graves glanced at me, then sort of took in the mood of the room, and dropped onto the bench so he could pull on his cowboy boots.

"Might be nice to see a little of the city before we leave," he said with hat calm drawl of his. "Wouldn't mind a beer."

Everyone was still dressing or undressing, on their way to getting cleaned up. But there was a tense expectation in the air.

Everyone was waiting to see what Lock would say.

He turned back toward the rest of the room, took a pretty quick read on the situation. "It'd have to be damn cheap beer."

"This is Redding," Troiter said. "That's the only kind of beer they have."

T2 high-fived him.

"I'll ask Coach." Lock slung his duffel over one shoulder and walked out of the locker room.

"Yes!" And here I thought Duncan couldn't look happier.

20

TURNED OUT COACH WAS already planning to take us to a place that was a little more upscale than a drive-thru. One of those family-friendly joints that had fake 1950s decor, real 1950s music, and vintage vinyl booths. The signs said they served home cooked meals and plain label beer.

Yep, the beer was cheap.

We were a loud bunch, most of the good mood still clinging even though we'd lost. None of the Rumblers were in the restaurant, not that anyone had really expected them to be.

Lock barely smiled and didn't order a beer. He looked like he was sitting on a pile of cactus.

I hadn't ordered a beer either.

Coach Clay and Assistant Coach Beauchamp sat across the restaurant from us on the stools at the bar, beers half-gone. They were partly keeping an eye on the team, and probably hoping for a minute's time away from all of us before we were sealed back into the six and a half hour bus ride.

Halfway through the grilled chicken quesadilla I'd ordered, I felt my phone vibrate. I pulled it out, thumb-swiped it.

I googled it.
Your team website sucks.
U play tonight!
Streaming.
Assholes!
Sorry u lost.
Rumblers suck.
Why r they laughing so much?

R they high?
Is that a thing?
I know u play next Friday.
I'll be there.
Got my own ticket, loser.
Want coffee?

I read them all, each of them popping up fast, because I'd been out of cell range on the ride here and apparently the 1950s internet in the restaurant had just decided to get cranking.

I waited a second after the coffee invite. Nothing more popped up. Well, except my pulse.

I texted back.

Yes, coffee. Anytime.

Her reply was immediate. *Wednesday after 2:00.*

Where?

Doodles

That was a little coffee shop near the Portland art museum that had started out as a food cart before it scored a tiny retail space that was rumored to be a haunted closet left over from an office remodel. There was no seating inside the shop, but outside there were a couple plastic chairs and nearby concrete planters you could sit on.

"Better hurry up." Duncan stole my fries. "Coach has that look."

"Which one?" I asked around the grilled chicken I shoved in my mouth.

"Could be two things." Three of my fries were plucked off my plate. I spun my plate so the fries were closer to me and picked up the knife in my left hand, holding it between us at wrist level while I continued to fork food in my face.

"One more fry and you bleed," I said.

He grinned. He knew I wouldn't stab him over French fries. Well, not hard.

"What look?" Coach was staring in our general direction. He looked determined and maybe thoughtful and possibly a little exasperated.

Like he was trying to figure out how a team full of losers was still in such a good mood. Or how a team full of talented guys and girls couldn't seem to pull a damn win when we had everything going for us.

His eyes caught mine. Lingered a little too long.

Or maybe he was just wondering if it was time to cut his losses and bring in some new players.

Maybe that disappointment was all for me.

I wasn't hungry anymore.

I finished my Coke and pushed the fries to Duncan, who ate them without question or pause.

"He's either trying to figure out how to punish us for our second loss of the season," Duncan mumbled through potatoes and grease, "or he's reworking the lineup and deciding who to permanently bench."

"Or he's tired of your face."

"This face?" Duncan batted his eyelashes. "Never happen. I am too damned adorable."

The door to the place opened up and the entire Rumblers team strolled in, singing some kind of ridiculous victory song about that's how winning is done. Every time they said the word "done" they sort of dipped down one shoulder and pointed to the ground.

It was annoying. And a little awesome.

It also made everyone in the place smile. Because of course it did.

Their coach and assistant coach wandered over and each shook Coach Clay's and Assistant Coach Beauchamps's hands, then settled down next to them and started what looked like an amiable conversation.

I guessed we weren't leaving yet.

"Yo!" Duncan stood and waved at the team, who were waiting for the hostess to take them to a table.

Several of the players looked his way and returned his grin, then waved him over amid shouts of "Donut! Get over here, you smooth groove!"

Smooth groove? Why did he get the cool nickname?

"Move." Duncan shoved at me and I got out of the booth so the idiot could bound over to his new friends who should be rivals.

They welcomed him in and one of the wingmen threw an arm over his shoulder and brought him along with the team as they were escorted to the back room, where apparently, there was a big enough table for the whole team.

"What is he doing?" Lock stopped next to my table and scowled.

"Hanging out with some of the guys on the Rumblers?"

He narrowed his eyes, flicked his glare at the far side of the place, then back to me. "He's your responsibility. Make sure he's on the bus in time."

"He's not going to miss the bus, Lock," I said. "He's not stupid."

And the look he gave me. The *look*.

He might not like me, might not like wizards, and okay, fine. I could deal with that. I could even respect it. But that look told me exactly what he thought about my friend. My brother.

He thought he was dumb, or irresponsible, or incapable.

Well, screw him. That was not going to stand with me.

"Duncan plays his ass off," I said. "He is as focused and determined to win as any person on the ice. Maybe more."

"He could do better."

"We could all do better," I countered.

"Yes," he said, "you could."

It was a challenge. We could have it out right here in the middle of the restaurant. People weren't looking our way yet. We weren't yelling yet. We weren't throwing punches.

But that's what was going to happen if I engaged.

I was a hockey player. All I knew was how to engage. Loudly.

I glanced toward Coach Clay. As if he felt my attention, his eyes ticked to me. Held a second.

There was something in that gaze. A sort of weighing curiosity. Maybe he was still trying to figure me out too. And maybe just like how Lock had judged Duncan, he was figuring me wrong.

Time I proved what I was. Time I proved it wasn't a bad thing to have a wizard on the team.

I shoulder-checked Lock as I stormed toward the door.

"Hazard," Lock said. "Where you going?"

"To get some air." Because I had control. Because no matter how much my anger, and the magic in me, wanted to prove a point, the thing he needed to understand was that I was in control.

I ruled my life. Not my magic. Not my anger.

I strode out of the restaurant into the cool night and kept walking. My thoughts rolled and tangled, a mash of hockey plays, magic, a headless wizard doll, and texts from a girl I really wanted to get to know better. It was a mess, my life, but the longer I walked, breathed, and put distance between me and Captain Judgment, the better I felt.

I just needed some time to think. Some time alone. I shoved my hands into my hoodie pockets and turned down the next block. Unlike the corner where the diner sat, this part of town was rougher, dirtier. It wasn't that things slowly got more rundown, more tagged up. It was like a line had been drawn in the road.

Light behind me, darkness ahead.

I didn't even hear the footsteps until I had jagged through several narrow streets and one dead end. The streetlights were out here, and the neighborhood had gone from good-enough to broken-down.

How far had I walked, anyway? And who from the team had followed me?

"Look," I said, turning around. "I just want a little time..."

Five guys were walking my way. None of them were from the Thunderheads. None of them were from the Rumblers. None of them looked friendly.

"Hey," the taller one of the group called out. "We just want to ask you a question."

Yeah, I bet. The only questions in their body language was "how much money are you carrying" and "how hard do we have to beat you to get it?"

Hell.

"I don't have any cash on me. I don't even have my wallet." That was back at the diner in my duffel.

"Sure," a guy with a shaved head said. "We're just gonna have to see for ourselves. Wizard."

Shit. Was he a sensitive? Good guesser? I couldn't be famous enough to be recognized on the street.

They wanted money. If not that, they wanted blood.

Choices: fight, run, *or use magic.*

I'd gotten through every other problem in my life without using magic, I could get through this too.

The men moved like they'd done this before, cutting off my way forward. Behind me was a broken warehouse. I glanced back, and hey, a couple more men were walking our way.

I wasn't getting out of this without a fight. Seven against one. Bad odds. I was fit, I knew how to fight, but seven to one?

I squared my shoulders and spread my stance, ready to run. Ready to fight.

Magic could be a weapon. That's what everyone was afraid of. That magic would maim, kill.

That a wizard like me who lived and breathed violence would lose control.

"I don't have anything you want. All I have on me is my phone." I pulled it out of my pocket. It wasn't a great phone. Not enough of a phone for seven guys to get all worked up about.

They closed in, casually spreading out in a circle around me. "Well, ain't that too bad." the first man said. This close, I could see his teeth were rotted stumps and his jeans were stained and ripped. He was not a marked.

I glanced at the others. None of them were marked. Well, maybe the bald one who had known I was a wizard.

That was good. That was an advantage. Seven unmarked was a lot different than facing down seven shifters.

"Since you don't got nothing for us," rotted teeth said, "we're gonna have to make you pay another way."

In the movies, this is the part where each guy comes forward, one at a time, does his fancy fight moves and the hero beats him down.

In real life, all seven rushed me.

I'm an athlete. I grew up with a brother who liked to shift into a wolf bigger and heavier than me and tackle me from out of the shadows. I could hold my own in a fight.

Any fight.

I ducked, punched a kneecap, pushed up and slammed another guy in the groin, 'cause no one ever expects the hits to come in low.

Two down and screaming. Five to go.

I pivoted and pushed, slipping free of the rain of fists pummeling my back: twisting, turning, fast. Out of their grabbing hands. Out of the ring of bodies.

Magic was right there. Easy as a thought. As if it were as much a part of me as oxygen and blood.

I needed time. Wanted them slow. Heavy.

I lifted a hand and that kindling behind my chest caught a dark, smoky fire.

Weights around their ankles, weights around their wrists. Heavy, heavy, heavy.

Magic rippled out across the pavement like a heat wave that distorted and sparked dull silver. And then…

…and then the men yelped and swore. They slowed from a run to a staggering stumble, arms locked low by their sides, legs stiff and unwieldy.

Just like that, I danced out of their reach. Now all I had to do was get far enough away before the magic exhausted me. I didn't know how long I had. Maybe a couple minutes, maybe a few more.

But as soon as I cut the spell, I'd be winded, and weak. They, on the other hand, would be fine. Angry.

I could knock them out. That thought sloshed through my brain, bright like a fire burning.

But if I did it wrong, too hard, they could die. If I was too easy with it, they'd just chase me down and beat me anyway.

Crap. I had not thought this out. I should have thrown a different spell. I should have used magic better, smarter.

A low, nearby snarl went screechy haywire then dumped down into a huffing growl. Even with adrenalin and magic fire-hosing through my veins, a chill of fear swamped me.

That sound was animal. Feral. That sound was danger. That sound was death.

My attackers all froze. "Cat," one of them said, eyes too wide, head turning to take in the doors and broken windows around us.

The sound had come from behind me. And no, I wasn't about to turn my back on these assholes to see what kind of cat was out hunting.

All I wanted was a chance to run.

But first I had to cut the spell. Then I'd need to barf. Then, maybe then, I'd be able to run.

The cat snarled again, closer, making noise because it wanted us to know it was out to kill.

My brain was working too slowly. I knew I needed to make a decision. Cut the spell and hope the cat didn't notice me? Didn't notice any of us? Throw another spell? Pass out and forget the whole thing?

The men were yelling. At me. Oh. They wanted me to let them go. Let them run.

Funny. It was funny how that's what I'd wanted from them just a minute ago.

Funny enough I laughed.

Laughed as they tried to run away from me.

But then I was out of air and needed to bend at the waist to catch my breath. Magic was pouring, burning. I was floating, up, up, up.

Something hot and furred moved up beside me, leaning against my side. From my bent position, I was staring right into a pair of familiar blue eyes.

Jaguar. Male. Pissed off.

Lock.

Ears flattened against his round head, and Lock hunched down, ready to attack.

"Hold on," I said. "Wait." I pushed up so I was straight again, and waved my hand like I was throwing something. "Get the fuck outta here," I said. "He will tear you apart."

I thought about scissors and cutting the flow of magic. I thought about water and pouring it over the fire inside of me. Anything to stop the magic.

The crack of the spell ending hit like a fist to the chest. No, a kick. A donkey kick. My bones bent with it and I couldn't breathe.

Lock growled, an engine-deep warning pressing all up beside me, lending me his strength, while I tried to breathe.

My attackers hadn't stayed around to see how this would work out. They were gone, walking fast because they'd probably heard that myth about a cat attacking you if you ran.

I collapsed onto my hands and knees, my head hanging. Finally, finally, got my breathing back. "You shouldn't have followed me," I said, rocking onto my heels.

He huffed another growl, still looking for a fight, still close to me. Protective.

At least this time there were no cameras. If Coach Clay found out I'd almost gotten mugged, and Lock had shifted and threatened non-marked, there would be hell to pay.

"This was not my best idea." I groaned as I pushed up to my feet.

Lock made a sort of snarly-talky sound like he was calling me an idiot.

The world blackened then brightened again. Okay. I just needed to make it back to the diner. I could do this.

Lock fell into step beside me and nudged me in the right direction as I staggered down the street.

"Where did you leave your clothes?" The cold air felt good against my fevered skin. My back was hotter than the rest of me, bruises I couldn't feel yet spreading under my skin. I couldn't feel my feet, and a part of me was still floating, floating.

I dropped my hand and Lock put his shoulder beneath it, keeping me focused on moving forward, focused on him being there with me. He was strong, warm, alive. He was part of the ground, the earth, the world I should be tied to.

Lock must have taken a shortcut back. I felt like I blinked. Once. Twice. And then there was the neon sign of the diner. He lifted his head, sniffed, then trotted over to a trash can at the edge of an ally. His clothes were folded neatly on top of the lid.

I didn't see any water or food. We'd need both pretty fast. Leaving Lock post-shift when he was the most vulnerable, wasn't an option.

"My duffel's in there. I have bars. Water. Wait for me, okay?"

He huffed at his clothes, then sat, staring at me.

Now would be a great time to read minds.

I didn't have that magic.

"You want me to wait? Wait with you?"

He stood, stared at me, stared at his clothes stared at me. At my *hands*.

Oh, yeah. That made sense. I should carry his stuff and when we got to the diner, closer to food, he'd shift back.

"Sorry, Captain. My brain isn't good. Floating." I gathered his clothes and followed him down the street. He paced to the side of the diner, and I placed his clothes on top of a stack of boxes there.

"Wait for me." I walked into the heat, noise, salt, grease, to Duncan's bag which he'd left alongside mine at the table, pulled out four heavy bars and two bottles of water. Fumbled to shove them in my pockets. Walked out as the world went watery and started slipping away.

Lock sat against the building in human form, dressed. He was hunch shouldered, his eyes red and barely open. Felidae shifters fought migraines after a shift.

He looked like he was about to barf.

"Here." I broke the seal on the water, slumped down next to him and pressed it to his hand. Then I opened a bar and gave that to him too.

He breathed through his mouth like he couldn't stand the stink of the food in his hands, but then drained the water until it was gone.

I opened water for myself, drank half of it, and worked on tearing open another bar, my hands trembling and weak. The wrapper tore and I ate the bar around it fast, almost choking in my hurry.

Lock picked up a bar off the ground next to me, opened it, dropped it in my lap, and took the last bar for himself.

"Why didn't you knock them out? With magic?" Lock's voice was steady. He was already recovering from shift. Even his eyes looked less red.

"I've never… I don't use it like that."

"I've seen you use magic."

"To save other people. I don't…" I shook my head. I wasn't floating anymore. And being back on the ground was such a relief, I just wanted to curl up here and sleep. "For myself? It's not what I do."

"They were going to beat the crap out of you, Hazard."

"I would have gotten away. I was going to run. I'm fast."

He stared at me for a long moment, his eyes still radiating the glow from his shift.

"You're not that fast."

"Why did you follow me?" I couldn't figure out why he, of all people, had stood beside me. He didn't like me. And unless he knew those guys were going to jump me—doubtful—there wasn't any reason he should have followed.

"You left without your shadow." He chewed the last of the bar, swallowed. "Without Spark," he clarified like I didn't know who he was talking about.

"So?"

"We're a team, Hazard." He sighed and rubbed his fingers over his forehead.

The door swung open and Duncan bounded out.

"Hey!" Then, after he got a look at both me and Lock on the ground, "What happened? Are you okay, Ran? Did you do something to him, because so help me, Lock, I will lay you out."

I reached up for Duncan's hand and he pulled me onto my feet. "He didn't do anything. I'm fine. Just got some air."

Duncan tipped his head, sniffing, trying to sense my lie. Probably sensing a lot of other things too. Like my fight-or-flight sweat and that Lock had just shifted.

He'd know I'd been in a fight. But he would smell the other men on me, not on Lock. So I was pretty sure he'd figure out that Lock and I hadn't gotten into a fight.

"What. Happened?" And those eyes, usually so clear and green, went hard as stone, dark, flashing. Duncan was no longer happy. No longer fun. He was dead fucking serious.

"Hazard got jumped by a couple assholes," Lock said as he pushed away from the wall and moved to go back inside. "He handled it just as I got there. But Hazard? Next time don't hold back. Denying what you are and getting killed won't do any of us any good either."

Then he disappeared into the diner leaving me standing next to my very angry best friend.

"Could he hate everything about me any more?"

"You got jumped?"

"Like would it kill him to make up his mind? First he wants me to never use magic. Now he wants me to use it better?"

"*Jumped?*"

"I took a walk. Some guys wanted my wallet. Which I didn't have on me." I shrugged. "Lock showed up. It all turned out fine."

"You used magic."

"Yeah."

"What did you do?"

"I just...slowed them down. So I could get away. It worked."

Those eyes were still hard. The kind of eyes that would make other wolves lay down and show their belly. I wondered if he knew he was doing that.

"You're lying."

"It did work. But I fatigued pretty fast. That's when Lock showed up. They all ran away."

"Jesus, Hazard. I leave you alone for two minutes." He dragged his fingers over his head and tugged on his hair. "Need me to beat someone up for you? 'Cause I really want to punch something."

I squeezed his arm. "It's over. I shouldn't have walked off alone in a city I don't know. Lock had my back. 'Because we're a team, Hazard.'" I made quotey fingers.

We both stared at the diner as if the puzzle of Laakkonen would suddenly become clear.

"I got nothing," Duncan said.

I grunted.

"Coach says we're loading up in five minutes."

"Right." I started toward the diner.

Duncan's big hand landed on the back of my neck, and gave me a little shake.

"Next time, I go with you."

"Yeah, yeah."

His grip tightened. "I mean it." A lot of wolf in those words. I knew better than to argue.

"Next time you go with me."

"Good."

The diner doors swung open and the team poured out, some laughing, but most already thumbing through their phones, getting ready for the long drive home.

Lock looked right past me like I didn't even exist. No surprise there.

21

WEDNESDAY AT TWO O'CLOCK. I leaned on a concrete planter outside Doodles. It was cloudy and cold, but at least it wasn't raining.

Genevieve was late.

I checked my phone again. Nothing. Thought about texting her. Decided to wait.

I pulled my coat tighter and people watched, trying to pick out what kind of jobs they might have, what kinds of lives they might be living.

It was pretty easy to spot the marked. Especially the shifters. There was just something about the way they walked: cat shifters sort of extra fluid, wolf shifters with a straight spine and heightened attention to the space around them. Sensitives were harder to spot—actually impossible to spot.

The wizards were pretty obvious. Thin to an extreme, but not in the way someone whose body has been devoured by drug abuse or illness was thin. Wizards looked like a wick about to catch fire, or a wire about to go electric. Bodies might be frail, but their stride was definite, decisive, confident.

I wondered if anyone would pick me as a wizard out of a crowd. My body was a lot bulkier, physically stronger than most wizards. But did my stride reveal confidence? Strength?

Those guys in Redding had spotted me, what I was.

I took a few steps, paced one way, paced back just to test it out. I walked past some windows and watched myself in the reflection.

All I saw was a guy walking awkwardly and staring at himself.

Not helpful.

"Hey, Hockey Forty-Two."

I grinned and turned. Genevieve's hair was tucked up under a red beanie, so that just her bangs brushed her forehead. Her coat was mustard colored and sweatery. Then she smiled and all I could see were her eyes.

Soft, bright, full of something happy that I wanted to explore.

"Hey, Rock Star," I said. "Coffee?"

"Did you order?"

"I was waiting for you."

Her nose did that crinkle thing and her dimples dipped.

"Nice. Have you been here before?" She nodded at Doodle's front door.

"Once. It was good." I closed the distance between us until the sweet scent of flowers reached me. I inhaled deeply as we entered the coffee-filled warmth of the shop to stand behind eight other people.

Shelves on each side were filled with organic coffee, art supplies, and tea things. A community bulletin board took up prime real estate on the shelf to our right, covered in flyers and coupons and announcements.

There was no room for chairs or tables. There was barely enough room for the people leaving the shop to get by the people standing in line.

"How was the trip?" she asked.

"It was okay," I said. "Long drive."

"Sorry you lost."

"It happens. We'll break the streak."

"Two is a streak?"

"Two is the longest losing streak I want to be part of."

We moved to the side so a mother and a little boy could get out.

"Why did you say yes?" she asked.

"What?"

"Why did you agree to meet me for coffee?"

"You asked?"

She looked up at me from under her bangs. "And?"

"And I like you and want to get to know you better."

"Not just because I work at the testing clinic?"

"No? Why would that matter?"

She shrugged, but wouldn't look at me. "Some people… I've had some people think they could get me to adjust their records. Grade them upward for better job ratings."

"People do that? Have they met you? Assistant by day and rocker by night?"

"What does that have to do with anything?"

"I've only talked to you like two and a half times and I know you wouldn't lie at your job about something important like that."

"Right? Right!" she agreed. "Magical abilities aren't something you want to over or under estimate. It's important to get accurate data. Most wizards work really important life or death jobs. It's crazy to put someone underqualified into one of those positions. Wizards do important things. I mean, shifters do too, and so do sensitives, but wizards are using magic to save lives."

"Yeah," I agreed. "Most do, I guess."

She touched my arm, then let go just as quickly. "Not every wizard has to be a doctor, Random. Trust me, not everyone should be. I've tested wizard truck drivers, fishermen, actors, plumbers, and window washers. Lots of people are wizards."

"Sure," I said. "But wizards with high magical ability always do important things."

"Not always. What's this about? You don't think hockey is important? You want to be a doctor?"

I shrugged. "Hockey's important to me…"

"That's what matters." She crossed her arms over her chest. "Your life. Your choices. Hockey's what you love. Right?"

I nodded.

"Right. So it's important. Plus, I can't imagine you being a doctor. It's just…no."

"Hey, I could be a doctor. Could I be a doctor? How high did I rate?" We were at the counter now.

Genevieve gave me a puzzled look before ordering a caramel latte with whip.

I ordered an Americano and we shifted to one side, waiting for our drinks.

"You don't know?" She picked up her latte, handed me the Americano. We shuffled past the line and squeezed out of the shop. The sudden cold after the steam and heat from inside hit like a slap. I took a gulp of coffee.

"What my ability with magic was rated? Not really." I sat on the edge of a planter and she sat in the bright blue metal chair positioned next to it.

"He told you. I was there when he told you. Were you even listening?"

"I heard 'you passed' and then all I could think about was what an amazing assistant he had and that I loved her dimples and how her nose crinkled when she smiled, and if she'd say yes if I asked her out on a date."

She laughed. "You did not. He told you you passed and you went white as chalk and practically ran me over trying to get out of there."

"Hey. I offered you hockey tickets before I ran you over. I was going to ask you to coffee but chickened out."

"And…" She held up her cup. I held up mine and we clinked them in toast.

"You really got your own tickets to Friday's game?" I asked.

"Turns out I like contact sports on ice. Turns out I might like the men who play contact sports on ice too."

"Lots of men play."

"Well, maybe I just like the wizards who play contact sports on ice."

"Not so many of those." My heart was beating funny. Not painful. Happy.

"Only one," she agreed. "You really like my dimples?"

"It's one of the things I like about you. I was kind of hoping to see you again. Get to know some new things I'll like about you."

She smiled and looked down, maybe shy, maybe just happy with that answer. Finally, she nodded. "That would be nice."

She still wasn't looking at me, and I missed the brightness of her gaze. Time to change the subject away from the almost-dating we were almost-doing.

"Tell me about the band," I prompted.

Her gaze flicked up. Shy Genevieve was gone, replaced by a woman energized, excited. Rocker Genevieve was in the house.

"It's great, right? I mean we're still a little rough, but we're finally pulling it together. When Chad left—he was our drummer—I thought for sure that would be the end of us, but Shashone—she's our new drummer—is even more amazing.

"Downpour wants us there every week. That's our first steady gig. We're still looking for a place to record a couple of our songs, and then we'll have to get them out there so people can hear them, but we're making plans. We all really want this. To make it happen."

God, she was gorgeous when she talked about her band. It was like all the light of the day shone out from her skin, her eyes.

She wanted her band to succeed, and was determined to make it happen. She was looking to her future, had a plan, a goal. More than one plan and one goal. She was also working for a magic testing facility and I could tell she was passionate about that too. About making sure people used their skills in ways that would make a difference in the world.

She was not only planning for a life ahead of her, she was living her life. Right here and right now.

Right then and right there, with the wind cold enough to add a little red to her cheeks, and the coffee steaming in smoky curls between us, I knew I wanted to spend a lot more time with her.

My heart beat for that. The hope that maybe she would want this. Want us.

"Oh," I said. That one word came out soft and low, right from the center of my chest. Not where magic begins in me, but where my heart beat.

Was this how love began?

I thought if I ever fell in love it would be after I left hockey, when there would be room in my life for something that big, that wonderful.

But here she was, Genevieve unexpected, still talking like the whole world hadn't just shifted for me. Punctuating everything she said with a wave of her hand and poke of her fingers.

And there I was, the world fading away, nothing but this tight wire stretched between us, a path, a way of being, a possible future of going forward toward something and someone that scared crap out of me. But at the same time held me close, made me want in a way I could not turn away from.

Because I didn't want to turn away.

The what-ifs flooded in like a hurricane. What if I was the only one who felt like this? What if she didn't really like me? What if I screwed it up? What if I was wrong about her? What if this was a huge mistake? What if I didn't feel this way tomorrow, or the tomorrow after that?

What if this wasn't really anything like love?

That last one, I could answer. If it wasn't love, it was still something good. Something strong enough that I *needed* to follow it, pursue it, find out what it was.

And since I was a hockey player, I was all about leaning forward and taking the shot.

So I leaned forward.

Genevieve was saying something about a digital audio workstation and still waving her hand. As I leaned in, her words softened, slowed, stalled. Her eyes fixed on mine.

"What—"

"You're amazing," I breathed across her lips. I waited, long enough for her to push me away, long enough for her to say no, or turn her head, or ask me another question, or laugh me off.

But she held very still, and the cold of the day was suddenly gone, lost beneath the heat building in that sliver of space between us.

"Oh," she breathed. Just "oh." Like she had just noticed something. Like the world had suddenly shifted for her too.

And then I kissed her.

Gentle. Careful.

Her lips were soft and tasted of sugar and cream and caramel and coffee. The flowery perfume lingered this near to her, as did a deep, grounding need to touch her. I held my hands steady, though, wanting this slow, wanting to know what this one step felt like.

I didn't want to take a step further out on this tightrope if I had gotten it wrong, if she wasn't stepping out onto it with me.

Genevieve did not stay still for long. Just a moment. Then her lips moved with mine, a gentle exploration as she leaned forward and placed the palm of her hand against my neck, my racing pulse caught between us.

I wrapped one arm around her, around us, so that we would not fall.

22

SCREAMING. DUNCAN WAS SCREAMING.

Not his wolf howl. His voice, yelling like he was trying to cut through a tornado wind. Yelling for me.

The day, which I thought had been sunny just a minute ago, had gone black in a second. Clouds erupted across the sky, dark enough to trigger the streetlights to snap on, one after another down the endless road in front of me.

I was...outside the arena? Yes. The team should be here with me, but I couldn't find them. We were supposed to be driving to the game in Tacoma. It had been weeks since our first game against them.

We'd bagged our first win of the season against the tough team out of Bend, Oregon: the Brimstones, then lost the back-to-back to them the next day. We had Calgary's Rustlers tied up until overtime, which we lost in a heartbreaking shoot out. The Brass drove down from Vancouver, Canada, and shut us down hard on our home ice. No surprise there, since the Brass were reigning champs from last year.

But we were about to face our rivals again, the Tide.

Where was everyone?

A movement down the road caught my eye.

Dozens of figures materialized out of the storm. Coming my way. Fast.

It was the entire team of the Tide—all of them shifted, eyes burning hot, fangs flashing white—all of them running toward me.

The raging winds hardly touched them.

Duncan, I knew now, was at my back.

I knew he would shift into his wolf and stand in front of me, protecting me. Saving me.

I knew I'd watch him die. These were not odds we would win.

The shifters were ten yards away. Five.

Duncan growled and shifted, pushing past me, twice as big as I'd ever seen him, bracing between me and Tide, his teeth bared in challenge.

They would tear him to shreds. There were too many. They would kill him.

"Random!" Duncan yelled again. Which was weird because he couldn't talk in wolf form.

The shifters were *here, here, here.* I could smell them: heat and hatred like the alley in Redding. I could see them, muscles and claws and fur and scale.

They were power.

I was fear.

They leaped.

Death, death, death.

Duncan yelled. Pain in his snarl, blood pouring through his fur.

No.

No.

I might be fear. But I was also magic.

I pulled it to me, all the magic in the ground, the air, the sky. All the magic in the bodies around me.

Mine.

Mine.

Lightning snarled low across the sky following the paths magic carved through it to reach me.

Magic: blue, black, burning red, crackled across buildings, twisted down lampposts, exploded along wires. Light bulbs hissed, shattered, rained down glass and embers.

Magic: hot, an inferno, as my fury turned tornado winds into fire. Burning the flesh of Duncan's attackers.

A flick of my hand and raindrops became razor blades, a swift, deadly barrage slicing the Tide to ribbons.

And still Duncan was calling.

"Random!"

A wall of water hit me. Ice. Shocking. So *cold*.

I gasped because I hadn't been breathing. Or had been breathing too hard.

My eyes snapped open.

I was not outside the arena. I was not fighting the Tide's shifters.

I was in my bed.

Inhale, exhale while I grappled with this reality, this moment.

My room was heavy with magic, so thick in the air, I could choke on the sweetness of it, the sting of it in my nostrils and eyes.

I was also soaking wet and shivering.

"Random?" Duncan wore a pair of pajama bottoms and a holey T-shirt. He looked really worried, his hair stuck up like he'd just gotten out of bed, the corner of his mouth caught in his teeth.

Sean, in his ever-present after-hours robe and pajamas, stood just slightly in front and to one side of Duncan as if he were trying to protect him. From what?

From me?

Horror trotted fast fingers from my gut to my throat.

Kit was next to her husband. She also wore a robe. She held a plastic bowl dripping water onto the carpet.

"Hey." I blinked hard and locked my teeth so they would stop chattering. "Are we okay? Are you okay?"

"We're all fine," Sean soothed. "You can let go of the magic now, Random. Just let go."

Magic?

Storm clouds curled against the ceiling, pulsing with light. Rain fell, faint and weirdly insubstantial, like someone had scratched raindrop flecks in the air with a metal paintbrush.

My nightstand was littered with broken glass from my lamp, and the air smelled of fire and electricity.

But it was the razor blades gathered in snowdrifts against the edges of the floor that made my heart pound too hard, too fast.

I'd been dreaming those knives. I'd made them out of magic in my dream to save Duncan.

And I'd made them out of magic in real life too. I could have hurt Duncan, Mr. Spark, Mrs. Spark. I could have killed them.

"All the magic you pulled up, dude." Duncan waved at the room, like I couldn't see it. See it all. His hand was bleeding. He was bleeding. *Blood.*

I'd done that. I'd *hurt* him.

I made a high, whining sound in the back of my throat, suddenly unable to breathe.

I'd hurt Duncan with magic.

This had to be a nightmare. This had to be the real nightmare. I wanted to wake up, needed to wake up.

Now, now, now.

"Easy. Easy, son. Everything is all right." Sean crossed to my bed, reaching out as if to comfort me, gather me to him.

But I couldn't look away from the blood on Duncan's skin.

"You are seriously freaking out, Ran." Duncan lifted his hand. That's when he noticed the line of blood spinning down the center of his palm and trickling to his elbow.

"Oh, shit." He quickly turned his back to me, toward his mom. She grabbed a sock off the top of my dresser and started mopping up the blood, trying to find the source of the wound.

That sound came out of my throat again and I clutched at the blankets, scrambling back against the headboard.

I should leave. Save them. From me. From magic.

But I was frozen. Trapped.

"Random?" Mr. Spark again. Gentle. Patient. "Son, you had a bad dream. But we're all fine." The mattress dipped as he sat next to me.

"Duncan is fine. It's a scratch. I just need you to let go of the magic, okay?"

A warm hand cradled the side of my face, cupped my cheek and tipped my head so that I was forced to look away from Duncan and had to look into his dad's eyes instead.

He wasn't wearing his glasses. That's what I noticed. That one detail that showed just how quickly he'd rushed in here.

"Let go." He nodded. "Go ahead and break the spell."

I imagined scissors. Snipped. Everything in my room went silent.

It had been noisy? Yes. Wind. A storm. Rain falling like a thousand tiny ball bearings striking tin.

"Good." Mr. Spark's encouraging smile matched his voice. "You're fine, Random. We're fine. Duncan's fine."

My skin was too cold, too hot. I wanted to throw up. Wanted to escape this moment. To step out of my skin and never step back in again.

"Easy," he said. "Just keep your eyes on me. I've got you. You're okay. Drink this for me." A glass of water appeared in his hand.

I drank.

"Eat this." One of Duncan's meal bars was exchanged for the glass.

I chewed, swallowed, never breaking eye-contact with Mr. Spark. His eyes were warm and welcoming and my everything right now.

"Good. Very good. Okay, now you can lay back down."

I couldn't move. I was stuck as if someone had stitched all the edges of me into the fabric of the air.

"Shove over, Ran." Duncan pushed gently at my shoulder, urging me to the other side of my bed.

He'd done this so many times when we were kids—we both had—that I switched into automatic and moved over. He dropped down next to me, fiddled with the pillows then nudged me onto one.

Shouldn't the pillow be wet? The blankets too? I was pretty sure the ice water Mrs. Spark threw at me had been real. Why wasn't my bed wet?

"This?" Duncan shoved his hand in front of my face. "Is a Band-Aid."

I focused on the little beige strip of plastic pressed against the back of his hand. He picked at the edge of it and pulled it off, revealing a shallow cut maybe an inch long.

"It's not bleeding anymore. It's barely a paper cut. There isn't even any blood on the Band-Aid." He turned the plastic strip so I could see the white rectangle that had been pressed against his wound.

Then, he said the words I really needed to hear from him. "You're an idiot. I'm fine. I'd tell you if I wasn't."

That was our childhood promise. When we got hurt in the game, when we got hurt wrestling with each other, that's what we said when we were telling the whole truth about how bruised up and broken we were after a hit.

"Jesus. Duncan." I breathed and everything emptied out of me. The fear, the confusion, the shock, the guilt, leaving me a Random-shaped puddle in the middle of my bed. "I hurt you. I *hurt* you with magic."

He stretched out on his side facing me, tucked one arm under his head while still holding his hand annoyingly close to my eyes.

"This is a scratch. Tiny. Nothing to worry about."

Nothing? I'd lost control of magic and had used it to hurt someone. Used it to hurt *him*. My brother. My friend.

"Wh-what happened?"

"You were dreaming." Sean sat at my desk, Kit leaned against it. He had his arm around her hips. The bowl she'd been holding was gone and he had his glasses.

I'd lost some time during my freak out.

"You were sleeping," she said. "We heard something that sounded like thunder, and then glass breaking and other noises coming from your room."

"Dude," Duncan said, "it was amazing. Rain falling like glass out of this…this *sky*. Storm sky, and there was like little lightning bolts and *fire* and everything. So cool."

"It hurt you. I hurt you."

"You made magic so real I could smell the rain. So real, one of those bolts of lightning hit me."

"Wait. What? You were struck by lightning?"

"Hell, yes, I was struck. It stung too. *So* cool."

I covered my face with my hands and groaned.

He slapped my chest. "Seriously. Amazing. You should have magic nightmares more often. Do you think you can dream up a monster? Maybe Godzilla? A tiny Godzilla that destroys a tiny Tokyo?"

I groaned again. "You can't be serious."

"We could film it. Make some money. It would be sweet."
He settled down and did that thing where he flipped the pillow
over, folded it, unfolded it, then put it back in its original
position.

"Random," Sean said.

I'd sort of hoped he'd left. I moved my hands away from
my face and looked over at him.

"Are you okay to go back to sleep?"

"I'll stay here with him, Dad." Duncan yawned. "Shake him
if he starts weather wizarding."

"I thought you might." Sean smiled fondly at Duncan but
was still waiting for my answer.

"I'm not that tired."

That was a big fat lie. I *was* tired. Very tired. My clock
showed three in the morning. Kit hadn't even gotten home until
around midnight. Duncan and I had a road game tomorrow up
in Tacoma. Sean had an early shift.

I didn't want them to lose any more sleep because of me.

"I'll drift off."

"Do you want to talk about your dream?"

No. No, I most certainly did not want to talk about that.

From the look on Sean's face, he could tell. "All right.
That's all right." He pressed against his thighs and stood. "If you
decide you want to talk, any time, Ran, I'll brew the coffee."

"Thanks. Thank you."

Kit reached over and pressed her hand against my hand.
"We love you, Random. This was just a bad dream. Your magic
got wrapped up in it, but we are not concerned it's going to
happen again tonight."

I nodded. They might not be concerned, but I was.

She shook her head. "You are so stubborn. All right. I'm
getting some sleep. Someone better make me espresso in the
morning."

"That would be me," Sean said from the doorway. He held
his hand out and she went to him.

I took a moment to watch them lean into each other's space
like they were pulling up to a cozy fire. There was love between
them, given and received. It gave me hope that everything was

all right. That my home, my family, was still here no matter how much I changed.

If I had lost control… I shivered hard. It could have been so bad. So much worse.

"Shut up," Duncan said. "You're thinking too loud and you're worrying. You're not going to blow up the house with your mighty, mighty magic."

"You don't know that."

He grunted. He was still lying on his side, facing me, his eyes closed, my extra blanket from the bottom of the bed pulled up to his shoulders. He flopped his hand out without looking. It landed on my arm. "I got you. If you do magic, I'll know."

I just stared at him.

He finally opened his eyes, and it wasn't the sleepy gaze of my friend behind that look. It was the steady stare of his wolf.

On guard. Because of me.

"For you," he said. "I'll look out for you. I'll wake you up before anything disastrous happens."

"You wake me up if I do magic," I said. "Not just if it's disastrous."

He closed his eyes, a small smile on his mouth.

"Duncan. You wake me up the second I do magic."

Still nothing.

"Promise."

He slitted open one eye. "Promise I'll wake you up the second you use dangerous magic, or at least as soon as I've recorded enough on my phone to post online."

I kicked him and kept pushing. "Get out of my bed."

He laughed and used his weight and stupid height to stay right where he was, one hand braced on my headboard, one foot hooked under my footboard.

"Out!"

"I'll sleep on your floor. You know I will. And we have a game tomorrow. You don't want me to be tired for the game do you?" He batted his stupid eyelashes at me and I stopped shoving.

"The second I start using magic, you wake me up."

"Fine. I'll wake you up. The second. Promise. Jesus, Random. It was just a little lightning storm."

"You bled." I hated that my voice cracked.

"I bleed a lot more on the ice, and I do that for fun. Your magic scratched me a tiny bit. Then you woke right up."

"Did I?"

"Well, not when we called your name, but when Mom threw water on you—which, hilarious—you snapped right out of it."

He pointed over his shoulder at the nightstand next to him. "See that cup of water? All set to go. I am *so* ready to throw it in your face and not get in trouble for it." He gave me a big grin and I couldn't help it, I rolled my eyes.

"Don't enjoy this." But the tightness in my chest finally unwound and I settled beneath my quilt. Not the same quilt that had been on my bed when I first went to sleep. They must have done a change of blankets while I was in the middle of my panic attack. The new quilt was an older one from the hall closet. It smelled of the lemon freshener Sean kept in there.

Duncan dropped his hand on my arm again, a heavy, familiar weight. I closed my eyes, feeling like I'd never erase the image of Duncan, standing in my room, face confused, as blood dripped down his arm.

Turned out using magic and then panicking afterwards was exhausting.

Despite my best intentions, I fell asleep.

23

MORNING CAME TOO SOON, wrapped in the smells of sausage and strong coffee. I had to push Duncan out of bed, and he grumbled about it, so I took the shower first.

Kit was already off to work. Sean had of our plates ready, coffee steaming in travel mugs on the table.

"I did some preliminary research." He nodded toward one of the plates on the table.

I sat and started in on the food. I was starved.

"There are some classes you can take. The basic things to do when magic doesn't behave how you expect it to." He took a drink of his coffee.

"Kit is going to check in at the hospital and see if they're still doing the online meditation sessions that help ground and focus. Help with anxiety too. There are a couple apps she recommended. She uses them when her co-workers drive her nuts. You could do those on the road."

My stomach knotted and I put down my fork. "Maybe I shouldn't go."

Duncan strolled into the room and slapped the back of my head. "You're going, idiot. We don't have anyone to cover your position since Magee caught pneumonia, remember?"

"What if I lose control on the ice?"

Duncan flopped into a chair and stretched his long legs. He made a dismissive sound then folded a piece of toast in half and shoved it into his mouth.

"Is that something you're concerned about?" Sean asked.

I *was* worried about magic, especially since the whole thing last night. But I'd never lost control on the ice.

As long as I was awake, I could control the magic inside me. No matter what the team captain thought.

"I think. I don't think I'll lose control. But last night…"

Duncan chased the toast with a gulp of coffee and stabbed at the sausage.

"Last night was a bad dream. It happens. You're still you, Random. How many times I gotta say that? You're not out to hurt anyone. Magic won't hurt someone unless you want it to."

I raised my eyebrows.

"Yeah, yeah," Duncan said. "You hit if you have to, but hockey hurt isn't what I'm talking about. You flipped your shit over a tiny scratch last night. You aren't going to Hulk out and start breaking bones."

Sean's phone alarm rang.

"That's it, boys. Finish up. Are you packed?" He switched off the coffee maker, tucked his phone in his pocket and picked up his messenger bag that I knew carried an identical lunch to the one he'd made Kit this morning.

He was good with details like that.

"Packed last night," Duncan said around a mouthful of sausages. "Before the magic show." He stood, gathered his plate and mine.

I grabbed the toast before he whisked my plate away to the sink. He ran water. I picked up his travel mug.

"Random?" Sean asked.

"Packed."

I finished my toast, pulled on my coat and hoisted my duffel and gear bag over my shoulders.

Sean locked the house and walked with us through the gentle drizzle to Duncan's car.

Just like he had always done for away games he wasn't able to attend, he gave us both a warm hug.

"Good luck tonight. I'm sorry your mother and I won't be there but I'll be listening."

The league was underfunded enough that most of the games weren't televised. But a local radio station had a broadcaster who was a fan. He and a friend did their best to cover all the games in the Pacific Northwest and they streamed the broadcast.

"It's all good, Dad," Duncan said as Sean released him from the hug. "We'll be home tomorrow afternoon. With a win!"

"Don't jinx it," Sean chuckled. "Call me after the game."

Duncan sauntered around to the driver's side and Sean squeezed my shoulder. "You are a fine hockey player, Random. And a very strong wizard. Both of those things are good. I want you to hear me say that. Did you hear me say that, or should I repeat it?"

I nodded. "I heard."

He waited, searching my eyes one last time, then gave me a smile and another quick hug. "Good. Now go kick some ass."

I laughed. He so rarely swore, it always surprised me when he did.

"Yes, sir."

He winked, then strolled over to his car and ducked inside.

Duncan's Vega gave out a tortured groan, wheezed, and grudgingly kicked over.

I got in fast before the old thing gave up for good.

24

THE BUS RIDE TO Tacoma was tense. Playful shoves quickly shifted into arguments, friendly insults into snarls. Coach told everyone to settle down, which lasted until we crossed Oregon's border.

Then everyone went back to snarling and shoving again.

We'd only pulled one win out of a game and now we were headed to face our rivals, the Tide. It was the end of October. We had a lot of season left. We had time to turn things around.

But it felt like we'd never get over this losing streak.

We'd been practicing hard. Working on plays that would shut down the Tide's physicality and speed.

We were ready for this. Coach had told us so. Said it with confidence.

Nothing but a win was going to wash the bad mood off of us.

I put on my headphones, and flipped through my phone for music. A message pinged.

I didn't recognize the number. Opened the text.

It was a photo of a letter. A lot like the last letter I'd gotten. White paper, printed message.

YOU WERE WARNED. GET OUT OF THE LEAGUE OR PAY THE PRICE.

Beneath that, a grainy photo. It was the back alley in Redding. Seven guys closing in on someone. Closing in on me.

I was so shocked, I just stared at it as white noise filled my head.

Someone was following me? Someone had seen the fight?

Someone had sent those guys after me? To beat me up? Holy shit. That was some hard-core hate.

Duncan groaned loudly. "Traffic sucks."

He sat across the aisle from me. Like he needed distance. Like he was too restless to sit next to me. I thumbed out of the message and took a deep breath. The last thing I needed to do was panic. Duncan would sense that, and then it would ripple through the entire bus.

But Duncan was glaring out the window, his spine stiff. If he were a dog—not that he was, but still—he'd be barking his head off at whatever he was staring at out there.

"You're a wizard." He turned and pinned me with a look.

"So?"

"So do something about the traffic."

"Like what? Roll down the window and yell at people?"

A flash of humor lit his eyes, then faded beneath his scowl. "Just. Magic it somehow."

Other players had noticed our conversation. Not because we were talking all that loudly, but because the bus wasn't moving.

"Duncan, it doesn't work that way."

"You can make magic do anything you want. Make those cars hurry up."

"I can't control people. I can't…" I didn't even know what he thought I could do. "…push a car around or make the bus fly."

"Have you ever tried?"

I just blinked at him. His shoulders were inching up toward his ears and his head lowered. I'd known him long enough to know his body language. He was uncomfortable, tense, fighting a shift, begging for a brawl.

"No. I've never tried to levitate a bus. Are you sure you want to be on it when I give it my first shot?"

Someone behind us snickered. I kept a very straight face.

Duncan scowled at me.

"All right, Dunc," I sighed. "But you're the one who has to tell Coach why we flipped over on a tanker truck and exploded." I pushed my sleeves back and cracked my knuckles. I felt the weight of all the gazes shooting my way.

"One…" I chanted, "two…three!" I snapped my fingers.

Nothing happened.

Absolutely nothing.

Well, except Duncan jerked.

I grinned at him.

"Boo…boo!" That, from someone at the front of the bus.

"You suck!" That, from the back.

And then wads of paper and hoodies and candy wrappers flew my way.

I laughed, batting away everything that came at me.

And Duncan finally, finally smiled.

He also threw his shoe at me, but hey, at least he kept his dirty socks to himself.

25

"WELCOME TO HELL, BOYS." Watts strode into the Tide's visiting team changing room and dropped his gear on the floor by the bench. He wiped an arm across his forehead. "All the heat, none of the fun."

He was sweating. We were all sweating. It was so hot in the room, every time I breathed in my lungs burned and itched.

Our equipment manager, Roxanne, walked in and stopped dead. "What in the—" She glanced at the wall on either side of the door, maybe looking for some kind of thermostat control.

She stepped out of the room, muttering to herself, then came back and dropped a bag in front of the door to keep it propped open. "I'll be back. Keep the door open." She stormed away.

"Think this is something the Tide do to every visiting team?" Duncan shed his hoodie and T-shirt in one go. "Or do you think they saved it for us special?" He slogged over to the benches and dropped down to untie his shoes.

"It's West Hell." I shrugged.

Maybe the steam room stunt was the Tide pregaming themselves a little upper hand. Boil us in our own juices before we even hit the ice. Try to shake us up.

It wasn't legal, but hey, this was not the NHL. Lots of stuff like this happened in the WHHL.

"Assholes," Troiter grumbled.

"Suck it up, boys." Lock laughed. "A little heat won't kill us. Let's get it done and show them out there on the ice how much we appreciate their hospitality."

There were a couple wet high-fives and we all got to it, doggedly sweating through our pregame rituals and fighting our way into our gear.

When Assistant Coach Beauchamp and Coach Clay walked into the room, I leaned toward the whiff of non-sweltering air they'd brought in with them.

Coach Clay stood there a moment, his cool blue gaze taking in everything. His hair instantly went damp at his forehead and collar. "I see."

That was fury. Just those two words. I couldn't look away from him. I had never seen Coach look that angry.

His face flushed red, his eyes narrowed to dark slits.

"Has anyone from the Tide or arena staff come by?"

And oh, his voice was so, so mellow. So, so calm. So, so not hiding the rage that crackled just beneath the surface, the anger that tightened all his muscles.

I got a good look at what a force he must have been on the ice when he played. Every cell of him loaded for attack and hanging on a hairpin trigger. Violence under velvet calm.

"No one's come by," Lock said. "We can deal, Coach."

"No." Clay's pale, pale eyes flashed gold. "We do not deal. Not with this."

That last bit came out with a growl that was not human.

I held very still, not even breathing. He was as close to shifting as I'd ever seen him.

Graves was the only guy in the room who moved, standing up from where he had been sitting on the bench. Squaring off toward Clay.

Coach tracked Graves, who was geared up and seemed completely unaffected by the heat, the grim mood, and Coach's anger.

"Don't suppose this is gonna kill us, exactly, Clay," Graves noted.

Something about his voice. Something that buzzed in my ear and dug deep.

"We aren't animals." Coach's voice was still steady, but thicker than normal, graveled. "We won't be treated like animals."

Graves didn't reply, he just held Coach's gaze. If I hadn't been staring so hard at Coach I would have missed it, but his breathing changed. Calmed. And when I slid a look at Graves, I realized he was matching his inhale, exhale.

Weird. Was that weird? I checked how Duncan was reacting to this. Even though he wasn't a cat shifter, I could usually get a pretty good read on what was going on with shifters if I paid attention to him.

Duncan's head was tilted, as if he were listening to a faint sound. He was frowning at Coach and ignoring Graves.

No help there.

"No, Coach," Graves said. "We are not animals, are we?"

Coach lifted his chin a fraction and blinked. His eyebrow rose and…was that a *smile* almost tipping the edge of his mouth?

"I'll go have a word with the arena." Coach was all calm again. All man again and no cat.

How had Graves gotten him to snap out of his mood so quickly?

No one else in the room seemed to be taking any notice of their dynamic.

"Beauchamp, get them out of here and get them some water." Coach strode out of the changing room.

"All right boys and girls, get your gear and follow me." Beauchamp was a bear shifter, built like a concrete truck, all shoulders and chest, gray hair and beard.

He held open the door while we did what he said. Then he plowed down the corridor as if he alone could flatten any obstacle in our path. He might be in his late fifties, but he moved like a man at least a decade younger.

The cold air in the hall was like diving into snow melt. It took several breaths before my lungs could deal with the sudden change. I wasn't the only one wheezing, coughing, sneezing.

How hot had it been in there?

Assistant Coach opened random doors and stuck his head into rooms until he found an open room to his liking and waved us in.

Looked like an unused conference room, no chairs, but the tables were pushed against the walls. Assistant Coach

Beauchamp shut the door behind Roxanne who had her arms full of gear.

"Finish getting ready," he said. "We'll go out early to warm up."

We were a little sluggish and fumble-handed, but we got it done. He gave us a pregame talk, listing off the first line on the ice, and reminded us of how he wanted us to play: smart, and what he wanted us to do: stay on the puck and shoot the hell out of top side right because their goalie, a big Iowan named Johnson, was weak on that side.

Then he left to find where Leon had gone with our water.

My cell phone pinged and I swiped the screen.

Same unknown number.

This time there was no letter. There was just a picture of a stuffed toy. A little wolf. With its head torn off.

I stopped breathing.

My heart slapped thick, heavy thuds against my chest. Fight or flight.

I should leave. Leave here now. That photo was a threat.

Not against me.

Against Duncan.

Fury and terror rushed through me, catching the dry kindling in my chest on fire. I swiped my thumb over the image, erasing it, erasing the message, erasing it like doing just that would make it never come true.

Magic boiled through the air, sweet, sweet, sweet. Pushed hard to slip my control.

I was wizard enough to know that casting magic on the heels of a nightmare, under the stress of this upcoming game, after receiving a threat on my brother's life, in this too-small room with twenty restless and twitchy teammates would be a massive disaster.

A disaster that would be my fault.

I had used magic to hurt Duncan. What was stopping me from losing control and doing it again?

"Easy." Josky's voice filtered through the fog in my brain. She lumbered toward me, a bulky and commanding presence in her goalie gear. "Hazard. You need to step out? Get your head together?"

She could feel it. Magic. She was a sensitive. Knew I was losing it.

Just like in the nightmare.

Just like when I'd hurt Duncan.

Someone growled. Another person snarled. Reacting to my panic? Reacting to the magic.

Could I force them into a shift on accident?

That was one thing I did not want to test.

Josky shoved all up into my space. "You still with me, Hazard?" She crowded in front of me, her height and width blocking my view of half the people in the room.

I opened my mouth to say something but smoke came out instead of words.

It was...horrifying. No words, no air escaping me. That smoke was the magic. Magic burning me up from the inside out.

"Well, shit." Josky slapped her hand hard against my chest and then pressed so that I could feel the weight.

And the pain.

A blast of candy-sharp lightning rammed down my spine. The top of my head burned hot, too hot. The bottom of my feet went numb, tingling, cold, cold, cold.

My skin hummed, my vision suddenly so crisp that light hurt.

Magic that had filled me was flung to such far parts of my brain, of my body, that I felt tied together, pulled apart, by a million thin lines of magic. Those thin lines were not connected.

It was as if Josky had just cut a million wires on a million bombs inside me. Disabling magic.

It was...shocking. Sobering.

Terrifying.

"What?" I asked. "How?"

Josky's eyes were too wide and her lips pale. "Are you clear?" she asked, her voice papery. Her gaze was not quite tracking, not quite focused. "Are you better? Now?"

"Holy shit, Josky. What did you do?" I mean, I knew she was a sensitive, but I had never, and I mean *never* heard of a third-marked who could do...whatever the hell she'd just done.

Influenced magic. Changed it, channeled it, grounded it, disarmed it.

Sensitives were the eyes and ears that could sense magic. They weren't doers. They weren't changers.

They were observers. Witnesses.

They didn't get their hands dirty with magic because they couldn't do that. Right?

No. Because Josky had just rewired the magic in me. That was true. That was real. That was now. But *how?*

I came up so blank, my brain echoed.

The room came alive with motion and groans and growls and curses.

Half the team spun to face the walls, heads hanging as they fought the need to shift. A few of them took a knee, the hockey technique and position required to stay in control of the beasts inside them.

Whatever Josky had done, or maybe it was what I'd done, with magic had triggered the marked. The other unmarked in the room knew the drill and held very still.

Josky trembled hard. I closed my hands under her elbows and helped her to a chair. She moved blindly, her vision still not tracking.

"I'm," she whispered. "It's…I'm fine. Hazard. Don't move."

I'd already frozen in place.

Because when a room full of apex hunters were trying to outmuscle their human hosts the smart thing was to be quiet and invisible.

I stood with my back to Josky, between her and the team, just as she had stood between me and the team.

Got myself a front row seat at the we're-screwed-atorium.

Lock at my left had his back flat against the wall, his head tipped back, eyes closed. He was breathing steadily, but every exhale was peppered with the faintest of growls.

"Dammit, Ran," Duncan said at my right. "Just…don't…you…shit." I could literally feel how hard he was pushing his wolf back. He counted down from one hundred quietly, a trick he used to use as a kid when he needed to keep the beast at bay.

Okay, so maybe it wasn't Josky. Maybe they were reacting to magic. To me.

I could work with that. I cleared my throat.

Every head snapped my way, eyes glowing, flickering, features shift-edged and blurry.

I inhaled, lifted my hands slowly.

They watched me like I was stretched across bones they wanted to chew.

The magic in me was disconnected, but it was still there, scrambled up and distant, but mending, rushing back to connection points. Because I was a wizard. And that meant magic was always there inside me.

Like blood. Like oxygen.

Just like it was always inside the other marked. Shifters and sensitives.

Josky had done some sort of amazing thing when she cut all of magic's wires. I could do amazing things too.

And right now, I needed to be amazing.

"Breathe." It was barely loud enough for me to hear from across the room. Graves stood in the far corner, stance wide as if he were holding up the entire building.

"Breathe," he said again.

He inhaled, exhaled, loud enough, we could all hear it. Did it again. This time I saw a few of the guys breathe with him. Just like Coach had followed his cue.

What was he, the shifter whisperer?

Graves hummed, that slow, soft tune that he'd been whistling during our practices, during our games for months, the song as worn and familiar as a heartbeat.

The song about butchers strolling through town to kill people.

It settled the tension in the room, softened the sharp press of magic. Replaced it with a sense of belonging.

It told us we moved as one, breathed as one, fought as one.

It told us we fought together, and in that fight, were more than just human.

Even against magic.

The tension torqued down by degrees and the shifters settled, muscles unlocking, bodies relaxing.

I don't know when Graves stopped humming, but even Josky's shakes had eased off by the time I noticed it was silent in the room. The hard press of magic in my head and chest was gone. I felt like me. But I was raw inside. Unsettled.

Graves sniffed, then cleared his throat.

"All right. I'll see about the water. You all just take a minute." That was enough to snap everyone back to the here and now, enough to rouse us out of the strange thrall we'd all fallen under.

It had to be magic, right? I watched Graves move through the room. If I saw him on the street, I'd say he was a second-marked: wolf. But that wasn't a wolf thing he'd done.

Still, every gaze in the room followed him. Just like they would have followed an alpha. But he paused and stared at Duncan. Waiting for Duncan to acknowledge something.

Duncan frowned, tipped his head as if he could almost hear something, could almost understand whatever point Graves was trying to make.

Then Graves moved past him and out the door.

Just like that, everyone was moving again, everyone was breathing again, everyone was normal again.

"Jesus," Duncan exhaled. "That sucked."

"Marked have it locked down?" our captain asked. "Because if you're struggling with the shift right now, you need to say something. The last thing we need is for one of us to shift on the ice against the Tide."

Feet shuffled. Everyone met his searching gaze and nodded.

Even me.

But instead of looking away, Lock zeroed in and walked over to me.

"Don't blame him." Josky stood and shoved me to one side so she could get in the captain's face. And when a goalie decides to block something, she blocks something.

"He was doing something," Lock said. "I've been feeling it since the bus ride. You must have felt it too, Josky. And you know this never used to happen before he joined the team."

"What I felt was the whole team about to fall apart. Not just because Wiz is here. This was a long trip and that hot house reception was shit. So, with respect, Captain? Don't lay the blame on Hazard just because you got a problem with him."

I pushed at Josky, but she didn't budge. Seriously, why did people always think they had to stand up for me?

"It was me," I said.

Josky sighed, and moved to one side. She shook her head and then waved her hand between us as if telling us to work it out ourselves.

I saw Tomas Endler set his shoulders, then walk over to talk to Josky. I didn't think Josky had any idea how much Endler looked at her. Nor how he had to psych himself up every time he talked to her in his halting Spanish-laced English.

"Magic," I said. "That was my fault. But it won't happen again, Captain."

I was still scrambled inside. Magic was cut and weeping in me. A heaping wet mess I didn't want to touch and I didn't think I could pull on it if I tried.

Lock scowled then stiffed his fingers through his hair, pushing it off his forehead.

"All right. All right, Hazard. We had a hard ride. That steam room shit was bull. So let's just put this behind and look ahead. Keep it tight out there, right? Score some goals. Leave the magic behind."

It was more encouragement than I'd expected out of him. There was a reason he wore the C on his jersey.

"Right," I agreed.

He nodded and before walking away, smacked me on the shoulder. Like a teammate. Like a friend.

"All right, Boomers, let's get out there and show the Tide just how much we can turn up the heat."

26

DUNCAN SLID AROUND IN front of me blocking my view of the game. It was three minutes into the second period. We were down by two and waiting for a replay on a goalie interference call. "What is wrong with you?"

"Nothing. Move."

He bent to see my eyes, like he was looking for signs of concussion. "Talk. Now."

My head was hot, my breath short. I wasn't sick. Not physically sick. I was just...messed up inside. The magic in me snarled up. And my brain...I wasn't tracking like I should. Wasn't focused.

I'd forgotten something. Something important.

But I could play hockey. Had played plenty of times before when I'd been sick. This no different. This wouldn't be the reason Coach Clay would finally figure out he'd made a mistake to put me on the team.

Then hockey would be over. I would be over.

"Whoa," Duncan said. "I don't know where your head just went right then, but you are throwing off shit vibes. Take a break."

"I got it."

He dipped his head again and caught my gaze. Hard green, that gaze. "Get off the ice, Hazard. Really."

The ref announced that there was no goalie interference, and just like that, the game was back on.

"Crap." Duncan let go of me and took off across the ice. He'd probably expected me to skate to the boards, get off the ice.

Instead I sucked down a breath, and threw myself into the play.

We lost the faceoff and chased the puck to the corner. Graves slammed a Tide player into the boards and dug for the puck. Watts powered into the pile, followed by another Tide. The puck shot clear and Duncan was there to take it.

He was a few strides behind me, and I hustled toward the net, Steele on my heels.

I put on a burst of speed and scooped up Duncan's pass, juked, and popped the puck high left.

The *ping* of the puck hitting the crossbar, had me cursing.

I pushed after the puck, turned.

And watched Duncan get slammed into the glass from behind. Hard hit. Illegal as hell.

Steele looked up from Duncan's crumpled form and made kissing motions at me.

Duncan did not come up swinging. He pushed onto his knees and stayed there, hands and knees braced, head hanging.

There was blood pouring from his face.

Duncan was bleeding. Hurt.

Blood wasn't enough to call a foul in this league. If anything the sight of it, the sight of a player too hurt to get up to his skates right away sent the crowd into a frenzied roar.

But I remembered. Remembered the thing I'd forgotten. The thing that had triggered magic's burn in me.

The text. The beheaded wolf toy.

Son of a bitch.

Someone had threatened to hurt Duncan.

And now this. Now Steele had made him bleed.

Magic in me stuttered, unwieldy, messy. Lashing. A furious storm.

No.

Steele was barreling toward me. So were three other Tides. The hit hadn't been called. The puck was still in play. The game was still on.

I busted after the puck, twisted, got slammed into the boards at the hip.

Jerked back as a stick swung up and cracked into the side of my face.

Stars rattled across my vision. The puck was at my feet, my stick protecting it, trying to push it free to someone on my team.

"Stay the fuck down," a voice grunted as another stick jammed my ribs, hard enough to bust bone.

The two players crowding me were the same ones who had been in Downpour with Steele. The same two who had been in the parking garage.

I pushed back, grunting with pain and blinking away sweat. "Fuck yourself."

"What are you going to do, little wizard boy?" the Tide player, Zima, asked. "You gonna do magic little boy? Go ahead. Cast a spell."

"Take a fuckin' knee." That, from Catcher. He punched my kidneys hard enough, my lungs stopped working.

Please, like that was the first time I'd ever been hit.

"Go polish your skates, asshole." I twisted, shoved, and the puck popped free.

JJ was there to settle it and haul down the ice toward their net.

I looked for Duncan. He was slowly skating toward the bench, one hand against his nose, trying to keep the blood from getting everywhere.

He climbed over the boards, and said something to the Tide bench. One of players, the big tiger shifter, shouted something back at him.

I don't know what Duncan replied. But whatever it was, the other guy jumped over the boards and came at Duncan, swinging his stick at Duncan's head.

Duncan blocked with his arm and threw a fist at the guy's face.

The benches emptied as players from both teams jumped into the fight.

Duncan is hurt. Bleeding.

Magic thrummed through the air, thick and harsh.

Steele, just a few feet away from me on the ice, tore at his uniform as he skated toward the melee. He twisted his head to make eye contact with me, eyes wide, teeth bared.

For a moment, a breath, there was desperation there. Pleading. As if he were drowning, trying to yell out with no air in his lungs. And then that was gone.

No sanity. No man behind the beast. He was wild blood hunger. He was rage.

Finally free of his clothes, he fell on all fours and between one breath and the next, shifted into a snarling black panther, roaring for death.

He sprinted. Toward Duncan.

No!

Sirens blasted through the arena. The crowd screamed and cheered. An announcer ordered us all to take a knee.

Referees unholstered stun prods and beat hell toward the brawl.

More players were about to shift. Not just the Tide, but my team too. And when that happened…

…a wolf toy, head torn off…

No.

The world did that slow motion thing. Every detail went super-sharp: the arena, the ice, the lights streaming down hard and crisp.

I saw the breath of every player…

…magic like oxygen…

…exhaling gold and red, inhaling blue and purple. Could see magic moving through them, changing them, shaping them, like knuckles pressing wet clay.

The heartbeat of the crowd thumped. A susurration of a million wings fluttering, straining against the wind to rise.

Honey lacquered my tongue, spiced with mint, pepper, gasoline. Magic all around me. Magic inside me. Magic at my demand.

Waiting for me to tell it what to do.

I dragged my hands through the magic, already floating, drunk on it. Flying. Fingertips trailed smoking ribbons of white that sparked black and red at the edges, magic's ashes burning against my skin.

My mouth watered and every inch of my body went tight with need. I groaned.

This was what I was made for. This moment.

I drew magic to me, pulling it out of the air, out of the ice, out of the chanting crowd. Pulling it out of my teammates, their lungs, their breath.

Magic spun in lazy circles of color, humming against the ice like fingers dragged across glass, an ethereal, haunting song.

With a thought, it became a stream: fast, roaring, water rushing away from the shores and banks of the shifters and instead hurtling toward me, feeding the tornado of color and sound and taste and memories and power, endless power, that swirled and curled around me.

Up and up, magic following my hand that I lifted, trembling above me. The hand in which I clenched my hockey stick, like a sword, like the victor in a fight, raising a trophy.

Magic responded.

And it was brutal.

Magic poured around me, through me, over me, heavy, endless. Light and sound and color and pain shooting up, pulsing to the rafters, and out, out, out. Out of the enclosed stadium where it would disperse, but not before devouring me in the process.

It felt like it took forever.

One second. Two. Three.

And then…

…darkness.

And then…

…silence.

And then, because things never could go my way for once…

…agony.

I was blindsided by the tackle, fell all the way to the ice. Hit my head so hard, my helmet popped off.

"Stay down." I couldn't see. For the longest time, I couldn't see. When I could, I found Graves standing over me. Graves had tackled me. And he looked pissed.

"W-what?" I tried to push up, but everything under my palms, under my body was slick and wet.

Water where ice should be. Water under my ass and legs.

The arena wobbled and I blinked hard until it stabilized. Concussion? How hard had I hit my head? How hard had he tackled me?

Time had seemed to slow down from the moment he'd body slammed me. Now it sped up. Too fast.

I pushed again, trying to gain my feet, only to have Graves slam a palm into the middle of my chest and shove me back on my ass, hissing as he did so. He crouched over me. When had he moved?

"I said stay down. You're still burning." His voice was low and filled with a power that stopped me cold.

Burning?

Before I could blink or ask him what the hell he was saying, he had already twisted, his huge fist pulled back. "Sorry about this, kid."

I couldn't have dodged the punch to the face if I'd tried.

27

GRAVES'S HAND WAS BURNED.

I kept coming back to that. Second degree burns. I couldn't look away from the bandages, white and clean, that wrapped up his palm and fingers, like something a boxer wore before a fight.

"Listening to me, Hazard?"

I nodded, my gaze tracking in sticky little jumps up his T-shirt to his face.

Not a mark on him otherwise. I'd expected more damage when they'd told me he'd waded through a tornado of magic to find me in the center.

On fire.

Burning with magic.

Out of control.

"Duncan?" My voice was for crap, like I'd yelled it out. I swallowed against the hot scratchiness. I wanted water. But my arms felt like they were made of concrete. I didn't have the energy to pick up the glass on the hospital tray next to me.

"Doctors are still checking him out. Checking everyone. Both teams. He's with them. They're making sure there weren't any side effects or damage."

Damage. The word just sat there in the front of my brain, big enough I couldn't think around it. Damage because of me.

I had fucked up.

"You fucked up, kid."

I huffed a laugh, because: weird. Then I lifted my concrete arm up to wipe at the hot tears slipping down my face.

I didn't know why I was crying. I was numb. Couldn't feel anything. Except. Except…

…*damaged*.

I'd fucked up.

"Hey. C'mon. Back with me." Graves snapped his fingers and I stared at his bandaged hand again. Burned.

He pointed it at his face.

My gaze ticked up, following it.

"There has been no damage other than the fight. Bloody knuckles. Bruises. A couple broke noses. But what you did? That magic? They haven't found any damage caused by that. Hazard?"

Graves leaned forward and dropped his good hand on my arm above the taped I.V. line. "Listen. Listen to me now."

His voice did that thing, or maybe it was just his presence, the calmness of him, the steadiness of him. Whatever it was, my brain slipped out of the loop I hadn't been able to break and I could focus on him. Could really see him.

I heard the sounds of the hospital around me too, smelled the heavy antiseptics, the cleaning products, felt the stiff blanket scratching my chest.

"There you are." Did he look worried? Yes. Tired and pale too, the lines on his forehead deep, the lines at the corners of his eyes pinched.

He looked older. He looked…

…haunted, hollow…

……exhausted.

"No one was hurt." He nodded.

I nodded.

"Good," he praised. "You didn't hurt anyone. But pulling on that much magic…" He leaned back, drew his hand to rub at the back of his neck as he looked away from me.

"I don't even know what to say, or how you did it, but Hazard. Listen. I was there." He looked back at me, his dust-colored eyes bright, solemn.

"It didn't hurt. At all. That magic you used, that spell?" He wiped his hand over his mouth now, as if tasting a memory he wanted to forget.

Or wanted too hard to remember.

"There was no pain in it. Every marked slid out of their shift smoother than I've ever seen. Came out of it feeling fine. Not hungry, not weak. There was no pain. Not even for the sensitives. You didn't hurt anyone. Except yourself. And you did a job on that, son."

"The damage…" My voice gave out entirely.

Graves stood and moved around the bed to the table with water. The room was small, the doorway covered by a curtain. I thought we might be in an emergency room, not a regular hospital room. He picked up my cup of water and held it for me, angling the straw to my mouth.

"You were the only one damaged, Random."

Him using my first name made the comment softer, more personal, caring.

I swallowed water, and ignored the tears that started up again. The water was cool, clean, and did a lot to settle me.

"What happened? I don't r-remember."

His eyebrows shot up. He lifted the cup a little, offering me a second drink. I shook my head.

He eased back down into the chair again. "What do you last recall?"

"The game. The…Duncan hit by Steele. He was bleeding. Nose?"

"Not broken. Split lip. Few stitches. He's fine. That all you remember before you…" he waggled his fingers at me.

"He was chirping at the Tide's bench."

Graves chuckled. "Yeah, he was stirring up trouble. Got it too. Paski couldn't jump the boards fast enough to get to him."

"They shifted."

"They started to. Everyone started to."

"What happened?"

"You happened."

"Oh."

He waited. But really, what could I say to that?

"Want to tell me how you did that? How you pulled thirty shifters down out of the shift?"

The curtain to the little room pulled to one side and Duncan came barging in, all shoulders and hard jaw, bloody stitched lip, and determination.

"What in the hell were you thinking?" he screeched. "Just because you can use magic—all the damn magic in a block radius—doesn't mean that you should. Jesus Christ, Ran, you were on fire!"

He'd pushed past Graves like the defenseman wasn't taller and wider than him and grabbed my face with both of his hands. "You will never do that again in your life, understand?"

He rocked my head in a nod. "Yes, Duncan," he mimicked in a high tone, "I will never use magic and set myself on fire like a stupid ass again."

"You…okay?"

At the sound of my voice, he softened his grip on my head. "How badly are you hurt?"

He didn't wait for my answer. "Graves, how bad is he?"

"The nurses said he's stable. The doctor hasn't seen him yet, but since I'm a teammate and not a member of staff, they're not going to talk to me. Are you on his emergency contact list?"

"Yeah, I should be. So are my parents. I finally got reception out in the parking lot. They're driving up here. I've never heard Mom so close to hyperventilating."

"They saw the game?" Graves asked.

"Yeah. They always watch."

I made a small protesting noise, and both men swiveled hard looks at me.

"I didn't m-mean to…"

"It happened, Hazard," Graves said, not unkindly. "There's going to be fallout. Every second of that stunt was caught on national broadcast."

The sound I made this time was a groan. I closed my eyes, suddenly just tired. I didn't want to deal with it all. Mr. and Mrs. Spark. The team. The media. I just wanted to crawl under this scratchy blanket, hide, and never be heard from again.

Duncan gently patted the side of my face, and then the foot of the bed dipped as he made himself comfortable as close to me as possible.

He was quiet and so was I. Graves eventually left the room, the swish of the curtain pulling closed behind him.

I didn't want to talk.

"Dad and Mom were so scared," he said quietly. "The only info I could get on you was from Coach. He said you were stable and resting. I tried to talk Dad out of driving up here." He exhaled a soft laugh.

"Like talking to a pile of bricks. Nothing was going to stop them from being here."

I sighed, opened my eyes. "I'm sorry."

He scowled at me. "You need to stop saying that. Every time you use magic, you apologize for it. You're a wizard. You're gonna use magic."

He shifted around a bit—there really wasn't a lot of room for two big guys on this small bed. But Duncan needed the contact, the wolf in him wanting to know I was okay.

I needed the contact too. I felt hollowed out and fragile. I hated it.

"How burned am I?"

Duncan's eyebrows went up. "What I can see? None. Here." He stood, pulled back the blanket to look at my bare feet and legs, replaced it, then lifted the top of the blanket off my torso. He hooked a finger in the loose hospital gown I was wearing, glanced at my collarbones.

"No burns. You're bruised up from the game. Nothing weird. Well, I mean you always look weird to me, but not weirder."

"Jerk."

He grinned. "Weirdo."

"I don't understand."

"Poor little brain."

If I had the energy to flip him off, I would. Instead, I just swallowed and tried to steady my voice. "If I was really on fire…"

"You were." His expression fell and he dropped his hand on my leg, his wolf needing to know I was whole.

"Duncan. What happened?"

He gnawed at the stitches in his lip for a minute.

"I didn't see everything. I took that hit—not a big deal, but blood, you know? Decided to see if I could get a rise out of Paski before I got my face patched up. That tiger is just way too angry for this game and I hate how he's been crowding Josky."

A quick grin, and then Duncan was back to chewing on his lip.

"And?"

"And then everything just *happened.* Someone shoved, someone punched. It was good. Fun. The crowd went crazy. A couple of the guys were edging a shift. So it was going to go beast real fast.

"I glanced up. Saw you glaring at Steele. He was coming right at us, already catted out. You…uh…you went stone. Man, that's a stupid way to describe it, but you just became this hard figure, all punched shadows and bladed light.

"You glowed, dude. Then you lifted your hand, pointed at Steele. He was running, about to jump on the pile of us. But then. But then."

He shook his head and laughed, one huff of breath. His gaze held mine, the familiar clear hazel like rocks under river water.

"He turned back into a man. Like that." He snapped his fingers. "Nobody shifts that fast. *Nobody.* You should have seen the look on his face. So confused. It was hilarious."

"What about you?"

"What about me?"

"You were bleeding. Angry. Shifting."

He blew air between his lips. "Yeah. Yeah, I was all those things before you did that spell. That was a spell right?"

"I don't know."

He tipped his head and looked at me like I was the biggest idiot in the universe.

"You really should take some classes, Ran. Magic can be dangerous. You could hurt yourself."

"You think?" Even with a ruined voice, he caught the sarcasm.

"Hey, I'm not the one who lit myself on fire, magic boy."

"I wasn't on fire. No burns."

Duncan winced. He got up, found my water and waited until I could get my hand around it—slow, but I made it—before he sat back down.

"It was magic. Spinning like a goddamn tornado. You were in the center. At first, I could see through it, and then…there was just too much magic. It was all these colors. And bright. And dark. And solid. And loud. Just...I thought you were in the middle of a meat grinder. It happened so fast I couldn't get out of the scrum to reach you."

"How?"

"Graves. Blew across the ice like a demon. Bodied you out of the middle of that thing. You hit the ice and the tornado tore apart into ribbons.

"But magic was still burning out of you. Getting stronger. Brighter. You were burning up. You were on fire. So he hit you in the face."

"I remember that."

"You're going to have the black eye for that." He shrugged. "It worked. Magic was gone. Like that." He snapped his fingers again.

"His hand?"

"Burned when he punched you. Nothing's broken. The ice melted. Everyone pretty much lost their minds after that.

"There are reporters all over the place. They want to talk to you, but you know, that's not happening while you're in a hospital bed."

It was a lot to take in. I'd wanted to stop Steele from hurting my team. No, I'd wanted to stop Steele from hurting Duncan. From ripping his head off.

But I didn't even know if Steele had been behind that text. It could have been from anyone. Everyone knew I had a second-marked brother. It could have been an angry fan trying to get me off my game.

I groaned. "What is wrong with me? What was I thinking?"

"You were thinking you were going to knock Steele out of his shift, and keep the rest of us from throwing the game because we'd be down too many players.

"We lost anyway, but I get it. The Tide suck. If I were a wizard, I'd have done worse."

"Hazard?" The curtain pulled aside and a doctor in a white coat walked into the room.

The woman next to him was about my height and very thin, her eyes wide, dark, and mesmerizing. She had to be old enough to be my mother, but there wasn't a wrinkle on her soft brown skin. Her hair was a shocking white and pulled back in a hair clip thing.

She was a wizard.

Fear shot through me. I was glad they didn't have one of those heartbeat machines hooked up to me, because it would have been beeping like crazy.

The doctor glanced at the screen in his hand. "So you are the originator of this magic use, is that correct?"

"Yes."

The woman looked surprised at my answer. Could she read my mind? I hope she couldn't read my mind. Just in case I thought: *I'm sorry. I didn't mean for anyone to be hurt.*

She didn't react.

"Well, I'm Dr. Burling and this is Dr. Skopil. Dr. Skopil is also a wizard."

"I am very pleased to meet you, Mr. Hazard." She sounded sincere, but those eyes.

It felt like she could see all the things I was made of and was judging my inability to handle magic properly.

"We're going to need to do a few tests," Dr. Burling said. "So if your friend...?"

"Duncan," I said while Duncan said, "I'm staying."

"He's going," I croaked.

Duncan opened his mouth to argue, but I cut him off. "I'm fine. Call your parents and give them an update. Find out how the rest of the team is so you can tell me. Okay?"

He pulled his shoulders back and glared at the doctors, who didn't seem at all fazed by his behavior. They probably saw overprotective friends and relatives all the time.

"As soon as we're done," Dr. Skopil said, "we'll call you back in. Duncan, right?" She held her hand out for him and he shook it.

"Okay. Fine. But be careful with him, okay?"

"We're here to make sure he's well," she said. "We'll be very careful with him."

Duncan gave me one last look and then left me with the doctors.

"What kind of tests?" I asked.

"We'll check your vitals," Dr. Burling said. "We'll go over your blood tests. Things are looking good, Mr. Hazard. And of course we'll make sure that you're suffering no unexpected effects from the magic use."

"Do you remember using magic?" Dr. Skopil asked.

"Yes."

"How often do you use? Would you say once a week? More?"

"Almost never."

She nodded. I didn't think she believed me.

"Well, this was a large use and with that comes the weakness I'm sure you're familiar with, along with headaches, sleeplessness, fatigue, hunger, or lack of appetite. Alternately, it can come with cravings. For more magic. And that can be very dangerous, as you know.

"We want you to follow the standard recovery procedures that you've followed in the past. Do you have a friend or family member who can monitor you?"

"Yes."

She was talking quickly. My bell had been rung hard enough—thanks a lot, Graves—that it was pretty much all I could do to process the information she was telling me.

This wasn't the first time I'd been through an injury. I knew how to drink plenty of fluids and apply ice.

"Now, it was a...class two?" She glanced at her colleague.

He'd been quiet, studying something on the screen. "There's video." He handed her the screen.

She watched for a moment, while the doctor stared at me, eyes narrowed.

"How are you really feeling?" he asked.

"Tired. But okay. My voice?" I swallowed.

"Normal, I'd say from this kind of spellwork. It should clear up in a day or two." He positioned his stethoscope in his ears and then pushed the buttons on the bed so that the head of it rose.

"I'm going to listen to your heart and lungs."

I breathed when he told me to, sat up when asked. I also watched Dr. Skopil as she tapped the screen to play the video more than once. Her eyebrows were raised, but her face was otherwise frozen.

"Everything sounds good." Dr. Burling moved away from the bed and Dr. Skopil handed him the screen. They exchanged a look.

"I need to test a few things with magic, Mr. Hazard." Dr. Skopil's voice trembled as if she'd just seen something frightening. "This won't hurt. I am a diagnostic wizard."

I nodded.

She held up her hand, palm toward me. I thought she was going to touch me, but instead she slowly held her hand an inch or two away from my body as she traced over it from the top of my head down to my feet.

"There is no permanent damage. No...damage at all. Strain. But well within parameters for spellwork."

She folded her hands in front of herself and gave me a hard look. "What kind of wizard are you, Mr. Hazard?"

"The kind who plays hockey?"

She shook her head. "What category of magic?"

"I don't know."

It must have been the look on my face that made her believe me, because my voice was still a frog's butt.

"Your records are incomplete. All we have is a recent report from Dr. Phelps."

Uh-oh. I knew where this was going. They were going to keep me here to test me. I didn't know how long that would take, but I was not about to be stuck in a hospital a state away from my home with wizards and doctors who wanted to poke and prod.

I was tired, embarrassed by my behavior on the ice, and just wanted to go home.

"I'm not doing any more tests." I levered up until I was sitting unsupported. Swung my legs over the edge of the bed. "I'm not staying."

"Mr. Hazard," Dr. Burling said. "We need to keep you under observation for side effects."

I kept moving. "Going. Home."

Feet on the cold floor sent a hard chill through me. I braced one hand on the sidebar of the bed and grabbed the plastic bag with my clothes in it.

My jersey and pants. No socks.

I pulled out the pants.

"Mr. Hazard," Dr. Skopil said like she was having none of this. "You need to get back into bed immediately. You are too weak to leave."

Too weak? Ha! I'd felt worse after bag skates.

She wrapped her hand around my wrist to stop me.

A pop of magic, nothing more than a ping of light and the tiniest bit of heat snapped at her fingers.

She jerked her hand away.

It hadn't hurt either of us. But I hadn't made magic do that. I hadn't been thinking about magic at all.

"We need a suppresser," Skopil said. "Calm down, Mr. Hazard. Let us help you. Why don't you stay in bed while we finish looking over your teammates. It will take some time. You may as well rest here instead of in the lobby."

"No. Thanks." I kept going, kept moving. Got into my sweats. Got out of the hospital gown.

"Suppresser," Dr. Skopil repeated.

Dr. Burling tapped on the tablet.

I didn't know what or who a suppresser was, but I wasn't going to stand here to find out. I got the jersey over my head then had to stop to breathe.

My arms were heavy, my chest heaving like I'd just done laps.

I was wrung out. Exhausted.

I pushed, got my right hand in the sleeve. Got the left.

The curtain shoved aside and I looked up, ready to fight the suppresser.

"Random," Coach Clay strode into the crowded room. "Why are you out of bed?"

"You must be Coach Clay," Dr. Burling said. "Mr. Hazard is refusing to listen to our recommendations. He needs to rest. He's clearly exhausted."

"They want to. Test. Me." My voice was bad and getting worse. "I want. To go. Home."

I was pleading with him even though my voice was nearly gone. "Please, Coach," I whispered.

He measured the doctors, studied me, then made his decision. He was by my side in a fluid second. "Can you walk?"

I nodded. If it meant getting out of here, I could run. Well, maybe fast shuffle.

"Mr. Clay," Dr. Burling said, "Mr. Hazard shouldn't be out of bed at this time. He is too fatigued and if he doesn't receive rest and care, he could be permanently damaged."

That sounded horrible, but luckily, Coach wasn't listening to him. He slung his arm behind my back and under my arm. Then guided me to the bed.

Before I could protest, he handed me socks. "Put them on." Then he retrieved my shoes from under the chairs

Dr. Skopil shook her head. "Mr. Clay. There has been a misunderstanding. There are a few *routine* tests we still need to run before we can release Mr. Hazard."

"That so?" Coach bent and shoved my feet firmly into my shoes. "And that involves a suppresser in what way?"

I looked over the doctor's shoulders to a guy standing in the doorway. He was big—tall and wide—arms crossed over acres of chest. He had a weird sort of long-distance expression on his face.

Something way down deep inside me went still and cold. I had no idea what he was—wizard? sensitive?—but everything in me wanted to be far, far away from him.

"We are not the bad guys here," Burling said. "A suppresser is just a safety precaution. When a wizard pulls on magic that intense, we need to cover all of the possible outcomes."

"You will not use a suppresser on one of my players, doctor. You can hand me the form to sign for his release."

Burling just sighed. I guessed he'd had stubborn patients before. Maybe even stubborn hockey coaches. He handed Coach the screen.

Coach read it and signed. "I'll have our medical staff keep an eye on him until he can see his personal doctor. Thank you."

Coach helped me stand, and with his arm around me, we walked out of the room and through the maze of the ER. People stared at us as we walked by.

"The press is in the waiting room and there isn't another way through to the elevator. How do you want to play this, Hazard?"

I almost laughed because he was the coach. His job description was basically coming up with strategies.

"Go through them?" I suggested.

"Think you can walk on your own?"

"Yeah." I pulled my arm off his shoulder—he was too tall for me to be hanging there anyway—and stood still for a minute. Sweat salted my upper lip and dripped down the sides of my face. It took every ounce of energy I had just to stand.

I pulled my shoulders back. All I had to do was put one foot in front of the next until I got to the elevator.

"Don't answer any of their questions," Coach was saying. "Let me do the talking. Just keep moving. Ready?" He had one hand above the button to open the ER doors, the other strong and steady under my elbow.

I nodded.

The doors swung open and cameras flashed, a staccato of light.

Wow.

They shouted my name, repeating it as they surrounded us. A wall of bodies, pressing inward.

Cameras and microphones. Too many voices. Too many questions.

"Hey, Random. Random, over here! Can you tell us what happened out there?"

"Was this in response to Tabor Steele's hit on Duncan Spark?"

"Your team is the bottom of the pack this year. Are you frustrated with your inability to do your part?"

"The decision on whether you should be suspended for shutting down a game due to magic use is being discussed. Do you think you're a danger to players?"

Coach pushed through them, one hand digging into my elbow and propelling me forward.

I just kept walking and looking straight ahead. There had to be an elevator around here somewhere. After the longest hallway I'd ever had to walk, the doors appeared.

The crowd had followed us all the way, and were still asking questions.

Coach stabbed the elevator button. "I understand you all have a lot of questions. I will be holding a press conference after all of the players have been seen by medical staff."

A couple reporters tried to get between us and the elevator door.

Had they forgotten Coach was a player back when West Hell was even more blood and guts?

The elevator opened. Coach snarled and pushed people out of the way. A man who was miles of legs and arms stretched out of the crowd and held the door open for us.

"You're not getting an exclusive, Dart," Coach said as he walked me into the elevator.

The man positioned himself in front of the door, blocking the other reporters.

"You look like the butt end of hell, Clay, and he looks worse. When you're ready to talk, really talk, you know where I am." He reached in and punched the button, gave me a sort of puzzled smile, then turned and faced the crowd. "All right, all right. We all know how this goes. Get moving. Show's over."

The elevator closed. Only the two of us were in it.

Silence.

Thank God.

"Lean." Coach pressed me up against the wall, his hand against my shoulder, helping to keep me on my feet. I leaned.

I don't know where he got it from, but he handed me a sport drink.

I drank it dry. Wished the elevator ride were twice as long. And that there was a bed in it. And a million hours of sleep ahead of me.

"Just a little farther." The doors chimed open and I pushed off so we could move down the long corridor.

"Clay!"

Coach went tight in a way I couldn't process. Fight or flight? More like fight and fury.

A man in a suit stormed down the hallway toward us, fists clenched at his sides.

The guy had a seagull face. His cheekbones were sharp enough to point, his nose hooked above a narrow mouth and small chin. His hair was black and about a month past a decent haircut and curled across his forehead and at his nape.

He had an obvious scar puckering one cheek.

Coach Nowak, the man in charge of the Tide.

"What the hell kind of shit show are you running?" Nowak yelled. "That—" he stabbed a finger at me "—little publicity stunt of yours is a fucking menace. Either you throw him out of the game or I sure as hell will."

"Fuck off, Nowak."

Wow. I'd never heard Coach that angry. He started us forward again. I really wanted to help out more with that, but it was taking everything I had to just stay on my feet.

Nowak shot out a hand and clamped down on Coach's shoulder.

He leaned in, and I could feel the anger radiating off him like heat waves.

"I warned you, Elliott, but you didn't listen. This time you have crossed the line. If you want to destroy your reputation by parading your team around like some kind of bullshit NHL franchise, fine. That's on you. You want to turn West Hell into some kind of politically correct, discount, apologetic game for pansy-ass has-beens, good damn luck.

"But you bring in players who are unsafe, uncontrolled when they play *my* boys? You bring in a wizard with no control over his magic? I will tear this shit show you call a team apart and make sure you never work another day of your life."

Coach Clay hadn't moved. Hadn't flinched. The plateau between them stretched on and on and on.

"Nice talk, Don," Coach finally said. "All those multiple syllable words almost made you sound smart." Then he pushed, physically moving the man out of his way as he carried me forward.

Everything was getting a little dark at the edges, and my breathing was going funny. I was losing my grip on reality. Was about to go under.

"Coach," I gasped.

There were more hands, arms wrapped around me, steadying and carrying me. Even with my iffy vision, I knew some of those hands belonged to Leon, Assistant Coach Beauchamp, Graves, and Duncan.

I was manhandled into a chair, my head pushed down between my knees while Leon told me to breathe nice and slow.

"Okay," Coach said. "That's all of us here. Everyone settle and listen up. There will be consequences for that debacle tonight. The WHHL has already contacted me and let me know they are coming up with some new rules about wizards on teams. At this point, they're going to let me know how many games Mr. Hazard will be suspended for, and how many games we will forfeit."

Everyone groaned and cussed.

I tried to lift my head to protest. I'd been the one who had fucked up, not my teammates. They shouldn't suffer for my stupidity. Forfeiting even a couple games could kill our standing for the playoffs this year.

A hand on the back of my head stilled me. Leon again.

"Breathe," he ordered.

"Don't blame it all on Hazard, Coach," Duncan said. "He wasn't the only one who might have pushed it a little too far tonight."

"Might have, Mr. Spark? Is that how you saw this, because if you thought tonight *might have* been a little too far, you need to gather your gear and get the hell off of my team."

Ouch. I knew that tone of voice. We were so screwed.

"Was it a little too far, Mr. Spark?" Coach went on.

"No, sir." Duncan's hand on my shoulder tightened. "It was a lot too far."

I swallowed hard and tried to talk, but my voice had checked out for good.

"As soon as I hold the press conference I *should not* have to hold to explain why my team, who *should* be setting the bar for the professional behavior the Western Hybrid Hockey League, instead lost their heads in a rival game for *nothing*, we'll get down to what individual discipline will be required."

He exhaled a hard breath. "I need you all to listen to me. I'm angry. I'm frustrated. I know you are too. But this ends now. Right here. We do not stoop to their level. We do not lose our heads. We force them to rise up and meet us. On our battlefield, on our terms.

"I am not saying the animals within us are wrong. What we are, every part of us, makes us better fighters, better warriors, better competitors. But this was not a time to resort to magic.

"We must play better, think better, and handle magic better than any other team out there. I want to see this team rise to something better than what is expected of us. I expect discipline. I expect brute force and balls-out skill, backed up by intelligence and un-fucking-breakable focus.

"That's what makes us the Thunderheads. That's what makes us a team. I want that. I want your best every damn time you step on the ice."

"Some of us already give our best, Coach," Lock said. "Every time."

Jerk. I mean, he wasn't wrong. But still: jerk.

"All or nothing, Mr. Laakkonen," Coach said. "We are a team. What one of us chooses, we all choose. What one of us does, we all do. When one of us falls, we are all there to back him or her up. What we do *not* do, is let our tempers, our beasts, our magic, our fear, or our anger get the better of us." He eyed each of us.

"We don't fall apart the first time someone pulls a dirty move. We fight back, *as hockey players*, not as animals. "If we can't be better than the beasts inside of us, then we've already lost. And if we're ever going to gain the respect of the world, if we're going to become something more than a freak show, if we're ever going to be seen as a hockey club that is every damn bit as good as the NHL, then we play it hard and we play it right.

"It's time you step up and prove me right. Now get on the bus. While I deal with this shit show press conference. Coach Beauchamp. Show them the way out."

I heard him leave, which was saying something, because he was always silent on his feet.

There was a general exhale and then Assistant Coast Beauchamp spoke, his deep rumble a relief. "All right boys and girls. You heard Coach Clay. Let's get this show on the road. If we run into any reporters, keep your mouth shut. If you can't do that, say something positive about the game, and about our rivals. Do us right, hear?"

Leon tapped the back of my head. "Think you can sit up without passing out?"

I lifted my face off my knees. The room stuttered and swayed then settled. I'd never been so tired in my life.

"Should I." I cleared my throat, because all that came out was a whisper. "Press interview?"

Leon squinted to where coach had left. "He didn't tell you to go with him. And with that voice, you're not going to do any good anyway. I'm sure you'll get a chance to smile at the cameras back home."

Great.

28

THE THUNDERHEADS HAD TO forfeit that game, and the next two. That made the Redding Rumblers and the Nampa Hunters happy, but it shot the hell out of our record. If we continued this losing streak, there wasn't going to be much chance we'd reach the playoffs.

Coach told me over the phone, "You pulled magic out of a block radius. Completely stripped it."

"They can measure that?"

"Yes, Hazard. They can measure that."

"Was anyone hurt?"

"No. Well, you. The league has passed down your punishment."

"Oh."

"Five games. You'll be off the ice for the next five."

"Oh."

"Hazard?"

"Yeah?"

"If you do that again, it won't just be the league dropping you from games. Do I make myself clear?"

"Yes, sir."

"One more thing. They want you to attend a training class. For wizards."

"Oh."

He sighed. "Don't sound so sad, Hazard. This will help you control your magic. This is good. It's the missing piece of your training I didn't even think about for you."

"Yes, sir."

Because I was that different from all his other players. That strange.

"How's your recovery?"

That pull on magic had done something to me. Broke something inside me in a way I didn't understand. I was weak, exhausted. My appetite was dead, my strength shot.

"Good, Coach."

There was silence. Then another sigh.

"Don't lie to me, Random. You see your doctor?"

"Yes, Coach." Sean had taken me and stayed so he would know what my recovery would require. Turned out it was more than ice and elevation.

"Are you following his advice?"

Sleep was the big thing. Had to get a lot of it. After that, no strenuous physical or mental activity. Lots of food, fluids.

No hockey for two weeks.

And absolutely no magic use.

If I never used magic again in my life, it would be fine with me.

"Yes, Coach."

"Good. If you need anything from me, call."

"Yes, Coach."

"Random?"

"Yes?"

"You're still a part of this team. Still a Thunderhead. We just have to take these steps to make sure there are no more mistakes going forward."

"Yes, Coach."

I hung up.

"Move over." Duncan dropped a pillow next to my shoulder. He stood by my bed glowering down at me like I'd done something personally to offend him.

I shook my head. My throat felt like I'd been practicing sword swallowing but had accidentally used a pitchfork. That was on fire. And covered in bees. And still in my throat.

"I'm sleeping with you."

He was really bossy tonight. I shook my head again.

"Just—" he blew out a breath. "Move, Random. I want to sleep."

So whiny. I closed my eyes and didn't move.

"You suck." He shouted: "Mom! Random won't move."

I heard her footsteps. "Random, are you okay?"

I opened my eyes. Gave her a thumbs up and put whatever I had left into a smile.

"Tell him to move." Duncan was still scowling at me, like I was some kind of obstacle he didn't know how to get over put in his way just to annoy him.

"He doesn't want you to sleep in here, Duncan," his mom said. She was watching me as she said it, checking to make sure she was correct. I gave her the thumbs up again.

"But I want to."

Yeah, Duncan was never going to take top scores on a debate team.

Kit looked at her son. "He needs all the sleep he can get, and you being in here complaining doesn't help with that."

"But—"

"No. Let him get some sleep without worrying about you stealing his covers or hogging the bed."

"I—"

"Not going to change my mind," she said. "And neither is Random. Go on." She pushed him toward the door, which was always funny to watch, because she was tiny next to him, but he looked like such a chastised three-year-old.

"Mom," he groaned.

"Out."

I smiled at the two of them. No matter how tired I was, just knowing they were there, such a part of my life, when it would have been easier a hundred times over to send me packing back to my absent mother and empty house, or out into the world on my own, made my chest warm.

This was my family. It was small and nothing close to normal. But it was mine and I loved it. Loved them. Even Duncan, who really needed a girlfriend so he could get all his wolf-pack cuddling needs out on her instead of me.

Kit came back and stood next to my bed. "Do you need anything, Random? Water? A bathroom break?"

I'd needed help getting to the bathroom, which sort of drove home how badly burned out I was. I shook my head. "Sleep."

She winced at the sound, then pressed her hand on my forehead, my cheek. She was a nurse, so she knew what she was doing. But I secretly hoped she was just touching me like that because she wanted to comfort me.

"You're going to be fine. I know you feel bad right now, but sleep is going to do wonders for you. Drink that water any time you wake up tonight. I'll check in on you a couple times, okay?"

She talked while her palm rested against my cheek, her gaze warm.

I nodded.

"Good-night, Random." She bent and brushed a quick kiss to my forehead. She hadn't done that since I was eleven.

She was worried about me. I hated that I'd made her feel that way.

I'd dragged my team down and worried the only people in the world who actually cared about me.

I had to fix this. All of it. But first I needed a plan. I closed my eyes to think and black waves of exhaustion swallowed me whole.

When I surfaced, it was the middle of the night. I didn't hear anyone awake in the house. Perfect.

I had a plan, and that plan started with me getting out of bed by myself, and walking to the bathroom down the hall.

Using magic had used up my body. That was the downside of being a wizard and it was why wizards had to be so careful with how much magic they used and how often.

I'd dealt with the side effects pretty well all the other times I'd used it, but sucking all the magic out of a city block, and then manipulating that magic had really hit me hard.

If I was going to be a part of the team, I needed to get my physical strength back.

I pushed the blanket down to my thighs and took my time sliding my legs over to the edge of the bed. Getting into a sitting position was no fun, but I did it.

Score.

For my next trick, I stood, bracing my hand on the wall, and then I started walking, slow, careful steps.

Blood pounded heavy and loud in my ears, and my breathing was all weird and ragged. There wasn't a lot of light in the room, so I could only assume my vision was still holding out.

I'd made it half a dozen steps when my bare foot landed on something squishy and warm.

"Ouch," Duncan said sleepily. "Get off my arm, Ran."

He was on my floor? Why was he on my floor?

"I couldn't sleep," I lied.

He made noise like he was rubbing his hand over his face, then grunted and stood. "Bathroom?"

"I can do it."

"Just…stop with the Vader whisper, dude. It sounds terrible." His big hand clamped onto my elbow. I tried to pull away, but he chuckled. "You are shaking so hard, I'm surprised your teeth aren't chattering. C'mon."

I didn't have the strength to pull away. He walked with me to the bathroom, hung out while I pissed and washed up, then took his place next to me, his hand under my elbow.

We started down the hall. He aimed us toward the bedroom, but I made a noise and leaned a little like I was on skates and could correct our angle.

"What?"

"Kitchen."

"I can get you food. Are you hungry? You should be hungry, because not to scare you dude, but you've lost at least twenty pounds since the game and it's only been two days."

I just kept walking to the kitchen. I was not hungry. But the only way to get back on my feet, was to be on my feet.

Duncan seemed confused when we paused, me leaning against the island, him with his head in the refrigerator naming off the contents in hopes I'd say yes to something. Finally: "Water?"

I was breathing too hard to answer, and there was a mosquito-buzz ringing in my ears, I flicked up a thumb in acknowledgment.

"You had water by your bed, Ran." He filled a plastic cup halfway. I took it gratefully, my hand shaking all to hell until he steadied it and helped me get the cup to my lips.

Drank it all down while Duncan watched.

"You think you can push this?" he said quietly. "Have you looked at yourself in a mirror? You're a skinny stick insect that's been drowned in the rain."

I flipped him off.

He grinned. "Yeah, like you could stop me from doing anything to you right now. I know you. I know you want to get better faster. That's why you just did a lap into the kitchen, right?" He bent a little to look into my eyes. "Right?"

"Yes."

"I don't think it's a good idea. Walking on a broken leg won't make it better faster."

"Not. Broken."

"You were on fire, Random. I think you keep forgetting that. Also, you forced two full hockey teams out of their shifts. Mid-shift. I looked that shit up. Nobody has ever done that. In the history of wizarding. And not just because they weren't into hockey. There's a stat on how many wizards have ever, once in their life, drawn someone down out of a shift. You know where you rank? Number one. No one's ever, *ever* stopped shift for more than one person at a time."

I inhaled, exhaled. This whole subject annoyed me.

"Don't roll your eyes at me. You did a huge, and just *so, so* stupid thing."

Changed my mind. It wasn't the subject that annoyed me. It was him.

"And when we do a huge, stupid thing, we have to take it easy and recover smart. Because if you want to get back out there on the ice this year, you'd better be smart about taking care of your body. Are you listening to me?"

I nodded. He was making sense. Even if I didn't like it.

"Wow, how weird is it that you finally agree with me?" He crowded my space and pulled me up, draping my arm over his shoulder. When I tried to pull away, he just patted my arm. "Better let me do it this way. Otherwise I'm just gonna put you in a fireman's carry and lug you into your room like a bag of kibble."

I would have argued, but by the time I pulled together the energy for it, I was lying in my bed, the covers tossed over me, and Duncan settled beside me, triumphantly, eyes closed, hand on my arm, happy as a stupid clam.

29

IT TOOK ME A week to talk Duncan into sneaking me into the rink. We'd done nightly laps at the house, adding in the living room and the hall that led to the laundry room, and Sean and Kit's home office.

I walked some during the day too, short trips out to the mailbox, or to the end of the block and back.

I worked back up to three meals a day, and then three with snacks but still lost another ten pounds. Right when Kit was about to knock me out and drag me in to the doctor, my weight stabilized.

The team had drills six days straight. Their punishment for the forfeited games. Duncan had gone in every day at five in the morning, and staggered through the door by eight at night.

Coach was working them hard. Partly to keep them in shape but mostly because he'd decided the entire team needed to play better together. He ran them through new drills, mixed up the lines.

And when they left to play the Nampa Hunters Saturday without me, they won.

They won without me.

I watched the entire game alone in my bed. My chest felt hollowed out from me not being there with my team, but my heart was beating with hope. The Thunderheads looked…good. Clean. Sharp.

All the losses, all the screwups, all the penalties from the league had fired them up. They hit the ice like they had something to prove.

And they did just that.

I was glued to every shot, every play. Graves and Watson were human freight trains, playing a physical game that sent a clear message: Thunderheads were done playing around. They had come to the ice to win.

Lock was on fire and the team rallied to his drive. He scored a hat trick, putting the Thunderheads in the lead.

No matter what the Hunters threw at them, the Boomers just kept moving, pushing, digging, making smart plays.

The game ended with the Thunderheads taking the win 4-1.

I cheered, even though it was more of a croak, and clapped, even though I was alone in my room.

Lock and Graves and Josky took stars of the game, and I could not agree more.

Just a few minutes after that, my phone buzzed several times. Duncan.

Hell yes!

You better be hype!

King of the assist. Worship.

I beamed at my phone and texted back.

F-yeah. WTG!

His reply was swift. *All hail the Donut.*

I tapped out: *Hail. King of all breakfast pastries.*

A new message buzzed in. Not from Duncan, from Gen.

I had only answered one of her half-dozen worried messages since the game in Tacoma. Just to tell her I was sleeping to recover, and that I'd get in touch when I was back on my feet.

She worked for a doctor who did testing. She probably had a good idea of what using that amount of magic could do to a person.

It had been pretty impossible to have not heard about my big blowup.

It was still all over the internet. Someone had put it to music, someone had spliced it into a superhero movie. Biggest screwup in my life, and I was an instant meme.

Holy crap! Great game.

Wish u were there.

I smiled, because it was really nice of her to watch the game, and to be thinking

about me. I typed my reply, hit send.

Wish I was2. Happy4 the win. We need one.

When do u play?

Earliest? Next weekend. Reality? Who knows?

How u feeling?

Better.

Good. Coffee? Tell me when.

I hesitated. Maybe for a little too long.

Don't be a baby, Ran. We're still seeing each other as soon as u get over your man pain.

I actually barked out a laugh.

So romantic.

I sweated out the wait on that. Was she being romantic checking in on me or was this just a friend thing between us now? Her reply was almost instant.

U want romance u have to take me to coffee.

Deal.

Then, to make sure I was being totally honest:

Not well enough yet. Will text. Hopefully soon.

Good. Sleep. Eat. Don't set yourself on fire again, ok?

I sent her a smiley face and she sent one in return.

I cracked a huge yawn and lay back down on my bed. I was a wreck. Just watching the game had worn me out.

My phone buzzed.

Gen?

Were u texting ur girlfriend? Not Gen. Duncan.

Go celebrate

u were! u loooove her!

Leave me alone

u wanna kiiiissss her!

I turned my phone off and tossed it on the nightstand.

Idiot.

But I was smiling as I fell asleep.

"I STILL THINK THIS is a bad idea." Duncan grunted as he finished tying his skate.

"You can go home." My voice had almost recovered. Just some extra gravel to it like I was getting over a cold. I had to clear my throat a lot.

"And what, leave you here for the whole three hours of sleep I'd get before having to be back here for early skate?"

"You sure do complain a lot for a guy working his dream job."

Duncan beamed, and it lit up his face. "I do love this job. You, I'm having second thoughts about."

"Shut up. You love me." I held out a hand, and he stood in front of me and clasped it.

"Up." He tugged, and I got on my skates. My shoulders dropped and half of the tension I'd been lugging around for the last week disappeared.

This I knew. This I understood and loved. Hockey. Yes.

"You sure?" he asked.

"That you love me? Dude, you can't stay out of my bed."

"Shut up. I'd sleep alone if you'd stop trying to die on me. Think you can do the ice?"

I gave him back the biggest smile. "Let's find out."

TURNED OUT COACH HIT the ice in the middle of the night.

This was not something I knew.

It was not something Duncan knew.

It was something we both found out after we'd huffed our way down the corridors and suddenly realized we were not alone in the place.

"Shit," Duncan whispered. "If we duck out fast, he'll never see us."

"Not hiding." I took the last few steps, and then I was on the ice, the familiar shuck and grind of metal cutting a thin line, carrying me, setting me free.

I could breathe again. I could move again.

This was where I belonged.

I took it easy: step and glide, step and glide. Duncan was quickly at my side pacing me step for step.

We hadn't brought out our sticks or pucks. The idea was just to see how long I could skate. To get a feel for how bad my conditioning had slipped.

"So?" Duncan asked.

"What?"

"How are you doing, idiot?"

We were taking the rink in a nice slow lap. Hadn't even gone around it once.

"Good. Don't know how many laps. But good."

"He knows we're here."

"I know."

Coach was in the trapezoid at the end of the rink, his stick resting easily next to his skate as he watched us glide his way. He was in a worn-out Berkeley sweatshirt and sweatpants. His hair was a mess, like he'd been dragging his fingers through it, or like he'd just rolled out of bed and found himself here, on the ice.

He looked tired. And maybe annoyed.

He tracked my every move, his expression carefully blank. Judging me. Judging how I was moving, how I was breathing.

There was only one way to get over a bad patch in hockey—bad luck, bad calls, bad hits—push forward. It had been a philosophy that had served me pretty well so far in life, so I applied it to most everything.

I applied it now and skated right up to him. I stopped, breathing a little heavier than I would have preferred.

Still, for my first time back on the ice in a week, and considering I'd barely been able to go to the bathroom on my own a week ago, I was pretty proud of myself. Which is why I held my head high and met his gaze.

"Hey, Coach."

"Hazard." His eyes twitched to the side. "Spark. What are you two doing here in the middle of the night?"

Duncan opened his mouth but I moved so I was slightly in front of him.

"My idea. I needed to know. If I could do it. Duncan came, but I'd be here without him."

"What did the doctor say about this?"

"The doctor's not here, sir."

The corner of his mouth pressed upward and the steel in his eyes softened back to ocean blues. He rubbed his hair away from his forehead with one hand, and nodded at Duncan. "Go get your sticks. We'll do a little easy work."

Duncan took off like a shot.

"How are you really feeling, Random?"

I hadn't expected Coach to sound worried. But then, I hadn't given him any reason not to worry about me. That had to change. From here forward, I was going to be the last player he had to spend a late-night skate thinking about.

"Last week sucked."

Coach pushed off slowly, handling the puck on his stick as he went. I knew he wanted me to follow, so I fell into place on his left. We were going slower than snails through quicksand, but still, we were moving.

"You've dropped some weight."

"I've got that under control now. What I did...the magic...I want to apologize. I lost my head. It was unprofessional."

"Agreed." He tapped the puck, an easy back and forth, more automatic than planned. "Tell me why."

"Why?"

"You've played several games with us, Hazard. There have been fights. Why this time?"

I thought about it. Knew I couldn't really untangle it all unless I told him everything.

"I got a letter. Back at the first press conference when I got picked up. I didn't open it for a while, but when I did, it was a threat."

"What?"

"It said I didn't belong. Here. In West Hell. There was a picture of a wizard doll all torn up."

"Why didn't you tell me about this?"

"I thought it was just, you know, someone all bent out of shape about wizards in hockey. Just..." I shrugged.

"You're killing me here, Hazard. Okay, so what happened to the note?"

"It's at home."

"Did you tell anyone else about it? Spark?"

"No."

He sighed. "I need to see it. Bring it in to practice next time you come."

"Yes, Coach."

"What did that note have to do with the game in Tacoma?"

"I got another one. Well, a text. Right before the game."

"Same content?"

"No. This time it was a wolf doll with its head cut off."

He was quiet a moment. Finally: "Duncan?"

"I thought so. Yeah. And when Steele pounded him into the boards, that was a dirty hit. That was intent. And I thought...I thought..."

"You thought he was trying to kill your best friend. Your brother."

I swallowed, but didn't say anything. Tears stung the edges of my eyes and I didn't want Coach to know how raw I still was.

"Do you have any proof it was Steele?" Coach's voice was calm but there was something more to it. A banked fury. That comforted me more than I expected.

"No."

"Do you still have the text?"

"I...deleted it."

He looked over at me, then took a shot at the goal at the other end of the ice. Hit it dead on. Since it was night and the rink was officially closed, the light didn't go off.

"If that happens again, I need you to tell me. Immediately. The instant it happens." He waited, not moving across the ice to dig the puck out of the net, not doing anything.

I met his gaze.

One thing was clear about Elliott Clay, he was steady. Patient. But he did not stand for bullshit.

I owed him the truth or nothing. Owed that to the team.

"I'll tell you. I promise. Coach..." I swallowed to steady my voice. "I haven't been playing at my best. The whole getting kicked out of the NHL before I could even be a part of it was, uh, hard.

"But that's in the past. I know I can be a great player. I believe that. I've worked hard for that. I don't know how the magic I have fits in with that, but I'd give it up in a second if it meant I could play even one more minute of hockey."

He stared at me. A lot of cat in his gaze.

"Do you have a personal issue with Steele?"

That kind of threw me, but it made sense. It was only after Steele had shifted that I went magic crazy. "No. He doesn't like me, but I can handle that."

He dug the puck out of the net then started moving toward the goal. I followed along.

"Tell me this," he said as he moved the puck. "Do you want to be in this league? Play in this league for our cup, for the Broughton? An honest answer would be best here, Hazard."

He knew I had NHL aspirations. Dreams. But...there was something about the WHHL that was growing on me. I'd been quick to judge it as the very thing Coach Clay was trying to drag it up out of: a blood sport, a freak show, a parade of random exploitation.

Not hockey.

But I was wrong. It was very much hockey, in some ways, even more so.

We were doing everything the guys in the NHL were doing, with more stacked against us, and a hell of a lot less pay, support, and luxury accommodations.

This was hockey. Brutal. Beautiful. This was my game. This was my league. It was about time I accepted that.

I was a competitive guy. You had to be to play this kind of sport.

I wanted to prove that I was the best damn hockey player in the world.

I wanted to do that right here in West Hell on a team that was as good as or better than any non-marked team in the NHL.

"Yes," I said. "I want to set the WHHL on fire."

"You've done enough with fire, don't you think?"

"I mean, I want to win. Here. In West Hell. I want the Thunderheads to take the cup. And whatever I need to do to be a part of this team, to make that happen, I'll do."

"Anything?"

"Anything."

He nodded.

Duncan was back, coming our way slowly to give us time to talk. With his wolf ears, I knew he could hear us, even from across the ice. The only reason he hadn't heard Coach when we first got here was because Coach was very, very quiet on the ice.

Cat.

"Then you're going to train with me. Every day. You'll go on the road with us, and we'll train before or after games. I will give you homework. I'll be in your head, Hazard."

"Yes, sir, Coach."

"And I'll be pushing more than just your hockey skills. I'll push you. You're gonna miss your bed because you'll be asleep before you reach it, understand?"

"Yes, sir, Coach."

"I'm going to do the same with your magic. And if you pull one more asinine move like you did in Tacoma, the league won't have to decide if they should write up new rules to punish you. Understand?"

My heart was hammering. I was excited, happy, terrified, determined, and so very, very grateful.

"Yes, sir, Coach."

"Good. I want to see that note. I want to see any other things like that you receive. Not because you can't handle it, but because you are my player, Hazard. And I keep my players safe."

"Yes, Coach."

"Now get the hell off the ice and get some sleep. I'll see you tomorrow. An hour before early skate. You too, Mr. Spark."

Duncan gave me the I-hate-you eyes. "Yes, Coach." He glared at me all the way back to the locker room, but I could only grin.

30

I GAVE COACH THE crumpled letter while Duncan was in the bathroom. I still hadn't told Duncan or Mr. and Mrs. Spark about it yet. I'd done enough to make them worry and didn't want to add to the pile.

Coach read it, then closed his eyes and pinched the bridge of his nose.

"I need to report this to the commission. If you receive any more threats, this will be evidence."

"It's just a letter."

"I'm saying it's more. I need your permission for me to handle this."

I could hear Duncan heading toward Coach's office, yawning and groaning.

"Okay," I said. "If you think that's best."

"It is." He opened a drawer, flipped through paper there, and placed the envelope inside.

Duncan zombied his way through the door and into a chair, rubbing at his face with both palms.

"So what do you think about meditation?" Coach Clay leaned back in his chair turning one of those happy little rock guys over in his fingers.

"I've never tried it," I said.

"Well, today's your lucky day."

"Hippy shit," Duncan whispered a little too loudly. I elbowed him in the ribs to shut him up. He grumbled something about not enough coffee in the universe.

"I don't care if you think it's hippy shit, bullshit, or dumb shit, it is the shit that works." Coach set the little rock guy down on a pile of straightened paperclips.

"The game starts in our heads, gentlemen," he said. "It has to. Those of us who shift are always aware of the other side of us, the animal wanting its turn at the wheel. Those of us who cast spells are always aware of magic itself, looking for a door, a way to take a form in this world. Question, Hazard?"

"Those of us, Coach? Are you a wizard?"

"No. But you don't think you're the only wizard I've known, do you?"

As a matter of fact, yes, that's just what I'd thought. Which was stupid. Of course he knew other wizards. I was not a unique person in this world. Not because I was a wizard.

"Sorry," I mumbled.

Duncan snorted, then yawned extra long.

"Meditation," he said, trying to make his eyes extra wide and awake, even though I knew he'd gotten less than four hours of sleep a night over the last few days. "Sounds fascinating. Let's do it!"

Coach Clay just shook his head but there was a fondness in his eyes. Yeah, Duncan was a hard guy not to like.

Honestly, it wasn't too bad. I had expected to sit on the floor with our eyes closed in total silence or something. But Coach put on a soundtrack of ocean, rain and soft bells.

We stayed seated in his office. The chairs were pretty comfortable. Coach talked us through what we should be doing, what we should be paying attention to.

His voice was easy, the voice of someone who knew how to read poetry, or maybe sing. Or maybe just someone who knew how to boss around a hockey team.

"Let your tongue drop away from the roof of your mouth, I'm talking to you, Spark. Feel the outside corners of your eyes soften and sink like your face is made of warm wax, Hazard.

"Now, I want you to focus on the magic. Where it seats inside you. How much space it takes. What it feels like."

Duncan's breathing changed, getting a little more even and speeding up a tiny bit. I didn't know if my breathing changed, but I did as he said, and took a good long, hard mental look at the magic I'd spent all of my life ignoring.

Magic was color, flavor, smell, *song, song, song.*

It moved through me like lazy winds. Ink through oil, struck strings, hushed voices. It hummed, all of it becoming a song that shouldn't sound so beautiful, but did.

"It belongs to you," Coach said. "It will always belong in you. It is no more powerful than you give it permission to be. Stifling our mark, stifling the magic, only makes it push back. Makes it hungry. Denying that it has room in us, only makes it test the bars of our will.

"So I'll cut right to the chase now—wake up, Duncan—"

Duncan next to me jerked a little.

Heh.

"Take a nice deep breath. Both of you."

We did.

"Exhale. Feel that in your gut, in your lungs, in your shoulders, in your neck, in your head. Inhale as deeply as you can. Hold that breath. Feel that?"

Full lungs? I would have asked but he hadn't told us we could exhale yet. I cracked open one eye.

Coach was watching me. His eyebrow twitched and a smile crooked his lip.

Oops. Cover blown. I opened my eyes. Still held my breath, which felt a little silly.

"Past the tightness of your lungs, past the thoughts running in your head. Go ahead. Exhale. Feel it?"

We exhaled. I didn't know what I was supposed to feel. Curious? Light-headed?

"That's peace, gentlemen. That's you sitting there, in your own space, comfortable with your own company. That is you— marked, magic, man, hockey player, son, brother, soul. The next moment doesn't matter, the moment that just slipped away doesn't matter. Because you are here. Where you belong."

His eyes had a soft fire in them, as if this, this, *this* was the important thing he wanted me to hear. As if *this* was the one thing he wanted planted in my brain to take root.

"This is your real power. In this calm."

Duncan opened his eyes and tipped his head, staring at Coach. Duncan wasn't one of those guys who held still for very long. But he was focused like he rarely was off the ice.

"You'll remember it when you breathe," Coach told us. "This point. This peace. This control."

He clapped his hands—not too loud, just enough to snap us out of our lull. "Let's hit the ice and see if any of this hippy shit stuck."

We geared up and were out on the empty rink a few minutes later. Duncan skated at my side. I could tell he was staying close in case I fell.

Annoying. But kind of nice too.

Coach wasn't far behind us. Wearing his coaching jacket that was black and red, a whistle around his neck, he looked taller and broader shouldered than in his slouchy T-shirt.

He brought a bucket of pucks and dumped them on the ice.

"All right, gentlemen, let's see what you can do."

He spent the rest of the hour putting us through our paces. I only made it fifteen minutes at a very slow burn and nowhere near full speed or strength. My stick handling was clean, my reactions solid.

I was out of breath, out of stamina, but all the skill was still there. Ready. Waiting.

Coach seemed pleased. "That's it for you, Hazard."

The noise in the arena was picking up as other players from the team arrived for the required early skate. There'd be a home game against Moose Jaw Owls tomorrow, and everyone wanted to put another W on the board.

I wouldn't be playing. I was still kicked out until our next game against the Spokane Demons this weekend. But unless my stamina suddenly turned around, there was no way I'd make it through a shift of that game, much less three periods.

The players stepped out onto the ice. They looked surprised to see me there. I made my way over to the bench, where Roxanne lined up water bottles.

She gave me a nod. "Morning, Hazard. Good to see you on your feet."

"Thanks." My cheeks flushed with embarrassment. I expected anger from pretty much everyone on the team.

"Well look who we have here," Watson said, skidding up beside me. "If it isn't the man on fire himself."

"Watts."

"Wiz. You look terrible."

"Thanks." I drank water, then shifted so my back was to the boards and I could see the team. They were in various states of warming up, laps, shots, stick-handling, stretches. I knew they knew I was there. Now that I was facing the ice, they all made a point of skating past me.

"Welcome back, Wiz," JJ said as he soared by.

"Good to see you on your feet." That, from Troiter.

"Atta boy, Hazard," our first line right winger, Balstad the "Baller" said.

"Total bad ass, slinging magic like that," Tetreault said with a grin. He got close and grabbed me into a rough hug, which I wasn't expecting. "Never seen a wizard pull so ghetto. My sister wants your autograph."

I huffed a quick laugh and shook my head.

It was a chorus of similar welcomes, stick taps on the side of my leg, pats on my head as every player on the team came by.

I nodded, said hi or thanks, and tried to keep the lump in my throat from turning into tears and embarrassing me.

When Josky skated over, wide and bulky and powerful in her goalie gear, she stopped and punched my arm with hardly any weight behind it. I must really look bad if she was pulling her punches.

"Thought the doctors said you should stay off the ice."

"They did. But...you know how it is."

"No, I don't because I've never pulled down that much magic. For hell, Hazard. I practically dropped my panties watching you do your thing. Too bad you're not my type."

I laughed and shook my head. She was crazy.

"And," she went on, "I've never been ejected for five games. What were you thinking? You're a wizard. You're supposed to be smart. But no, you go out there and set the world on fire. Must be terrible for all the other wizards out there to see a noob like you show them up.

"They're going to throw you out of their First Marked club or something for being too good, too soon."

"Never liked that club much anyway," I said. "There any room in Third Marked club? I hear you sensitives do delicate things like knitting sweaters for featherless chickens and hugging forlorn trees."

"Bite my sensitive ass, jerk," she laughed. "You just earned yourself another dance, and no more standing there staring at your girlfriend when you're supposed to be dancing with this girl." She tapped her chest, then leaned in to get a water bottle.

"Glad you're back, you ass," she said a little quieter.

"Thanks. Me too. I don't know why everyone is being so cool about it."

She poured some water on the back of her neck. "We've all lost our shit on the ice. This sort of makes you part of the club now, you know?"

"Which club? The freak one?"

"The human one."

"Oh." I flushed hot. Maybe she was right. Maybe I'd sort of missed that with all of my whining about being a wizard. "Thanks for standing up for me back there. Before the game."

"Naw, it's cool," she said. "Anytime. I have a thing for fourth line."

Duncan skated to a stop, grabbed water. "What thing do you have for fourth line?"

"Pity," Josky said while she looked him up and down like he was just the biggest doofus on skates. "I pity you fourth liners. Too bad you can't score."

"You are so sassy when you first roll out of bed," Duncan said. "Just like your mama." He made big eyes and his mouth opened into a ridiculous "O."

Josky hit him and did not pull her punch. Duncan grunted. "Ow."

"Dick," she said. "Who's your roomie this weekend?"

"I'm sure I don't recall." Duncan rubbed his arm where a bruise was probably already spreading.

"All right. Well, I'm sure there won't be any payback for you shit-talking my *mother*. None at all."

"Crap."

She laughed and pushed off, heading toward the net so she could do some extra stretches before Coach called the drills.

"You okay?" Duncan asked.

"I'm good. Better now. Now I'm here."

His smile was quick and sharp. "They give you shit, you tell me."

"Don't need you to fight my fights, Dunc. They give shit, I give it right back. Go. Skate. Coach is glaring at you."

Duncan took off and I moved down to the door so I could sit on the bench. The skate had taken everything I had out of me. I was too tired to hop over the boards.

"Hazard."

I turned to the captain. Waited.

His gaze quickly cataloged me from toe to head. There was something in his expression that made him look worried and a little confused.

"I don't even know how you're standing," he finally said.

"I won't be in a minute." I smiled to take the edge off that truth.

He frowned at me.

"Uh, so…" I slid toward the door. "Congrats on the win. Good game."

His eyebrows did an extra dip, then he looked across the ice. When he looked back at me, he'd unclenched his jaw. So that was something.

"I misjudged you, and I was wrong."

Wow. That took a hell of a lot to just come out and say.

"You shut down that brawl in seconds. And no one was hurt, except you." He nodded once. "As a man, I appreciate your effort in trying to keep the team safe. But as your Captain?" His eyes went stern again.

"I don't want to see you sacrificing yourself like that unless we are on the edge of death and dismemberment. That fight would have blown itself out. There wasn't any reason for you to overreact like that."

I nodded.

But he hadn't seen Steele's eyes before he shifted, the drowning desperation that turned to hatred, rage. Steele hadn't had any control over his animal. Lock might not know it, but there could have been more than blood lost on that ice. There could have been lives.

Yes, I had overreacted. If I'd been better with magic, I could have pulled Steele out of his shift without having to hoover down a block's worth of power. Without pulling everyone else out of their shifts too.

"Was there?" Lock asked.

It took me a second to remember what we were talking about. Oh, right. He was asking me if there was some reason I overreacted.

"It was overkill," I admitted.

Truth.

"It wasn't because I was up in your face? Before the game?" he asked.

"No. That's sort of normal, right? I have no problem with that."

Coach blew the whistle and called everyone to center ice so he could break them up into drills.

Lock tapped his stick on the side of my ankle. "Okay. Good. Good. Because I'm your captain, too, Hazard. If there's something going on, you can tell me."

"Sure," I said. "Thanks."

He nodded and then he was off, halfway across the space to center ice without any effort in his stride.

I hadn't told him Steele had lost control of his shift. Partly because he and Steele used to be friends. Partly because pointing out someone had lost it in West Hell was the definition of redundant.

Even Josky had said everyone did it at least once.

That game was over. We'd hit the next one with fresh legs and fresh minds.

I lugged my tired, shaky body around to the bench and sat with a grateful sigh. I leaned my elbows against the boards and put all my remaining energy into staying awake to watch my team work hard and laugh hard, like a team should.

31

MY MANDATED MAGIC TRAINING was down in Salem, with two well-respected and currently retired teachers who had their master's in magic study, specializing in wizardry.

They were also both wizards.

Mrs. Able and Mrs. Strong headed up the Able & Strong wizardry training courses. Mr. Spark knew them from his college days before they'd gone to set the world standard with their innovative teaching techniques for the marked, and especially for the first-marked.

"Do you want me to come in with you?" Mr. Spark asked after he pulled up next to the quaint cottage-style house across from Bush Park.

"I'm good," I said. "See you in an hour?"

"Call if it lets out early."

I got out of the car, wandered up the curving walk and knocked on the door. There was a stone gargoyle on one corner of the porch. Someone had given it a knit hat.

The door swung inward and two women stood in the space.

I expected them to be a lot older. Grandmotherly. But they were about the same age as Mr. and Mrs. Spark.

One was tall, thin and pale, her heavy black hair long and smooth, her lipstick bright red. She reminded me of the mother from the Addam's Family.

"Random Hazard, I'm Mrs. Able." She nodded, almost a bow, but did not offer her hand.

The other woman was shorter by a head, her hair also black but kinky and free in a cloud around her slender face, her skin darker, her eyes deep set, the color of amber.

"I'm Mrs. Strong." She held out her hand and I took hers, shook.

"Look at you," Mrs. Strong said, still shaking my hand.

"Come in, Random, we may call you Random, might we?" Mrs. Able asked. "Or is there another name you prefer?"

"Random's fine." I crossed into the room. They walked backward deeper into the house, never looking away from me.

"We are going to have a hell of a lot of fun today," Mrs. Strong said. "Coffee or beer?"

It was ten in the morning. "Coffee's good, thank you."

"I see. Apparently only *some* of us are going to have fun." She chuckled and turned down a hall.

"Come right this way." Mrs. Able glided off toward the living room. I expected antiques and mystic frou-frou. But it was clean, modern, with several bookshelves, and a couple green leafy plants in the corners.

"Welcome to our classroom," she said, waving her hand out toward the room and offering me a choice of couch, chair, or love seat. I picked the couch.

She settled in the love seat.

Stared at me. Just. Stared.

I waited. Tried not to fidget. Fidgeted anyway.

Mrs. Strong returned with three beverages. Coffee for me, beer for herself, and something in a black mug that smelled like cinnamon and cloves for Mrs. Able.

Mrs. Strong slipped onto the loveseat next to Mrs. Able.

"We'll begin with a question that will guide every step of your training," Mrs. Able said. "You will need to be as honest as possible."

Sweat popped across my forehead and upper lip. This was it. This would make the difference in how I was trained to handle my magic. Make a difference in what kind of a wizard I could be.

I swallowed and nodded.

Mrs. Strong leaned forward, the beer dangling between her fingers. "Who was the greatest hockey player, and you can't choose Gretzky."

"You may choose Gordie Howe," Mrs. Able said.

Mrs. Strong made a dismissive noise. "Or you can make the right choice and pick Bobby Orr."

I blinked. Looked between both of them. They were absolutely not kidding.

"I'm going to have to go with Sidney Crosby."

They both gasped. Mrs. Strong booed me, while Mrs. Able laughed and held up her mug. "Gretzky it is."

I grinned.

"So who do you think it going to win the Stanley Cup this year?" Mrs. Strong asked.

I spent the rest of the hour talking and arguing with two smart, funny women who loved watching hockey, and who were very excited for my career.

But it wasn't all hockey and heckling. They'd also loaded me up with mental exercises and homework I had to finish before I saw them again next week.

No spells, though. No using magic. They'd been firm about that. They'd issued threats about that.

Said they'd curse my team.

Which…I didn't *think* curses were real, but I was not going to make a couple of hockey-loving master wizards angry enough to find out.

"How'd it go?" Mr. Spark asked as he made his way to the freeway north and home.

"They were, uh, nice."

He glanced over at me. "You mean frightening?"

I laughed. "They can't really read minds, can they?"

He shrugged and merged into traffic. "I could never prove they couldn't."

"I started thinking about testing out one of the spells they were explaining—a way to put a volume control on magic—and I swear they answered my questions as I thought of them.

"I like the idea of a volume control. It makes sense. Because that's what it was like last time. It was turned up too high, all the way to eleven before the game. And in the locker room, and then when Steele shifted and Duncan was fighting, it all went, so *loud* or maybe just *big* and I could feel it and hear it, and it was everywhere. I knew I had to take it all in, and make it do something else. Something different. Something quieter. That wouldn't get Duncan hurt."

I stopped because my throat was still sore.

"Is that what it was like? When you pulled on all that magic during the game? You haven't talked to me about it."

"I talked."

"Not really."

True.

"We have an hour until we're home," he said. "How about I pull off, get us some food, and you can fill me in. No judgment. No rules."

He'd said that to me since I was in first grade. He was the first adult in my life who had listened to me. He was good at it. The best. But we hadn't talked about my magic, because I'd been hiding it for so long.

"Yeah," I said. "Let's do that."

He took the exit to Keizer. We rolled through the Keizer Station, a collection of shops and restaurants right next to the Volcanoes baseball stadium.

We ordered burgers and fries at a drive-thru and were quickly back on the freeway.

Sean set the cruise control. "I'm ready when you are," he invited.

And so I talked about magic.

At first it came out of me in stops and starts, but eventually I just talked.

Started with getting kicked out of the NHL and finished it with the first time back on the ice with the team yesterday.

By the time we reached the house my brain had a kind of hum to it that I usually only felt after a good, hard game.

And I was exhausted.

"Anything else, son?" The engine clicked softly as rain fell in misty sheets against the windows.

I shook my head.

"Then I'm just going to say one last thing: I'm proud of you, Random. Life has knocked you off your feet many times since you were a child. And you have always picked yourself back up. I know how hard it is to lose your dream of playing in the NHL.

"But I am damn proud of you for not giving up on dreaming. You have something to give to this world: talent, joy, kindness. I know you will find a way to give those things no matter what happens in your life.

"I am grateful to know you, Random. No matter what you do with magic. No matter what you do with hockey. I'm proud of the man you've become."

And man, what was I supposed to say to that?

Mr. Spark leaned over and gave me a quick hug. "All right. Let's go see if there's dinner planned for tonight or if we're calling in pizza."

I breathed in, breathed out and tried to feel it like Coach had told me to.

This, right here. This moment shaping me, holding me. A pause. No worries from the past. No worries for the future. Just the words of the only dad I'd ever had grounding me to this world, telling me I belonged.

SEAN AND KIT SAT one row down from me, leaning toward each other and eating popcorn like this was just another nice evening on the couch instead of our first home game against the Owls.

I had never figured out how they could stay so calm about the games Duncan was playing in. Being in the seats instead of on the ice always made me sweaty and amped up.

We were just into the second period and the Moose Jaw Owls were playing that game where they seemed slow and smooth and all about defense. All about blocking not scoring until they suddenly turned on the burners, got possession of the puck, and flew across the ice to slap the puck into the net.

Their slow game threw off the rhythm of play. We were on our heels when they broke free and went on the attack.

Our D-men worked hard in front of the net.

Josky deflected a shot, a rebound and a second shot too.

The Owls kept at it, and finally jabbed the puck between her skate and the pipe.

Goal.

The crowd rushed to their feet shouting with frustration.

I was on my feet too, scowling. One point didn't mean the whole game, but it was a bad way to start the period.

"What kind of BS play was that?" a voice beside me asked.

Gen stood in the aisle, a beer in both hands.

"Hey, you're...hey," I said smoothly.

Her grin grew wicked. "Oh, like I didn't know you'd be at the first home game since the big blow out in Tacoma. Move over, Forty-two. You've got an extra seat."

"How did you find me?"

"Magic."

I moved over to the empty seat next to me.

She sat then handed me the beer. "Also, the JumboTron totally spotted you in the crowd glaring after that last goal. I thought tonight might be a beer kind of thing?"

"Yeah," I said. "Thank you. Thanks." I swigged down a couple gulps.

Sean twisted in his seat, not-very-subtly asking to be introduced, while Kit turned, her sharp gaze taking in Gen, me, our beer. Then a big ole smile spread across her face.

"Random," she cooed. "Why don't you introduce us to your friend here?"

I squirmed in my seat. I'd never seen that kind of calculating delight on her face before. It made me nervous.

"Mrs. Spark, this is Genevieve Brooks. Gen, this is Duncan's mom, Kit Spark."

"So happy to see you here, Genevieve," Kit said.

"Thanks." They shook hands.

Mr. Spark just kept eating popcorn and watching me like I was suddenly more interesting than his son down there trying to win a game. Why was he staring at me?

"Mr. Spark, this is Genevieve. Genevieve, Duncan's dad, Sean Spark."

"Wants some popcorn, Gen?" He held up the bag.

Gen scooped out a handful and smiled. "Thank you. Duncan's doing great tonight."

"He needs to remember JJ doesn't have Random's speed," he said. "But yes, he's doing well. How do you know our Random here?"

"Yes. How did you and our Random meet?" Kit asked.

Our Random? What was up with them?

"We met at the testing clinic," I said.

Yep. Just like a bucket of ice, even mentioning my magic cooled everybody's happy time.

"Oh, so you're the cute assistant and rock star Duncan told me Random can't stop talking about," Kit said, brightening.

"Is that right?" Gen panned a slow look my way. "Can't stop?"

"Uh, I…"

Why was it so hot in here? Was it always this hot in here? Half the building was filled with ice. It shouldn't be this hot in here.

"Well, just so you know," Sean said, "you are invited to spend Thanksgiving with us."

"Really?" Gen chewed popcorn and stared at me almost exactly the way Mr. Spark was looking at me—like I was suddenly super interesting and amusing. "Were you going to invite me to spend Thanksgiving with your family, Random?"

"M-maybe?" I hadn't even thought about it. Hadn't thought about much except hockey and magic, and whether I could ever deal with one without the other.

"Ooh. We made him stutter," said the woman I used to call Mother. "He only stutters when he's flustered. Or when he likes a girl."

"You're supposed to be on my side," I groaned.

Kit let out one of her laughs, the loud ones that made everyone turn to pay attention, and which made Sean give her that fond bemused look.

"Shhhh…" Kit waved her hand, looking scandalized. "We need to watch the game. But Gen, you really are welcome at our place for Thanksgiving. Stop by any time."

She turned back around and Sean winked, then draped his arm over his wife's shoulder so she could lean on him.

"I like them," Gen said low enough only I would hear.

"I used to, too," I said leaning toward her, but loud enough I knew the Sparks would hear me. "Before they got old and weird."

Kit giggled and there was something just so normal about all this, I felt my shoulders drop and I took another drink of beer.

Gen knocked her shoulder into mine. "Tell me about hockey. How did they even score that goal?" Her gaze was riveted on the ice, following the face-off, which we won.

"Refs didn't blow it dead, so the puck was still in play."

"I thought the Owls were slow."

"They are until they're really, really fast. A lot of cats on the team. They work well together."

"Yeah, they do. Bastards."

We clunked our plastic cups together and drank beer in companionable annoyance of the team with the angry owl on their jerseys.

"Thought you were going to call me for coffee," she said.

"I was. I'm still…"

"Exhausted?"

I glanced over at her. "Yeah. Getting better, but not all the way on my feet."

"It takes time. I see wizards going through tests every day. Remember when you asked me what your score was? What you rated?"

We both paused while the second line made a push toward the goal.

"Skate, skate, skate," I chanted quietly.

The crowd shouted, then let out a mighty groan when our left winger botched the rebound and the play moved quickly to the other zone.

"Crap. Their goalie sucks," Gen muttered.

We clunked cups again.

"How high?"

"I've never seen anyone score higher than you. Let that sink in a second, okay?"

I did. It didn't help me get my head around it. "You must not have that many people go through your office?"

"Everyone goes through our office. We're one of the most highly respected testing centers in the Northwest."

"Oh." I didn't know what to say.

"When you pulled that...whatever it was. Tornado? My mind was totally blown at how much magic you were burning through and how well you controlled it."

"Not that great on the control."

"You didn't die, so that's pretty great. No one else died either, so that's even better. Plus you pulled several dozen people down out of shift. That's..."

She went silent and watched as Duncan made a sweet stretch pass that JJ was there to handle. JJ might not have my speed, but he had good ice sense.

"When I first saw you get swallowed by magic, I thought you'd died," she said. "And dammit, Hazard, you do not get to die before we've had our third date."

I laughed. "Fair. And what's this right now? Number three?"

"No. It's our fourth."

I did some counting. She was wrong. This was either our second or our third.

"When did the third happen?" I asked.

"Never gonna happen." She smiled and there was that dimple and nose crinkle.

My heart stuttered and a flipped. She was amazing. I couldn't look away from her.

The crowd roared and leaped to their feet. From all the racket, I knew the Thunderheads had made a goal.

Gen didn't look away from me either. "I could probably do Thanksgiving."

"Good," I said, quietly enough it got lost in the crowd.

"Good," she said back, her eyes full and bright.

This, attraction, this whatever it was between us felt solid. New, and curious, but good. Real.

I might have said more. She might have said more, but just then the klaxon went off again.

Another goal?

"Goooal!" The announcer yelled out as the crowd went berserk.

"Hell, yes!" I whooped.

I grabbed her hand and we both got on our feet to yell and cheer.

WE TOOK THE WIN, putting one point over the Owls in a final score of 4-3. It was an exciting game, all fast plays and edge of your seat screaming in an arena vibrating with noise.

No shifts.

No magic.

Just good, hard hockey.

A real nail-biter.

That we *won!*

I lingered outside the changing room, unsure if I should leave the team alone and let them enjoy the victory without me. I had done nothing to help them win. Still, I wanted to at least congratulate them.

Gen was outside of the building with Mr. and Mrs. Spark. That seemed urgent and dangerous too, leaving them to tell her embarrassing things about me. I took a step away.

"We know you're out there, Wiz," Watts shouted.

I sighed. Wolves and their sense of smell.

"Get your magic ass in here and celebrate with us," Duncan whooped.

And really, how could I say no to that?

32

YOU HAVE A FAN club? A FAN CLUB???? Duncan texted.

You're high I replied.

The Wizzers? Hahahahhaa!

Bullshit. Where?

He was in Vancouver at an away game and sent me a link.

I groaned. The Wizzers was indeed a fan club, started by Mrs. Able and Mrs. Strong. I wasn't going to hear the end of this for days.

The Thunderheads won the next two games without me while I did my morning workouts, studied a lot, slept a lot, and tried to ignore the fan club which gained members by the day.

Then, finally, my two weeks of no-hockey was over.

I traveled with the team to Edmonton so we could play back-to-back games against the Sands. It was my first game back and it was also two in a row and I was nervous as hell.

I was a mess during pregame warm ups.

"You are playing in your head, dude," Duncan said as we waited our turn in the drill. "Like your body isn't even connected to the ice. Just...relax and do what you do. You got this."

I did not got this.

Graves skated up next to me, easy on his skates like a man who'd been born in them. "What's going on, Fan Club?"

I rolled my eyes at the nickname. Maybe Wiz wasn't all that bad.

"First game back. Just got some nerves. It'll work out."

He nodded. "I used to puke every night before a game. I ever tell you that?"

I smiled. I hadn't expected him to have a weakness, much less admit it. "No. How did you get over it?"

He shrugged one shoulder. "Didn't say I got over it."

"Wait. You puke before every game?"

"Not as often now, but yeah, often enough."

If he was a shifter, which I was still sort of doubtful about, going onto the ice with an empty stomach was terrible for him. If he shifted without the resources, he could black out or worse.

"You think I should, what? Clear my mind? Focus on my breathing and be in the moment?"

He gave me a weird look. "Who's been telling you that?"

"Coach. Able and Strong."

His eyebrows went up at the mention of my teachers' names. "The wizards? Have you met them?"

"They started my fan club," I said miserably.

He laughed, and it was a good deep sound.

He tapped my shoe with his stick, something the team had been doing more lately. "Look, it doesn't have to be complicated, Hazard. You know hockey. Nothing else matters today. We'll win or we won't. You're not going to make that much of a difference."

"Hey!"

He grinned. "You *could* make a difference, and you damn well better step up as the year goes on, but kid, this is a long, hard grind. All you gotta do *today* is show up and try not to lose track of which end of the ice you're supposed to be shooting at."

"Those are some low expectations of me."

"You have some unbelievably high expectations of yourself, NHL. Stop thinking you're so special. You're just a hockey player, just like the rest of us. Shoot the puck at the right net. Everything else will fall into place."

He tapped my foot again and pushed off to get in position for the passing drill.

And, yeah, I felt better.

We tromped the Sands on their home ice. I pulled it together and managed to play a decent game, though I was exhausted by the end.

But it was a good kind of exhausted. It was the best.

And the next day? We did it again. Two wins in a row on the road and a six game win streak. That was something to be proud of.

The bus ride home was a party. Lots of singing, lots of laughing, lots of crowing about which plays were the best, which players were the best.

Coach left us to it, even while Assistant Coach Beaumont shook his head and looked exasperated. Yes, they were great wins, but it wasn't like we'd brought home the Cup or anything.

We were halfway through November and there was a lot of year left. Still, we were finally finding our rhythm. We were working together in a way we hadn't even gotten close to at the beginning of the season.

On top of that, we only had one more game before we got four days off over Thanksgiving. And that game was against the Tide, so we were all feeling competitive as hell.

MY PHONE PINGED THE next morning. I didn't recognize the number.

I know you have a game against the Tide tonight. I know you've received threats. Meet me at the restaurant across from the stadium at noon. I have answers.

Who is this?

There was no reply.

I must have decided to go, and decided not to go a million times before breakfast. But by the time noon swung around, I made excuses to Duncan about getting myself to pre-skate on my own, and was outside the restaurant.

I walked in. Scanned the lunch crowd.

A man stood from a table near the back.

Coach Nowak. He waved me over like he expected me to follow his orders, then sat back down and went back to eating.

This didn't make any sense. I had no idea why he would want to meet me. But it couldn't be a coincidence that he was there, waiting for me to walk through the door, and had waved me over. The text this morning had to be from him. Which meant he had answers about who was sending the threats.

267

I walked to the table, sat down across from him.

This felt wrong, like talking to the opposing team was illegal or something. It wasn't. Not really. Players got traded from team to team all the time. But still, something was off about a coach wanting to see me. Wanting to see me about the threatening letters I hadn't told anyone but Coach Clay about.

"Glad you're here, Hazard. Food?" He pointed toward the menu on the table in front of me. I shook my head.

"Why did you want to see me?"

He sawed off a bite of steak and chewed before answering. "I thought it was time to clear the air with you, Random, may I call you Random?"

"I'd prefer Hazard."

His eyes narrowed, and he leaned back. "Well, here's how things are going to go, *Random*."

Ass.

"You're going to sit there and listen. All the way through to the end of what I have to say. You're going to keep your mouth shut. Then you and I will have a better understanding of what needs to happen about those threats you've been getting."

"Maybe you should talk to Coach."

He took another bite, chewed, swallowed. "Oh, I will. But right now, I'm talking to you." He lifted his beer, took a drink. "I don't like your kind. Wizards. And I don't like your kind in the middle of my game. I wanted you out. But that didn't happen. And I am man enough to see that having a wizard in the league filled seats. Ticket sales are up. That's good." He pointed his fork at me.

"You have to understand where you fit in this league, though. You're not a hockey player. Not really. You're a novelty. A fad. Just like Pop Rocks. Interesting now. Forgotten tomorrow.

"Now that I've realized that, well, you will remain in the game. As long as you're interesting? You'll be tolerated. After that? It's over."

"You can't—"

"Your coach is in debt. Buying that team put him under a financial load that will end him. He is too proud to take the help people have offered. Which means he's a season or two away from being out on the street.

"Your assistant coach is a year from retiring, and that third owner doesn't give a damn about hockey. I've been in this game and the game behind it—the game of making money—for years. I know how to grease the wheels. I know how to win."

There were rumors Coach Nowak was dirty. That he had thrown games. It sounded like he was all but admitting it.

"I have people, you understand? People?" He tipped his beer again. "All down the line and all up the line, working for me. People who make sure my ability to make money isn't impeded."

"Are you telling me you blackmail people? Bet on games?"

"Mouth. Shut." He glared at me, eyes pebble hard.

I took a drink of water, trying to cool the anger rising under my skin. West Hell had a bad enough reputation I could absolutely believe Coach Nowak was dirty. I hated that he was bragging about it. Bragging about how he used this league to profit.

He waited a minute more, then started up again, like we sat down to lunch every week to shoot the shit.

"People. Let's say you sent a letter to the commission to complain you've been threatened. Let's say there's a man who made sure that letter never made it there. I have those people. You following?"

Son of a bitch. He was behind it. He was behind those letters, the threats. I nodded.

"Let's say you go for a walk after a game, and a few local boys give you a hard time. I have people. I'm a planner, Random. A leader. I like to keep tabs on all the loose ends.

"And you are a loose end that needs to be tied down. Here's what's going to happen. You're going to play hard tonight. You will allow the plays to come down as they may. No magic. No interfering. You're just there to do what you can for your team and *no one else.*"

I frowned because now he wasn't making sense. I was always there to play for my team. What the hell was he talking about?"

"Why would I do what you want?" I asked, instead.

"Because if you don't, I will destroy Clay's life, will destroy Beauchamp's retirement, and will tear every Thunderheads player down so far, they'll have to dig for days to find air.

"Don't think I can? I have dirt on every person in this league. Your captain? Want to know why he hates wizards? Hates you? No, don't look at me like that, I'm going to tell you.

"He had a friend who was a wizard. Names don't matter. What matters is that he and the wizard used to pal around with Steele. Until that terrible accident, *magical* accident that killed Steele's mother. Of course there was a cover up. No one was prosecuted for the crime. His wizard friend disappeared in the wind."

His face brightened with a smile. It was a gleeful, angry thing, like he'd found a handful of salt and was enjoying rubbing it in an open wound.

"Didn't know that did you, Random? Well, now you do. And that's just a taste of what I know." He seemed to rediscover his appetite and shoveled food in his mouth.

I vibrated with anger. He could be bluffing, but the sickening feeling in my gut told me he was telling the truth.

"And if I go to the authorities?"

"All the way up the line," he said around a mouthful of buttered potatoes. "In the league, out of the league." He shrugged. "I have people."

Which meant there was no one I could turn to. Not even the police. And I wasn't sure what I could accuse him of doing. He hadn't actually admitted to threatening me, although I was sure he was behind the letter, the text, and the guys jumping me in Redding.

But if he had destroyed the letter, there was no evidence to back me up.

"So why did you bring me here?" I asked.

He looked surprised. Sat back again and wiped his mouth with a clean cloth napkin. "I brought you here to tell you I expect you to play hockey tonight, Random. Just like you said you wanted to. With no magic involved. Isn't that what you want too? Isn't that what you said when they kicked you out of the NHL?"

I refused to nod. I stood, and walked away.

Behind me, his laugh rang out.

COACH NOWAK WAS DIRTY.

He was behind the threats. And now that he'd decided I was a fad, useful for filling the arenas, those threats were over.

But the thing that confused the hell out of me was asking, no, *telling* me that all he wanted me to do was to play hockey. To let the game fall as it may.

Since that was what I always did anyway, the entire lunch encounter made little sense. What was his angle? What was I missing?

"Their captain is a wrecking crew tonight," Duncan said.

I watched Tabor Steele, the centerman with the C on his chest. He was tall, somewhere in the stretch above six foot where I stopped paying attention because it was all atmosphere at that point.

And he had speed. He was putting himself everywhere the puck was headed. Making plays like this was the only game of the year that would count.

I expected him to be on the first line but Nowak was mixing it up and giving him extra minutes. At this rate, he'd wind up playing a lot of fourth line.

We'd already been in on the ice a lot together. Looked like we were going to get more of the same.

So when I took my next shift, I was not surprised that he was all up in my face.

Of course, along with his face came his elbows, his stick, his cheap shots, and his mouth. There was something extra angry about his play. Extra desperate.

I wondered what dirt Nowak had on him, and I wondered what he used it for.

Duncan felt the level of desperation radiating off Steele and was slinging insults even though he was supposed to be dealing with his own man, Zima.

I swung past Duncan while we were setting up for a new face-off.

"Keep it easy, Donuts. Pay attention to your man. I don't need your protection."

"Something." He shook his head. "Something's different with him. It's making my skin itch."

I glanced over at the visiting team bench. At Nowak.

He stood with arms crossed over his suit jacket, glaring at the ice. Glaring at me.

"What?" Duncan asked.

I shook my head and got in place. The music was too loud, the crowd was too loud. I didn't know what to tell him anyway. Nowak was a problem. Duncan knew that. Steele was a problem. Duncan knew that too.

"Play smart," I said.

He tipped his head like he was considering my request. "How about I play to win?"

And then there was hockey. It was a rhythm, a battle.

Absolute focus on the puck, on the ice, on the players around me, as the roar and chant of the crowd faded, faded.

It was sweat and hits and cussing and pain. It was speed, and freedom, and brutal grace. I forgot about Nowak. Forgot about Steele's weird vibes. The only thing in my mind, in my heart was winning this with my team.

By the third period the game had leveled off at 2-2. We had twenty minutes to bury the puck one more time, and win this thing.

Our crowd was worked up to a froth. They jeered at the refs, cheered every time we made a run at the net, groaned when we missed shots.

That energy fueled us, lifted us.

It was its own kind of magic.

Fifteen minutes went by scoreless and as those minutes ticked down, the intensity ratcheted up.

Every Thunderhead out there was an electrical current I was a part of, a loop I completed and fed. Our team pushed and retreated and fought like a heart beating, beating, beating.

The Tide were their own heartbeat, the rapid rush of prey, the pounding tempo of predator. On our heels, in our faces. No punches pulled.

They were out to break, bend, bruise.

We brawled for the puck, unafraid to make a man bleed.

Watts took a stick to the face the refs missed, and had to go back to the locker room so Leon could patch him up.

Tetreault got hammered into the boards so hard, it took him several long, grueling seconds to get back on his feet again. He skated over to the bench for a change, bent in half.

Graves threw down gloves and started a fight with the guy who had bodied Tetreault. The crowd went insane, cheering out his nick name: Grave Digger.

Nothing like a little fair and honest hockey fight to get the fans on your side.

Both fighters got sent to the penalty box, but not before Graves gave the guy a black eye that was already swelling shut.

Oh, yeah. This was fun!

Penalty minutes meant we were playing four-on-four, both teams a man short. Covering that much ice this late in the game was grueling work.

Steele and I ended up behind the net, fighting for the puck. He had been on my ass all period, shoving, punching, slamming me with stick or fist every chance he got.

And it felt like his chances were endless.

"Trash. Washout," he snarled. "Your magic doesn't mean anything out here, little man. Get off the ice, hack. You're weak. Nothing. Let the real players play."

He slammed the back of my head, follow it up with a pop to the side of the neck.

Magic in me roiled in an angry, nauseating wash of power.

I breathed. I centered. Just like Coach said. I held magic back before it blew.

"Kiss my magic ass, Steele."

Maybe not all that original, but my stamina was bottoming out fast, and I wasn't going to waste my breath thinking up brilliant insults.

Steele jammed the puck out from between my skates and made a breakaway to our net.

I scrambled after him. Forced a pass that went wide.

Minutes ticked down. Graves and the other player were sprung from the sin bin.

Two minutes of game left.

If we were going to break this tie, it had better be soon. It had better be now.

We subbed out, waited our turn, then were back on the ice before I could do anything more than catch my breath.

One minute left.

Another hot face-off and we were flying, pushing, every muscle, every burst of speed, every hit aimed at the net.

And then I saw it, our chance to score. Their goalie was a frickin' brick wall, wider than he was tall. But he couldn't see JJ through the traffic of bodies in his way.

Before I could get to the puck, one of the Tide was on it.

That player, Paski, wound back for the shot. He put shifter muscle into it, practically bending his stick in half.

It should have been a pass. Away from the net. But it was a sniper shot across the ice.

Fast, fast, fast.

My brain fired a warning.

Everything, *everything* slowed.

Steele was in the way of that shot. He'd been tangled up with another player, hadn't twisted around to see the play. Was moving. Right into the line of the puck that flew high.

It would hit him. Side of the neck. Side of the head.

His helmet wouldn't save him. His face gear wouldn't save him.

I didn't know why. But I looked over to Coach Nowak.

And he was smiling. The bastard was smiling.

This was what he wanted. What he'd ordered me to do at lunch. Just let the game play out. Don't use magic. Don't be anything out there on the ice except another hockey player.

Just let a man get hit by a career-ending shot.

I could save Steele.

My enemy.

My rival.

The man who wanted me dead.

What was I supposed to do about that?

A thousand options ran through my head, a thousand images.

My empty house, my adopted brother, my loving family. And between it all, holding it together with sharp, smooth punches of a needle through the stiff edges of reality, was hockey.

This game, these brotherhoods. The laughter, the wins, the losses. Friends who were more than friends. Miraculous moments shared and so fleeting, fleeting, fleeting.

A thousand thousand split-second decisions.

Some I'd won, some I'd lost.

That moment, that final moment when I'd pulled on magic, when I'd saved my teammate from ending his NHL career and had instead ended mine.

I'd made a choice then: Save him.

Because teammate, or stranger, or enemy, he was a part of this. A part of the game I loved.

The game that had saved me. The game that could save other people too. The game that was still my life even though I'd thought I'd lost it.

The game that had given me not one family, but many.

Sometimes life and death come down to a split-second decision.

This time it was mine to make.

I reached deep inside me, felt magic hovering there, waiting for me to call it out, waiting for me to shape reality with endless possibilities.

It was a part of me. No shame in that.

In fact there was joy.

The kindling behind my heart caught fire. Not a bonfire, just a flame. Something easy, something strong, something I coaxed with threaded ribbons of light to reach, spin, fly.

And catch the puck in a net of magic, stopping it dead in the air right in front of Steele.

Time clicked back up to normal speed. Steele jerked and ducked the instant he finally saw the puck glowing in the magic net right in front of his eyes.

The arena went silent.

And then the crowd rolled with an avalanche of sound.

Refs blew whistles, game play was brought to a halt.

Lock skated over and told me to drop the magic, and wait by the bench while the refs reviewed the play.

I untangled the magic with a tug of a string. The puck fell flat on the ice with a smack.

The crowd cheered even louder, a chanting force of "Wi-zard! Wi-zard! Wi-zard!" that rang in my bones.

I held up a hand in acknowledgement and coasted over to the bench where Leon passed me water, and players held out their hands for high fives.

My teammates repeated "nice work," "nice save," "good catch," and Coach Clay nodded and leaned forward to yell over the crowd.

"Good work, Hazard. Don't care how they rule, you made the right choice."

I nodded, drank water, and scarfed down half a bar Leon shoved at me.

The refs were going over the replay, and they had contacted the league's situation room for their review and to get a ruling on whether or not that was illegal use of magic on the ice.

I watched Coach Nowak, who was watching the play on the screens behind the bench.

He looked furious.

Someone might mistake that for anger at his player for almost braining a teammate. But I knew better.

He had planned to take Steele out. He had ordered Paski to do it.

I could see the irritation, the agitation in Paski's movements as he skated slow circles near his teammates. He was not looking at his coach. He was not apologizing to Steele.

This was all kinds of messed up.

The ref finally skated to center ice to make the announcement on the call.

The crowd went silent.

"We have an illegal use of magic on equipment. Two minute penalty."

The crowd jeered and booed, then broke out into the *wi-zard* chant as I skated to the penalty box. I didn't care that I'd taken the foul.

Those were the rules. I was not supposed to use magic to affect the ice, the players, or the equipment.

But I wouldn't change my decision.

I'd saved a man's life. I was certain I would make that same choice again and again and never once regret it.

I clomped into the box and leaned forward, watching my team face-off against the Tide.

We had less than a minute on the clock to break a tie. The face-off was where we'd left, in the circle near the Tide's goalie.

We had to win this. We needed to win this.

God, I hoped we won this.

I took a deep breath. Held it.

The ref dropped the puck. Lock won the battle and tapped the puck out to Duncan.

Duncan passed to Graves, who passed to Watts, who juked to open up a lane and passed it back to Graves.

Ten seconds.

Graves offloaded it back to Duncan who chipped it around two Tides to get it on Lock's stick.

Lock wound back and fired the puck at the net.

It was a second. Less than that.

Three players between him and the net. No room for the puck to get through.

And then…

…like there was nothing but open space between a forest of skates…

…goal!

The lights went off, the crowd went crazy.

Every Thunderhead on the bench jumped to their feet, pounding the boards and shouting.

I jumped out of the penalty box and joined the celebration.

It took everything the refs had to get us back in position to let that final second slip off the clock. When that was done, all that was left was joy.

Thunderheads poured over the boards, piled on top of each other, slapping backs, helmets, laughing. Josky, helmet thrown off, skated across the ice to pile drive into the celebration.

We'd won.

Holy shit, we'd won.

That's when I caught Steele's gaze. He looked shocked. Not at the goal. He wasn't even looking at the rest of my team, or his own.

He was just looking at me, as if he couldn't understand what had just happened.

I gave him a quick salute with my stick. Then he was hurried off the ice with the rest of the Tide.

I skated out to center ice with the rest of my team and held my stick high in salute, in gratitude, for our crowd.

33

THE CELEBRATION IN THE locker room was loud enough and happy enough, you'd have thought we just took home the Stanley Cup, not defeated our rivals for the first time on our home ice.

We were ridiculously happy with ourselves. Coach told us all to bask in it and then get some rest before the next game on Monday.

We'd won this one, but we had a long road ahead of us to the playoffs. If we made those, and I really thought we had a shot at it, then we had a long, hard haul to the Broughton Cup.

But none of that mattered. Tonight was all ours.

By the time I stumbled out of the lockers to meet Gen and Sean and Kit outside the arena, I was giddy with laughter, drunk on the win even though all we'd had in the changing room were energy drinks and soda.

I was halfway down the main hall, the sound of my teammates singing that annoying winner song the Rumblers had sang fading behind me.

We needed our own victory song. And really, since half the team couldn't carry a tune if it was taped to their hands, we should just leave the singing to the Rumblers.

Duncan was staying behind for the song. I'd gotten a crazy stream of congratulations from my fan club (yes, I kind of liked it) and a more personal congrats from Mrs. Able and Mrs. Strong, which was a selfie of the both of them grinning from ear to ear wearing shirts with 42 on the front, and holding up their fingers in a number one gesture.

They'd been in the audience. Which was humbling and cool.

But it was the message from Gen asking me when I was going to be outside so we could start celebrating that got me moving.

"Hazard?" Steele stepped out from the hallway shadows, blocking my path.

I stopped. Sighed. Did he really think I was going to do some kind of showdown at the O.K. Corral now? Here?

"Steele," I said evenly. "Good game."

He nodded a little jerkily, then exhaled all in one fast blast. "I want to apologize for being an ass." He rubbed his hand over his head. "That shit you threw last game. Pulling magic. It was...creepy."

I wouldn't call it creepy, but okay. I could see his point. It must have been really weird to have something step in and take over the magic you'd lived with all your life and pull you out of a shift.

"I shouldn't have done that," I said. "It won't happen again."

Never. Because the recovery time sucked.

"But tonight. I don't know how you caught that puck. Don't know why." He winced and looked off over his shoulder. "But thank you. Thank you."

Wow. I never thought I'd hear that out of him.

"You're welcome. It wasn't personal. None of this—" I waved a finger between the two of us "—is personal. We both want the same thing, yeah? Good hockey. Can't do that if someone's in a hospital."

He nodded. "Agreed. So. Good luck out there."

"Oh, naw. We don't need luck. We're going to bulldoze this league straight to the Broughton Cup."

His smile was fast and genuine. Competition was the language all hockey players spoke fluently. "Good luck because you'll have to get through us first."

"What, like tonight?"

"One fluke of a game. We'll take you next time, just like we took you last time."

"We forfeited," I reminded him.

"We still won."

True.

I grinned.

"Steele!" A voice boomed down the hall. Coach Nowak. He looked just as angry as the last time I'd seen him. Or really, as angry as every time I'd seen him. I didn't think he had any other mood. Even when his team won, he still looked like he had a mouth full of rusted tin cans.

"Get your ass on the bus, Mr. Steele."

Steele ducked his head like he was expecting to get the back of the man's hand and headed toward the exit.

Nowak considered him while Steele walked away. His eyes were flat and hard. Sweat trickled down his temple, and his hands clenched and unclenched.

"You want my advice, Hazard?"

"Not at all," I said pleasantly. "Because I'm not going to take it anyway. I think tonight proved that."

The scowl on his face could have boiled stone.

"Get the hell out of this league," he snarled.

"You make one move on me or the people I care about and I will go to the authorities and tell them everything. I showed that letter to a lot of people. And I still have your text. You put Paski up to that hit. You wanted Steele out of the game. And I can prove it."

I was lying, but he didn't know that.

"No one will believe you."

"I'm the first wizard in hockey and I've saved two lives before we're halfway through the season. You really think I can't get people to listen to me? Important people? You think I won't take a lie detector test? You think I won't offer myself to the mental search of a wizard who can read minds? You think I won't go to the press?"

I thought he was going to yell, but when he spoke it was a hoarse whisper.

"You. Will. Fail. You're nothing but a fad. Pop Rocks." Then he turned and stormed away.

"I'm the guy who's going to see that you lose, Nowak. Every. Time. Until your stink is scrubbed off this league for good."

I watched him disappear around the corner and only let down my guard after I'd counted to twenty. I was dizzy with relief.

That was a win. And I knew it wouldn't be the last.

"Wi-zard!" Duncan called out from behind me.

"Hey," he said, "let's go celebrate until we can't see straight!" He dropped his arm across my shoulders.

"How great was that?" he asked, hopped up on energy drinks and the win. "It was so great that's how great it was! You were great, *I* was great! Probably greater than you because, dude, I was so great. Why did you take a hit for that Tide asshole? But still, you did magic, and it was *whoa* and *what* and *boom* in his face and so great. And we scored with one damn second left and it was so...so..."

"Great?" I suggested as we moved down the hallway.

"Exactly! Great! I love winning! I love hockey. And I love *you* most of all buddy!"

He planted a big sloppy wet kiss on the side of my face, then jogged ahead of me whooping and jumping to try and hit the ceiling.

I smiled and followed him.

Out of the arena, out into the cool rainy evening where my family and girlfriend greeted us with handfuls of popcorn thrown in the air and loud cheers.

Like we were heroes. Like we were magic.

And maybe for this night, for this moment, we were.

34

"OKAY," DUNCAN SAID, RESTING his stick near his skate and leaning on it. "Bring it, Wiz."

"You didn't even get to pick your own name?" Gen asked next to me.

She had on a pair of figure skating skates, and she knew how to use them. Apparently, along with rock and roll, and cross-stitch anarchy (whatever that was) she could skate.

"It's a hockey thing," I said. "You never pick your own nickname. And just for the record, I kind of hate Wiz."

"Aw." She caught my hand and skated backward. I went with her, guiding her by leaning a bit to avoid a couple little kids who were all speed and no skill. "But I like it."

"Well, maybe I do like it now."

"That happened suddenly."

"Some of the best things do."

She smiled like I hoped she would, all bright and hopeful, with that sweet, wicked dimple action.

"Really?" Duncan skated up next to me and jabbed his stick under my skate hoping to trip me.

He'd been trying to knock me down like that since we were eight and it never worked.

"I thought you two lovebirds came out here so Ran could show off his sweet, sweet magic skills."

"We did." I guided us all over to the side where there was less traffic. It was the middle of the week, early morning, and most of the skaters were under the age of six. The ice would really get busy soon, since we were in the middle of the mall on a public rink.

The big Christmas tree had been set up in the middle of the rink, and three stories above us, the moody blue and gray of an Oregon winter sky filled the glass ceiling. I had been working hard with Mrs. Able and Mrs. Strong and I wanted to show off how far I'd come.

And because, well, I could. "Ready?"

"Yes, already," Duncan said. "Go."

I reached out for magic, drawing it through me like a breath, the honey weight and sweetness filling my mouth.

I didn't fight it, or worry if I would use it wrong, or right. Didn't worry if it made me more or less of a hockey player because hockey was always going to be a part of me. And so was magic.

A good part of me.

And instead of using it only for life and death, I had worked to find ways I could use it for something fun. Something beautiful. Something just for the three of us. For joy.

I had learned how to handle it so it didn't burn me out immediately. So I stayed grounded, clearheaded, and could enjoy it.

I held an image in my mind and gave it to magic like setting a rock skipping over waves.

The whole world—well, our little part of it—changed.

A night sky arced above us, stars burning and twinkling in silver and gold. Snow dusted down around us, in blue and pink and white, like feathers and dandelion wishes.

The little kids on the ice all started laughing and screaming, turning with their arms spread wide, their faces tipped to the sky, tongues out to catch the snow.

It would melt and taste like honey.

"That's it?" Duncan asked. "You can make it snow? So?"

But he couldn't fool me. His smile was bright and he had gathered up a little pile of snow next to the puck he'd brought along with us to the rink. He liked it when I did magic. A lot.

"I can do this too." I glanced at the puck and sent it skittering across the ice to smack into the glass around the rink, then back out onto the ice where it traced a figure eight in the snow.

He tipped his head and stared at the puck for a minute. Snow caught in his hair, like an exploded pillow had smacked feathers all over his head. He looked ridiculous.

"Can you do that during a game?"

"I shouldn't. Penalty, remember?"

"True," he allowed, still not looking away from the puck. "But during practice. Just to freak the other team out a little?"

"Maybe just a little."

"Hazard. You are a brother like no other." He glanced at me and he was happiness and strength and joy and the reason I even had a chance to be standing here, happy and whole. "We are going to get into so much trouble!"

I laughed and he skated off to retrieve the puck.

A little kid threw a snowball at him and Duncan jumped right into the game of chase and dodge, perfectly at home with the five-year-olds.

God, I loved him.

"It's amazing," Gen said. "Seriously, Random. Don't let it go to your head, but you are…this is amazing." She tipped her head up and caught a snowflake, then laughed. "It's sweet."

"I thought about making it taste like turkey just to screw with Duncan." I pushed off, bringing her with me this time.

She followed, her steps falling into perfect rhythm with mine. "Why didn't you? That would have been hilarious."

The snow sang out like little bells as it struck the ice. We glided around a kid making snow angels with his dad while the stars above glittered and spun.

"Because I wanted to do this. For you."

"Me?"

I nodded. "I want to do a lot of things for you. Until I somehow find the way to tell you how incredible I think you are. How real and funny and smart and…perfect."

She leaned in, filling all the space between us, eyes bright, lips curved in a gentle smile. "You know what makes this so wonderful?"

I raised an eyebrow. "It's magic?"

"No. What makes this wonderful is it's you. Bright, unexpected, thoughtful. And just a little amazing."

"Just a little?"

She shrugged. "Well, I haven't seen all the ways you're going to tell me I rock yet." And then she tipped her face up. Not to catch snow. Not to skate.

But to move close, closer until there was no space between us. Until I could see the kindle of joy in her eyes.

She kissed me, soft, hopeful. Asking me questions neither of us were brave enough to say yet: *Us? Yes? Forever?*

I kissed her back, holding her tight and giving her the only answers in me: *Yes. Yes. Yes.*

Her lips tasted like honey and magic and promises. Like laughter and hope and song.

And in this moment we became something new. Something to explore, to build, to share.

Here, I belonged.

I breathed, and she breathed, and it was everything.

It was life.

It was victory.

It was magic.

Coming Soon

SPARK
West Hell Magic - 2

Duncan Spark's life can't get any better, but it's about to get much worse...

DUNCAN SPARK IS AN unapologetic hockey player and gleeful wolf shifter. Playing hockey in the West Hell freak league with his wizard brother, Hazard, is a dream come true. He's got family, teammates, pack.

But when a rival team swoops in to steal Hazard, Duncan's world is blown apart. Duncan throws himself into the line of fire to save his brother, and volunteers to take Hazard's place.

Surrounded by enemies on a team that hates him, Duncan is a wolf without a pack. But everyone knows that backing a wolf into a corner only makes it more dangerous.

ACKNOWLEDGMENT

THIS BOOK WOULDN'T BE nearly as strong without the effort of several generous people.

I'd like to thank my amazing cover designer, Kanaxa Designs, who came in with creative guns a-blazing and captured Hazard perfectly in this absolutely fabulous cover.

Thank you also to my wonderful copy editor, Kimberly Cannon, for not only catching my grammatical errors but for also keeping an eye on the hockey rules. I'm so glad you laughed at that one part where you-know-who was mentioned.

Big thanks to my sharp-eyed beta readers Dejsha Knight, Christy Keyes, and Evil Eye Editing, and to the extraordinarily vigilant proofreader, Eileen Hicks. Thanks also go out to Indigo Chick Designs for the skillful formatting of the print edition of this book.

To Karen Mahoney, Rinda Elliott, Jenna Glass, Lilith Saintcrow, Keri Arthur, and Rachel Vincent, each of you are amazing authors. Thank you for your unflagging behind-the-scenes support. Dames forever.

Shout-out to my hockey sisters Deanne Hicks and Dejsha Knight. It wouldn't be the same if I couldn't share the joy and excitement with you. Let's knit more hats!

This book might not have happened without the enthusiasm of my husband, Russ Monk. Thanks for all the games, trips, and keeping track of the stats. I owe you one for those two months I made you listen to my never-ending list of possible team names. I might also owe you one for making your GPS app sing in a boy-band voice while we navigated Canada. I love you.

To my sons, Kameron Monk and Konner Monk, thank you for your encouragement, hockey good-humor, and being the best part of my life. I love you both.

And to you, my dear reader. Thank you for strapping on your skates and pushing off onto the ice to give Hazard's world a try. I certainly hope you've enjoyed the game!

ABOUT THE AUTHOR

DEVON MONK is a national bestselling writer of urban fantasy. Her series include West Hell Magic, Ordinary Magic, House Immortal, Allie Beckstrom, Broken Magic, and Shame and Terric. She also writes the Age of Steam steampunk series, and the occasional short story which can be found in her collection: A Cup of Normal, and in various anthologies. She has one husband, two sons, and lives in Oregon. When not writing, Devon is drinking too much coffee, watching hockey, or knitting silly things.

Want to read more from Devon?
Follow her online or sign up for her newsletter at:
http://www.devonmonk.com.